HIDDEN IN LEGEND

An Elven Heritage Collection

CHRISSY WISSLER

Blue Cedar Publishing

Blue Cedar Publishing
P.O. Box 5275
Torrance, CA 90510

❀ Created with Vellum

ALSO BY CHRISSY WISSLER

Elven Heritage Series

Hidden in Mist

Hidden in Truth

Hidden in Shadow

Hidden in Fire

Hidden in Flight

Hidden in Spirit

Hidden in Desire

Hidden in Memory

Hidden in Time: Novel

Hidden in Lore: Collection #1

Hidden in Myth: Collection #2

Hidden in Legend: Collection #3

Little League Series

Swing Away: A Little League Novel

Prom Dates & Softball Bats

Throw Like a Girl, Catch a Date

Fly Away

No Crying in Softball

More to Life than Softball

A Pitcher's Unexpected Date

A Catcher's Christmas Wish

Stolen Bases, Stolen Kisses

Softball Baby

Off-Balance
Batter-Up Pucker-Up: Collection
Everlasting: Collection
All or Nothing: Collection

Home Run Series
Home Run

Romance Video Game Series
Second Chance: Novel
Anything Possible
Changing Perspective

Enchantment Avenue
Searching for Sanctuary: Novel
Dragons in Preschool: Short Novel
The Blessings Bridge
Pixie Dust Cupcakes
Christmas Weather Witch
Unfreeze a Heart
More than Nurture

INTRODUCTION

The first time I finished an Elven Heritage story and wrote those words 'the end'... I knew it wasn't actually *the end*.

Far, far from it.

I knew I was actually staring at a series and a character... both who I just fell in love with. Kate, who's just full of sass and voice and trying so hard to find her place in a world that actually has no place for her (as if any teenager feels differently). I knew, without a doubt, Kate and this world of lost elves was one I'd keep returning to, if only so *I* could find out what happens next.

Of course, life often has ideas of its own and with the addition of my own Kate into my life, the birth of my daughter (also Kate—yes, I love the name *that* much), and then her brother who followed a few years after, these stories slipped into my 'to-write' stack.

Waiting, but never forgotten.

In fact, every so often my husband (also my first reader) would comment, "Are you ever going to get back to your Elven Heritage stories?"

The answer was always a definitive: YES.

The challenge was putting the *world* back into my head. The characters, the magic, those thoughts and ideas and how they fit together into some bigger puzzle. Of course, I was still being mom at the time (and still am) but life got a tab bit easier, to the point where I could... you know... think about Kate and and her story and these elves...

And where the heck they were taking me next.

I know a little of that now, as you'll see in the forthcoming novel, *Hidden in Time*, but I also knew that, for readers, the best thing I could do was to give you a place where all of Kate's stories were, in one giant collection.

Which is exactly what this is.

Now, there are two previous collection. *Hidden in Lore* contains stories one through four, and *Hidden in Myth* has five through eight. But this one, this one right here, has all eight just for you. Just so you can read from one story to the next, because really, they *all* are one story.

I hope you enjoy going on this journey with me, of learning who Kate is and her heritage, and just what the heck she's gonna do about the magic that seems pretty darn determined to wake up.

—Chrissy Wissler
Torrance, CA
May, 2018

HIDDEN IN MIST

An Elven Heritage Short Story

There was no way Kate was setting foot in that forest.

Not with those pines...those trees practically drenched in mist. No, as if the mist were seeping from their trunks and branches.

As if they were one and the same.

Their needles so dark they looked almost black. Disappearing right into that mist and farther up...so far up she couldn't see where the trees stopped and the sky began.

That gray, moody sky.

If she just gave it a minute, she was sure it'd open up and drop buckets of water on her, her mom, and this crazy idea about hiking at Mount Rainier when, as far as she was concerned, it was still in the middle of winter.

Even if there was no snow...right at this particular spot.

Kate gripped the worn, fraying strap of her backpack. Hands cold, numbed. She almost wished for the heavy, pressing weight of books. Of her classmates. Of what they said behind her back.

Whispering.

Cold, unwelcoming eyes slanting towards her.

Just like that forest.

Not to mention the single, itsy-bitsy trail cutting into that forest—boot-packed dirt mostly covered with green stuff and leaves—that she was supposed to follow. As if this were no problem. Head right into the creepy forest that was sending her stomach twisting.

Making the hairs on her neck stand up on edge.

She felt it.

Really.

She wasn't crazy.

Those trees were actually bending towards her. She could hear the creaking of bark as it twisted.

Turned to her.

Her breath puffed out in a white, cloudy mist.

Her mom was crazy. Insane. This place was supposed to make her feel better?

But seriously, if the creepy factor wasn't gonna clue her mom in, you'd think the emergency vehicles and rescue guys behind her would do the trick.

But no.

Not her mother.

Kate glanced over her shoulder. The dozens of men and even a few dogs, making their way to the visitor center and back country office. Two buildings that looked like they'd fought tooth, nail, and floorboard for this spot in the forest. Their brown coat of paint, now flaking and peeling, was clearly the loser of that battle.

There were a lot of rescue workers, she noticed. All with strained faces. Conversations nonexistent.

Part of her wanted to know what had happened. Was it a rescue or a recovery?

But the other half, the part of her that looked at this forest, part of Mount Rainier and the National Park, with its misty claws and twisty trees, that half...didn't want to know.

Was afraid to know.

Every parking space was taken. Vans marked "Search and Rescue" parked on the squishy mountain grass. In between long, skinny trunks of pines. Squeezed in so close there was barely any room to open a door.

Felt just like this forest.

With all the trees.

Pressed around her. Bending towards her.

Reaching.

She wasn't imagining things...was she?

Kate's hands reached up. Automatically. Without thinking. Slipped free strands of blond hair from her ponytail. Covered her ears.

Different. Weird. Freak.

Kate shoved the memories—Heather's words—as far from her as she could. Stomped her boots. Her toes still numb even with the double layering of scratchy wool socks.

She was fine. Totally normal.

There was nothing wrong with her.

Just like there was nothing wrong with the creepy forest of doom.

She gave that forest another look before turning, half hoping she could convince her mom this wasn't such a great idea.

Not that the three-hour drive from Seattle had done a thing. Seattle, where they'd been living only a few short months before the whispers started again and her mom, as usual, got this strange look on her face. This constant uneasiness that drained her of color, making her look all hollow-like. At least until she'd decided to come on this stupid hike in the first place and then bam, there was rosiness in her cheeks again.

Which still didn't change the fact that in a month, maybe two, her mom would throw in the towel and they'd head back to Montana. 'Cause no matter what her mom did, she couldn't escape.

Kate headed up the gravel road—which turned into a cobblestone path (though, to be honest, at least half the stones were MIA). There was her mother, fully decked out in hiking gear (which Kate hadn't known they'd even owned), sporting a warm, purple jacket with matching pants. A jacket that hugged her curves in all the right places...nothing like Kate's bulging jacket, which had a thing for making her look like a whale and not like a filling out (slowly) teenage girl.

Her mother, who was determined—for whatever reason—to see this little mother-daughter hike through.

Even though her mother hated the forest. Hated trees.

Except right now. Apparently.

Her mom was making her way closer to the command center (the only park visitor that Kate could see) and the thick throng of rescue guys in jackets (bulkier than hers, if it were possible). They didn't seem to notice her mom. Not with walkie-talkies glued to their hands and all eyes focused on the linebacker standing in front of a map, leading the charge.

A map that had a couple dozen pins of different colors. None, Kate had a feeling, that were good.

Her chest tightened. Felt like her heart squeezed between beats.

Why couldn't they just leave? Forget this stupid trip that was doing —absolutely—nothing to help Kate forget. Couldn't. Not when she could easily hear the visitor center's creaking welcome sign. Could hear it so well, it was as if she stood underneath it and not at the tail end of the parking lot. Or the muted, hushed conversation taking place at the command center as plans were made for another day of search. And recovery.

To find the missing girl.

Alice.

That was her name. A girl who'd been last seen near Indian Henry's Hunting Ground Trail, following right behind her friends, and then was gone. No trace. No sign. Nothing.

Kate bit her lip. Tried to keep from listening.

Couldn't.

Just like before. With Heather, who she'd thought, even for a moment, was her friend. Not best friend, but the first person who'd given Kate a smile and showed her where her locker was, and home-room, and the fastest way out of school as soon as the ear-splitting bell rang.

The tall man with pretty impressive football shoulders, sporting a piratical eye patch, stepped forward, and the rest of the Search and Recovery group came to him. Silent, watchful, as if they were all under some sort of spell. Probably fear for the girl. Alice. His face was a road map of wrinkles and scars, one jagged one running right through his eyebrows and straight on down. She'd a feeling there was no eye there, just an eye patch. Why she thought that, or why she just *knew*, she had no idea. It was just a feeling, just this... certainty.

"We've searched the twenty-three miles where Alice was last seen," he said. "Both man- and dog-teams. The kids say she was last spotted here."

He pointed to a blue pin, finger just as huge as those arms.

"So far, the canines haven't caught a scent. No sign either. Not anywhere off the trail. No broken branches. No footprints."

He focused his attention on each man and then the one or two women awaiting their orders. Then stopped suddenly. Kate realized her mother lingered on the outskirts of the group, just outside of normal hearing range, but he wasn't looking at her mother.

No. He was looking at Kate.

Saw Kate, and only Kate.

Single eye met hers. Green or gray or hazel...she couldn't tell, the color kept shifting.

But his gaze didn't. It held right there, right on her, and he just kept on staring across the heads of all his workers as if he knew...

That she could hear.

Kate swerved on her boots, digging into that half cobblestone, half gravel path. Fast. She dug her now-numb hands deeper into her jacket pockets as if all that would stop the voices. As if she ran far enough and stuck her fingers in her ears, it would all go away.

Poof.

Like magic.

His voice continued, following her. "The helicopter hasn't seen her either. It'd help if the weather held, but that fog..."

Deep. Baritone. As if it knew it was delivering bad news but did it anyway. Had to.

"I'll be honest. It's not looking good."

Kate's throat closed. Locked the air in her chest. Even as the fear tightened. Held on.

It was happening again. Just like at school.

Kate made a beeline for the bathroom. Passed the half-collapsed wood bench with its neon-green moss covering it from top to bottom. Practically ran across the cobblestone path with its missing stones.

She didn't care. She kept running.

All that mattered were flushing toilets, locking stalls, and being at the other end of the visitor center. Away, far away, from the rescue center.

But then she heard another sound. Slow, shuffling boots over squishy grass, but lighter, not as heavy as the rescue workers, because these were made by younger someones. Half their age. Her age, in fact. She could tell all this just by the sound of boots sticking to the moist earth, almost as if the earth, the forest, wanted them to stay.

Wanted to keep them.

Kate looked back, stopped. Couldn't help herself. And, she'd been right: they were her age. All of them maybe a year or two older, but definitely seniors, while she was just squeaking in as a junior. They didn't look like anyone at her school, though, not the way their bodies shuffled along, as if they were sleepwalking as they came out of a small wooden building. It was as if their bodies were moving but they hadn't quite realized it. Eyes red-rimmed. Black circles fading into eye sockets. Haggard. Exhausted.

Seeming to fade right before her eyes, as if all the colors that belonged to them were disappearing.

Kate picked up her pace. Needed to. But she wasn't fast enough, couldn't get far enough.

Because she heard them just fine too.

How they should have watched out for Alice. Kept her partnered up with someone. Given her a compass instead of making her lug the extra water as a joke. Should have stayed put, together, when the fog rolled in instead of hiking through it, even when it covered the ground, the trees, until all they could see was the murky grayness.

And shadows.

Kate squeezed her eyes closed. She wasn't hearing any of this. Couldn't be.

Except she was.

"There you are," her mother said.

With Kate's head bent low—not to mention her closed eyes (probably not the smartest of moves)—she nearly walked right into her mother. Who had appeared before Kate. Silent.

As if she'd materialized right out of thin air.

Kate slid to a stop.

Sort of.

Her boot, barely broken in as it was, caught on some stone—one of the handful of stones actually still in the path. She pitched forward, would have gone headfirst into the rain-soaked, mushy grass if her mother hadn't caught her.

Easily.

Gracefully.

So nothing at all like Kate.

"Oh! There, there. You're all right. So clumsy, my Kate, even now."

Her mom stood there, a hesitant, almost relieved smile on her face even as she righted Kate. How was it possible that they were related— mother, daughter—and yet her mom looked as if she was meant to be there, like as if was comfortable in her body, with who she was?

Nothing at all like Kate.

"I'm sorry. I thought you heard me."

"I didn't," Kate muttered. "Hear you, I mean."

"Oh, well. That's good." Again, there was the smile.

Which was weird. Because her mom was the one person whom Kate never seemed to hear. Not that she told her mom that. Or about the kids at school...every school she ever went to. No, it was better to keep it to herself, better to just try and hide and blend in. Her mom wouldn't understand, not as graceful and beautiful as she was. And besides, not hearing her mom was a good thing, right? Like, maybe she wasn't a freak; maybe all her classmates were wrong about her.

It should have made her feel better.

It didn't.

Not when Kate was finally starting to piece together these little oddities. Starting to wonder...about herself. About her mom.

What if Heather was right?

"I'm...glad we're here," her mom said.

She sure as heck didn't look glad.

"It's been a while since I've been hiking. Maybe I missed it."

Again, didn't look like she missed it.

"Anyway, this will be good for you too. To get away from your friends, from school. Clear your mind."

Kate knew, simply knew, that her mom was lying to her. This whole impromptu trip was a lie. She didn't know how or why, just that it was. Her mom hated the forest. Anything that looked like a tree, even if it was only two feet high, she wanted nothing to do with. And yet, the moment she'd heard about Heather at school (not from Kate) telling everyone how weird Kate was, how she'd overheard a private conversation, one that had been impossible to hear, her mom had swooped on in and plucked Kate right out of there.

And then insisted they come here, to Mount Rainer.

Her mom patted Kate's arms, wiping away invisible dirt or dust or whatever that brown stuff decked out all over the ground was, acting as if Kate were covered in it, when she wasn't.

"And you should be more careful," her mom said. "I don't want you to get hurt. A lot can happen out here, you know."

It was almost as if her mom couldn't stop moving, as if she was nervous.

"I want to go home," Kate said. "I don't like this place."

Her mom's hands finally slowed. Stilled.

"I know, sweetie, I know. It's...a little uncomfortable at first. But I think you need to be here."

"Why?"

"I just...I just know. And who knows, maybe we'll both get some answers and figure out what we want to do next."

Right. As if that wasn't a dodge.

"Sure, Mom, whatever." Kate pushed her away. "As if being in this creepy forest is going to give me all the answers, like how to stop the whole school saying I'm weird. That I'm a freak when we both know I am."

It was the first time, ever, she'd said this to her mom. But she couldn't help it. Her chest hurt as if it was just going to tear right open.

"That wasn't what I—"

But Kate wasn't listening. She was heading back to the car...with or without her mom.

She couldn't stay here. Had to run. Had to get far, far from this freaky forest with its tall, reaching and bending trees. From her mother who knew—knew—why she was weird, why she wasn't normal like everyone else, and still pretended otherwise. Like how Kate could still hear those voices, the teens, whose words slapped and yapped at her steps, just like the soaking, water-moist ground. Mud and upturned grass that clung to her boots, refusing to let go.

Just like the voices.

"They won't tell us, but it's true."

It was a girl's voice, breaking, catching.

"They don't think they'll find Alice. Not alive."

Not alive.

Kate focused on breathing.

Her mom followed right behind her. Her mom, who didn't carry along the slurping, sucking of boots on grass like Kate did.

Or like any normal person did.

God, it was as if she couldn't be fully weird and cool and beautiful like her mom. No. Instead, she just had to be weird and gangly and just...just wrong.

"I know you don't like this, being here," her mom said. "I don't either. Trust me. We will go on this hike and be done with it. It will be good for you. You know I don't like trees much—"

"You hate them."

"Well, yes, but even still, I need to come out here to.. think. I did it when I was your age and it helped me understand."

"Are you going to tell me about it?"

Her mom stumbled a moment, which was a first.

"No."

"Fine. Then I'm going home."

"What I'm trying to say, please, just wait a moment."

She reached for Kate's arm but Kate jerked it away, smooth and graceful, which was so not Kate's normal mode.

Her mom huffed. "Okay, fine, I understand. You're mad. All I'm trying to say is the forest helped me move on, and besides, you're always asking to get away from the city, and—"

Oh my God! She just didn't to get it.

"What about that girl?" Kate asked.

"Girl? You mean Heather? Honey, I'm sure it was just a misunderstanding. She probably didn't realize just how close you were and I'm sure it was embarrassing, what you heard, to say the least. She'll forgive you once she realizes you only had her best interests—"

"I'm not talking about Heather!"

Kate stopped, kicking up clumps of dirt, and faced her mom. She snapped her hands on whale-shaped hips (thanks to the butt-ugly jacket). She just...just wanted to scream at her mother to actually listen to what she was saying.

To just tell her the truth already.

There was something weird about her. About this forest.

"Alice," Kate snapped. "I'm talking about the girl lost in the woods. Her name is Alice. You know, the girl who disappeared right before her friends in some strange fog? With shadows. Who those rescuer-guys aren't sure they can find. What if something like that happens again, huh? To me?"

"Alice?"

Her mom's had gone pale. Her face. Neck. Even her hands were bone-white.

"Where—where did hear that?"

"From over there...." Kate jerked her head to the command center.

Her mom followed the movement, eyes widening further.

She must be tracking the distance, calculating, trying to understand what Kate was saying....

Then she saw a brief moment of horror—no, fear—cloud her mom face.

"Are you telling me, that...that you could hear them?"

Oh, God. Hadn't she learned to keep her mouth shut? Hadn't school and Heather and everyone before taught her anything?

"I mean," Kate muttered, "I just overheard it, when I was passing by."

"Katherine Silver. Can you hear them?"

Kate's shoulders shot back. Back taut and straight. "And what if I could? What would you do then? Tell me the truth? Explain why everyone, even my closest friend, thinks I'm a freak?"

"You're not a freak. There's nothing wrong with you."

Except her mom closed her eyes. Shivered.

There was a sudden gust of wind. Cold. Biting. As if it had been carried right on down the slopes of Mount Rainier to slice through this small glade, this small opening in a forest that wasn't happy...as if that unhappiness had actually come even further, as if across a great, great distance.

And yet...it was this forest, this one right here, that didn't want them here, didn't want Kate here. She didn't know how she knew, she just knew, right down to her bones. Because...she was different.

"Mom," she whispered. "You know, don't you? You know what's wrong with me."

But her mom didn't answer. Not really.

Not like Kate expected anything else.

"There's...there's nothing wrong with you. And besides, what else would I do, huh? If you were so very different from everyone else? I would go on. We'd go on. Together. Just like we're going to do with this hike."

"That wasn't what I asked."

"I know."

Her mom reached out. Tugged one of Kate's free strands of hair, but didn't tuck it behind her ear. Instead, she just left it there...to hang. To cover that slight, delicate tip of her ear, barely different than anyone else's, but enough.

She didn't meet Kate's gaze.

"This is the only way," her mom said. "Trust me."

The only way.

Her words hummed in Kate's chest. Followed her. Licked at her boots the moment her feet finally touched that winding, half-eaten path—which her mom had the nerve to call a "trail." She glanced back at the visitor center one last time, at all the those rescue workers, the teens who looked drawn and faded, until her gaze landed on the one-eyed man who was, even now, watching her.

The need to run came over her again. It hit so hard and fast her knees practically buckled. Would have, if her mom hadn't been standing there. Beside her. Digging her fingers into that whale-shaped down jacket.

Keeping her upright.

As if she'd known.

She gazed down at Kate with that same strained smile she'd plastered on since they drove into the park. Since Kate had "told" her about the voices.

"See?" her mom said. Whispered. As if she didn't want to draw any attention. "There's nothing to be afraid of. We'll go on our hike and those boys will find that girl."

Kate doubted it. Just like she doubted her mom—very much—that there was nothing to fear.

A forest with pine trees so thick Kate couldn't see where one ended and another began. Their long, spindly limbs bowing down, deep green moss hanging off branches in long tendrils, practically touching the trail.

"It'll be fine." Her mom patted Kate's shoulder. "You'll see. We'll go on our hike, get some fresh air, and get some answers."

And yet, she still didn't say *what* answers, and Kate knew, without a doubt, that she never would.

At least if her mom could help it.

Her mom trudged into that forest without a backward glance. Her back so straight and tall it was as if someone—probably a tree—were pulling her by the hair to keep her upright, to keep her going. As if the very last thing she wanted in the world was to go in there, yet she went anyway.

Kate had no choice but to follow...and hoped to God they'd be out soon.

Before the forest decided to eat them. Just like it had Alice.

As far as Kate was concerned, this forest really had it out for her.

She tossed her backpack—smudged from top to bottom in neon-green moss, mud, and something that she was absolutely not going to look at—over the second—*second*—giant-sized log that just happened to have fallen right onto the path.

Err, trail.

It was as if the forest really, really wanted her gone. Wanted her zipping out of that park without a second glance.

Except, of course, Kate had no freakin' choice.

She scrambled over the ucky, rotting log. Wished her legs were an inch or two longer, and did her very best to not look at the squirmy, scuttling things as they dove for safe hidey-places under rough bark and broken, moss-drenched limbs. Her pants, of course, caught on one of those branches and took a good chunk of bark with it—along with dirt and white, finger-sized sluggy-looking things, trailing a path of slime—

"Eww. Gross!" Kate slapped at her knees.

Not with her bare hands…that would be pointless.

She used her sleeve instead.

Pushed and wiped—anything to get the things off her. She also did her very best not to scream like a little girl. This was the worst, absolutely worst idea her mother had ever, ever had.

"What's wrong?"

Yes, her mom, who was a good league or so ahead of Kate, barely breaking a sweat and looking as if she'd just gone for a short jaunt in the woods because not a hair from her long, perfectly plaited braid was loose or out of place. She also didn't have any bugs crawling over her pants either. Her legs being the inch or two Kate had needed to clear the log.

"Nothing." Kate slapped at her knees. "I'm fine."

Totally fine. So fine she was ready to go home…even if that meant going back to school. Anything was better than this forest. With its bugs.

With eyes that tracked her every move. Every breath.

Kate shivered, and for once, it had nothing to do with the biting wind that cut down this trail like it owned it. Made those pine needles dance and twist and rustle.

She had no idea how her mom could stand it. Any of it. Acting like everything was A-Okay.

Up ahead, her mom adjusted her own backpack. Took a long drink from her canteen, and then gave Kate a smile. A warm one filled with a ton of relief.

"You're doing great, you know? We're almost done with the loop and then, then we can go home. We don't have to come back."

"Uh-huh. Sure."

Kate plucked leaves, pine needles, and spare chunks of bark from her ponytail. Yeah. Real great. She was a regular Mountain Woman. It wasn't until she pulled out a crumpled maple leaf that she paused. Realized that she'd not only heard her mom just fine...but her mom had heard her.

Kate's head snapped up. Mouth open. Could she hear her mom? From here? And did she...did she actually just tell her mom that she could?

"Mom?"

Her mom stood there, halfway down the trail and nearly out of sight. Face so pale her smile and all that warmth totally gone.

She just looked at Kate...not in horror, but in resignation. As if she'd tried so hard...to pretend, deny Kate didn't know, but in the end, she'd failed anyway.

Kate could hear her and now, well, now they both knew.

"Oh, Kate, I'm so sorry. For all of this."

"Sorry? Why do you have to be sorry? You know, instead of feeling sorry, why don't you just tell me what the hell is going on? You know, like who the hell I am, instead of lying—"

An eagle screamed.

Loud. Shrill. Desperate.

At least Kate thought it was an eagle. She didn't exactly have much experience in this whole nature department. But it sounded—no, felt—as if it was just overhead.

The forest, right then, it...changed. Shifted, became something else, something other. That same other she'd sensed back at the visitor center, listening to the one-eyed guy and his hunt for Alice. The forest, with its pines and deadened summer trees, crept closer. Branches bending. Creaking. A mist, no, a fog slunk around the downed log. Up and over. Kissed her ankles, raising to her knees.

Kate's grip on her backpack tightened.

She couldn't tear her eyes from the fog. So cold. Colder than the snow-heavy wind from the giant mountain itself.

A cold, which felt like death.

The fog touched her chin. Gentle. Inviting. Pulled her gaze upward to the sky.

To see.

Kate stared up into a sea of branches. Sharp, deep green pine needles. They danced and swayed as another cold wind ripped between them. Arched overhead as if they were one wave.

Or more like a hand...reaching for her.

She heard her mom in the distance.

Calling her name.

Yelling.

But it was only a dim hum, and fading by the minute.

The eagle screamed again. Sharper this time.

Kate saw a small opening between the needles, the fingers. Glimpsed brilliant white feathers.

Then, gone again.

But it was enough. Enough to break the cold, cold grip the forest had over her. The cold that had creaked into her arms, legs, into her mind. Into her heart.

She couldn't see her mom. Not the trail. Not even that granite boulder.

"Mom!"

Kate jumped forward. Tripped—over a gnarling, twisted root. One that hadn't been there before.

She fell. Couldn't stop herself. Not even when her hands, braced to catch her on the boot-trampled trail but instead...landed on a blanket of freezing cold fog.

And a soft, bleached field of moss.

Kate's whole weight—and apparently her backpack's—smacked into the ground and onto Kate's poor hands. Hands and wrists that were absolutely not meant to take that kind of pounding. Certainly not the tiny rocks and branch slivers that dug into her palms.

She immediately twisted, rolled onto her side to take the pressure off. Held her hands close to her chest and gazed upward into a world of smoky-gray fog.

No trees towered above her with moss dripping from its branches. No sun, either. Not even wind, or the breath of one.

She swallowed a yell.

Then, a cry.

Not so much because of her wrists (which hurt like something else), but because of where she wasn't.

She lay on a bed of moss. And it wasn't like the kind of moss she'd seen earlier all along their hike. The kind that glared so bright and green it could blind you, or looked like it'd glow when the lights went out. That moss, with its glow-worm feel, didn't look like this.

Not like this at all.

Kate leaned closer to the tiny leafed thing that hadn't a speck of color. As if its color was gone. Stolen.

Its life leached right out, leaving this gray, wilted thing behind.

It hadn't been a dream.

She wasn't on the trail. Not anymore.

She strained to see. To catch even the smallest hint of tree, the trail, or her mother. Nothing but fog. It clung to her hands, slithered into her mouth. Made her breath puff out in white, freezing mists.

"Mom?"

Her voice, quiet, shaky, echoed about the small moss field.

No answer.

Not even the stirring of moist earth drifted to her. Only this gray world stared back at her. Glared at her.

As if daring her to keep up hope.

Her hands brushed the hard, rough dirt and the color-bleached moss. She hugged her knees to her chest. Rocked.

She was alone. All alone.

Just like at school.

Could practically hear Heather, her voice whispering right into Kate's ear. Telling her again, and again, that no one would speak with her or dare be seen with her.

A freak.

Kate buried her head in her arms. Squeezed her eyes closed. Anything to keep out the rolling fog. The faded, gray world.

Anything to keep from remembering, anything to keep the

memory far away from her. But it leached right on out, just like her own color, and there was nothing she could do to stop it. Only relive it.

"How dare you?"

Heather had stormed into the girls' locker room. Brown eyes narrowed, red-rimmed, face blotched as if she'd been crying. As if... she'd been humiliated.

"How dare you say those things about me? About Kent?"

"I wasn't. I didn't—I'm sorry, but I just heard him. At the soccer field with the team and I-I didn't want to not tell you. That he was only using you for, for—"

For sex.

Heather's face got even redder.

"I tried telling you."

But she couldn't. Not when she saw how much Heather cared for Kent, and why would she listen to Kate? The new girl. The one who'd been around only for a few months. So, Kate'd told another of Heather's friends, someone she thought she could trust.

"That's it, then? You just 'heard' him say those things about me? From the stands? Seriously, Kate? You really think I'm going to believe that lie?"

Heather came forward. Slapped Kate so hard in the chest she felt it right to her bones. She stumbled back. The back of her head smacked into a metal locker. It hurt, but not as much as Heather's words.

Those cut deep.

"Or is what he said true? That you're just a liar. Or, are you some freak with superpower hearing?"

Kate didn't answer.

But the fog did.

It pulsed around her, creeping closer. Growing colder. Hummed to her, told her how Heather was no different than her mom. Her mom, who knew there was something...off about Kate.

Knew, and yet, didn't tell her.

Kate buried her head deeper. Felt herself falling further into the fog and not caring.

Why should she?

Why, when the people she cared about most abandoned her?

Wings ruffled. Fluttered.

Kate's eyes drifted opened. Slowly. As if she were shoving, pushing against a current determined to take her far, far from home. Her memory, the day with Heather, held on. Fought to stay with her.

She felt tears run hot down her cheeks.

Actually, it was the only thing she felt now. Her hands, numb. Feet too. Even her heart.

Kate lifted her hands. Even they looked dim. Fading. As if the fog was already workings its way into her. Deeper and deeper.

Was this what had happened to Alice? Was she even Alice anymore, or just some husk of herself, rocking herself back and forth in the gray moss and crying?

Crying.

Just like Kate.

Kate wiped her eyes. Then harder when the tears wouldn't stop.

Another fluttering of wings. Just above her? As if...they were growing more concerned. Desperate.

Kate pushed to her feet. Shoved her backpack behind her. Winced as the small cuts on her palms pulled and burned, and cursed. Well, if she could feel pain, if she could get mad, then she'd get through this.

Somehow.

Every step took concentration. Strength. As if she waded through a swamp of black, sucking, rotting tar—not the springy gray moss. Sweat dotted her forehead, beaded, and then got swept up by the touches of cold fog.

She shivered, but kept going. Focused on putting one foot in front of the other. Followed, as best she could, the sound of wings. Thought, maybe, she heard a soft sob in the distance.

Kate peered, but still just saw waves of gray rolling over moss and long-leafed bushes. No way to even tell if she was going in circles. Or heading towards the trail.

Another sob.

Softer this time.

Weaker.

Could it be...?

Kate turned in the direction of the sound. The fog swirled about her ankles. Became thicker. Harder to see—and that was saying something.

She tightened her grip on her backpack. The strap dug into her palm, imprinting it, helping her focus.

But Heather's words pulled at her again. Yanked her back. Wanted her to sink further into the fog and the mist, to forget everything but how she would never fit in, would never be normal.

"I never want to see you again. You're not welcome in this school, in my home. You should just go. Go!"

"What's worse?" Kate asked aloud, asked outside of her memory. Asked the words she'd been too afraid to say at the time. "That you believed I was lying? Or that I was telling the truth?"

Maybe Heather was right.

That she was different.

A freak.

But that didn't mean she had to give up. Not now.

Another sob drifted to her. Found a crack through that thick, gray fog. Drifted to her, then a rustle. Like leaves bending and parting.

Not Heather, Kate knew, because Heather wasn't here.

"Alice?"

A pause, then...

"Stop. Just stop. Please."

Kate's knees nearly buckled. Relief, so sweet and powerful, nearly undid her. Made her fear want to let loose because she actually wasn't alone in this nightmare gray world.

"Hold on!" Kate called back—or tried to. Her voice seemed lost, muffled by the mist. "I'm coming. Just, just keep making noise."

Any kind of noise.

But Alice heard. And she did.

"Just go away. I don't need to hear anymore. I can't hear anymore."

Alice's voice was definitely faint, but it was enough.

Enough for someone like Kate.

She trampled over moss. Nearly ran into a tree that practically materialized before her, swept up right out of that fog—but Kate was on her toes now. Desperation pulling at her, driving her.

She wasn't alone.

A small glade appeared. Surrounded by a ring of blacker-than-night trees with branches that were bowed so low they were scraping the back of a short, chubby girl...who was curled up in the center.

"Alice?"

The girl glanced up. Her face, her hands, just as gray as the moss. Eyes just as black as those trees. "Are you here to taunt me too? To tell me how fat I am? How ugly and revolting?"

"What? Of course not! I heard you and—"

"Because I've heard it all! Slow and fat. I knew they were making fun of me. Laughing that all I was good for was to carry the water and their stupid bag of Snickers."

A sob broke out. Wracked through her body.

The branches lowered. Bent and twisted. They reached for Alice.

"They thought it'd be funny if I ate the whole thing myself. Well, I didn't! I didn't."

A gnarled, twisted, and forked branch passed right into Alice— then faded, as if they were becoming one.

"Alice, listen to me." Kate took a step forward. Boots crushed the dry, parched earth and moss. "There's nothing wrong with you."

Kate pushed through the dense branches to reach Alice. Snapped and broke any that were dumb enough to touch her.

"There's nothing wrong with you, just like there's nothing wrong with me."

Alice lifted her tear-streaked face. Gazed at Kate as if she wasn't sure if Kate was real. She blinked. Once. Then twice. "What...what do you mean?"

"Who cares if we're different? Who cares if we don't look like the Heathers or the popular girls of the world? Who cares if we're a little overweight or just have stupid-ass, crazy good-hearing that's just seriously not natural?"

A clawed-looking tree limb grasped Kate's arm.

She yanked herself free. Spun.

Snapped it, clean in two.

Kate reached Alice. Stood over her, hands on her hips and mad as all hell. "Me? I'm done caring because if I didn't have these weird ears and weird hearing I would never have found you."

"You...you aren't a memory."

"No. But I am really, really glad to meet you." Kate knelt beside Alice. Held out her hand. "I'm Kate."

Alice, who was still on the ground, blinked up at Kate as if this whole thing was a really cruel joke. But a pink tinge was coming to her face.

Kate really, really hoped that it was hope. They'd need some to actually get out of this creepy-ass forest.

Alice reached up. Took Kate's hand. A hand that was way, way to cold to be natural.

"How did you found me?" Alice asked.

"I heard you."

Alice looked like she didn't believe her. That was fine too.

And, for the first time ever, it was.

"Do you really think we can get out of here?" Alice asked.

"Absolutely."

How exactly they'd get out, well, that was another matter. One not worth voicing right at this moment.

"Can you stand?"

Alice, who'd been out here for a few days, actually looked pretty good. Other than the practically-no-color part. Even her shirt, pants, and jacket had gone gray. As if they were the first things to get bleached of life.

Kate swallowed. Didn't want to think about what would have happened if her eagle hadn't led her to Alice....

"That's right," Kate whispered.

"What is?"

"We just might have some help after all."

Kate gazed into those dark trees with those branches—now starting to sway and bend their way. Clearly none to happy about losing their next meal.

"Eagle?"

Wings arched out. Stretching. Flapping.

But something else answered as well.

Chittering. Creeping.

Kate yanked Alice upright. "Can you run?"

"Yes, I...I'm not very fast. My friends weren't lying about that. About my weight."

"Good. But I won't leave you. No matter what happens."

Kate tightened her grip on Alice. Swung her backpack over her shoulder, but ready to ditch it—or throw it—at any of the creepy crawlers that even thought about coming after them.

"That guy at the visitor center said we should stay put. If we ever got lost."

"That's probably great advice. Normally. But I'm not about to let this stupid forest, or its stupid fog, take me. Or you."

Out of the corner of her eye, she glimpsed dark shapes moving. Slithering towards them.

Shadows.

Wings lurched from a branch. Her eagle? He was above her, this time, definitely above her. She heard him take flight and out...out of this fog?

The hell with it. Freak or not, she was out of here.

Together.

"Come on! This way." Kate pulled Alice after her.

"But how do you know?"

"I just do."

And she did. She could hear.

Kate pushed her sluggish feet against the thick, dim, and gray moss. Running and pulling Alice with her.

Followed after her eagle, heard his wings high above, as if he were leading the way out of this gray, shady world.

She kept her eyes narrowed. Strained to see through the fog... ducked as a branch came into view.

Nearly tripped over another root.

Kate's breath puffed out. Harder this time to breathe. Colder, too. Like the fog, this forest, someone, some conscious, was doing everything to hold them, to mar them down right here, right to this place....

The ground sloped down.

She hadn't seen. The fog, that sneaky, cheating fog, had hidden it from her.

Both she and Alice tumbled down, down. Slid. Fell. Kate's legs slammed hard into the dry, parched ground. She felt the impact roll through her limbs. Alice nearly went down again, but Kate yanked her upright.

They had to keep going.

Moist, rain-touched air drifted to her. Slim snatches of green pierced through the gray.

Nearly out.

But the shadows kept up with them. Darted in and out from the slim, dead trunks of trees. Clawed at them. Taking bits and pieces of them. Life, memory, hope. They didn't let up either. The shadows, and whoever had sent them, trying desperately to convince her that she didn't belong, would never belong in that world with its beautiful and totally normal people.

Kate just ran. Just followed the fluttering, beating of eagle's wings, guiding her. For the first time, trusting in who she was.

Not normal, but different.

Even if her mom had lied. Had kept the truth—whatever it was—from her. But no more. She was done with the lies, done with the pretending. Now, now she wanted answers. After they got out of here alive, that was.

The wind from their running pushed the hair back from Kate's face.

From her ears.

She saw Alice glance up at her. Saw that slight widening of her eyes, which Kate was glad to see were turning to a starling blue. And still, she couldn't help but remember Heather that day, when Heather had confronted Kate and she'd been so very, very angry. And afraid.

As if sensing her thoughts, Alice squeezed Kate's hand. She whispered, a bare breath passing from her lips, "Thank you. However you found me, thank you."

"You're welcome."

Kate's ears, with their slight tip at the ends. Not fully curved, not like most people. It was just a slight difference, but a difference.

And it didn't matter. Whoever Kate was, whatever she was, didn't matter. Being different would get them both home.

It did.

Together, they got back to her mom, Alice's friends, and the search-and-rescue guys. And the one with the single eye, the color that couldn't seem to stick, hazel and blue and then yellow—Kate really just didn't care, she practically flung Alice into his arms. But for a moment, so fast and brief, she swore she thought he grinned at her. A grin that was both joyful and knowing. As if he'd known exactly where they'd been...a world of shadows and mist. She wanted to ask, opened her mouth to demand what the hell was going on—shadow world? Deadly, life-sucking mist?—but then, he and Alice were gone. Simply whisked back to the visitor's center in a throng of over-stuffed jackets and protective rescue workers. Probably an IV and bags of fluids and electrolytes for Alice. And, Kate sincerely hoped, some real food for surviving on her own for so long.

Of course, this left Kate and her mom together.

Alone.

Kate's chest was heaving, as if her lungs couldn't pull enough breath in...the breath that was oh-so-wonderfully warm and filled with life and colors! Sweat dotted her forehead, sliding down, but somehow still freezing cold. She didn't care. She'd made it out of there, and, if she were honest, came out with more than she'd had before.

She reached up, touched the tip of her ear. Yes, she was different, but maybe...maybe different wasn't all that bad. Maybe.

Her mom stood there, her whole body shaking as if she were the one who'd come running out of the shadowy, mist world.

"You came back." Her mom's voice was barely a whisper. "You made it back."

"I did."

"Niflheim. How did this...how can it be?"

Her mom took another shaking breath. Tears slid from her eyes, and they didn't stop, even as she pulled Kate into her arms. In fact, it felt as if her mom was more scared now than when Kate and Alice had stumbled out of the fog.

Kate pulled back slightly. Met her mother's eyes. "You know where I was? You know what happened to me?"

Her mom closed her eyes.

"I want the truth now. No more lies. No more pretending."

"I...I can't."

Kate almost pulled away, almost ran right back into that forest to demand answers from someone, even if it was only a creepy-ass forest, but...her mom held her there, as if she knew.

"But," her mom said, "I will take you to someone who can, who...might know."

"Who?"

"Your grandmother."

Kate didn't bother to ask questions, knew damn well her mom wasn't going to answer them. Hell, she knew only a handful's worth about Grandma as it was, because Mom refused to speak of her. But, if this was the first step to Kate finding answers, to understanding where she'd just come from and what had just happened, she'd take it.

"When?" Kate asked.

"Soon. I promise."

Kate gazed once more into the forest, which now felt innocent, with just the usual mist from the rains that clung to the air, dripping down off pines and branches. That moist wetness of leaves and dirt and life.

All totally normal.

Except for Kate...and what she'd just seen, lived through, and then...found her way out of again.

Normal, but different. The question was: Would she accept it or keep fighting, keep pretending, just like her mom was still trying, desperately, to do?

Honestly, she didn't know.

She just wished she could go back to who she was, before Heather outed her to the whole school, before coming here, and yet...at the same time, she knew she couldn't. Never again. Because what had happened to her, to Alice, in that shadow world—it was real. And someone, for some reason, had been trying to kill her.

Or get her to wake up.

Kate wrapped her arms around her middle and shivered.

HIDDEN IN TRUTH

An Elven Heritage Short Story

The freezing-chill Montana air zipped into the closet-sized grocery store as soon as the glass doors, moving at about the pace of a snail—maybe two snails racing neck-to-neck—creaked opened, and then closed again. All those canned vegetables and peaches, piled almost to that stained ceiling, didn't seem to mind the cold. Sure they rattled a bit, just 'cause they were piled so high, vaguely threatening to toppling over with a loud crash, but that was all.

Nothing at all like Kate, standing there, her poor hands whiter than they'd ever been in her life, clutching her Cap'n Crunch cereal box and truly considering just abandoning it and heading back to Grandma's behemoth truck, a truck that barely ran, but hey, at least it still had heat.

'Cause her simple long-sleeved shirt? Yeah, it wasn't exactly the best protection against late-spring winds, apparently.

Nor were her jeans, especially the holes ripped in her knees.

She was shaking from head to toe, so cold that she'd lost her sense of smell about five seconds stepping outside the truck, and wondering why stubbornness ran in her gene pool...and caused her to leave her perfectly good, new sweater in the truck. Okay, the chances of the sweater actually being warm, and you know, *useful*, were pretty darn slim. But hey, it was a nice shade of pink that really went with her tone, and at least it gave the hope that she might, you know, stay warm.

Not that she'd been prepared for this weather. The cold, how it lingered in the air even after the sun finally decided to creep up into the sky, how it settled in your bones and just kinda hung about all day long.

Seriously, how *could* she have prepared when her mom had literally sprang from nowhere: Oh boy! Let's go visit Montana and meet the grandmother you'd had never met in your life.

(The same grandmother, by the way, that her mom had sworn she was never, ever gonna meet.)

All of which would have been fine, or mostly fine, except for the really cold part, if she wasn't standing there in the cereal aisle, the giant-sized (and camping-sized) boxes of Golden Grahams and Lucky Charms and the nasty, fake-wheat-healthy stuff towering over her, staring at her, practically *begging* that she take it and liberate it from this dusty hole of a grocery store (where they'd probably been parked on the shelves for at least three years). The staring, begging cereal, she could handle.

The boy staring at *her*, not so much.

Kate ducked behind the Cap'n Crunch cereal box. Her loose blond hair fell over her shoulders, the tangles getting worse even as she attempted some kind of secret-spy move. Which was, honestly, really dumb, and if she'd had a half second to think instead of react, she would have calmly set the cereal down, turned, and walked away. But she was not a calm person. She was a person used to hiding, a person forced to hide.

She barely kept from reaching up. From touching that slight tip to her ears.

Different. Always, different.

Just as she'd always hid who she was, something she didn't understand and had no hope of understanding because her mother had refused to speak of it. Even now. Even after what happened a month ago when she and her mom went hiking around Mount Rainier.

Kate had always hidden who she was, that slight difference that followed her no matter where she went, no matter who she met, what county or what state, it didn't matter. She was different and there was nothing, nothing at all, try as she (and her mom) might, would ever change that.

Not to mention how impossible it was to hide the deep blush that had brightened instantly when she saw the boy, standing just down the aisle from her (near the Lucky Charms), and those gray eyes of his instantly zeroing in on her.

And then, not leaving.

Which meant she looked like a blinking red stop sign. The kind found in those upscale housing communities where people needed actual lights because they were "special" and they couldn't just, you know, *read* a stupid sign.

Hoping like hell the boy had moved on, Kate peered around her cereal box.

Nope. Still there.

Still staring, too.

Tall, lanky body, probably around her age—seventeen, maybe eighteen—holey jeans and all. His head was cocked to the side, a small smile tugging at his lips, and...joy practically dancing in his eyes.

All of that would have been kinda fine, if not for the way her heart pounded and her face heated. And there was this pull, a pull from some place deep down, some place she was afraid to even acknowledge was there, that it existed. Because she suddenly remembered that day in the woods, the hike with her mom that had started her on this cold-ass journey to Montana. How Kate had found herself lost in this misty, freezing-cold world. A world of no colors.

Kate gripped the cereal box harder, her fingers bending the cardboard.

She would not remember. She would *not* think about that day.

Instead, she focused on the boy and looked behind her, thinking for sure he was looking at someone else, 'cause that was the *only* time she got smiles like that...

Except there was no one.

Besides Grandma, anyway. Grandma in her floral dress that came to her shins, who didn't even attempt to hide the mud-splattered hiking boots. She didn't have a coat or a sweater on either, but if she was cold, she didn't show it in the slightest. Certainly not in the way she grinned and went about with that booming voice of her, talking so loud the people in the next county could hear.

Now, sure, boys were common in grocery stores, even this one, Lighthome Groceries, which was about the size of a bathroom and still managed to stock floor-to-ceiling what the big chains carried.

Generally, though, boys moved on and did what they came for. Buying Cheetos, hot dogs, beer (though this one certainly didn't like he hit the twenty-one age yet, even the fake-ID age).

But he was still standing there, hands tucked in his pockets, just... watching her.

Which he'd been doing the moment she'd walked in those doors.

Her grandmother, whom she'd only just met for the first time, like, *ever*, and who was making Kate seriously, seriously reconsider her mom's sanity about coming to this back-end-of-nowhere town at the furthest little tip of Montana. You've probably heard of Glacier National Park and Whitefish, a big-old fancy ski resort for the rich (and people who saved big time for vacations).

But Lighthome? Probably not.

Lighthome, a town of like, fifty, that even Google had never heard of before. Seriously. It was that small. But hey, they had a grocery store, at least.

Finally tired of being stared at (and tired of looking like an idiot just standing there and blushing), Kate turned to her grandmother. "Who's that?"

Okay, fine...she *might* still be hiding behind the cereal box.

Grandma, on the other hand, didn't bother hiding anything. Not her obvious stare and certainly not her booming voice.

"Who?"

Grandma wheeled around, floral dress flapping about her scarred knees, boots leaving giant clumps of dried-up mud on the equally stained checkered floor.

"That?" Grandma asked. "That's a boy. I thought you could tell the difference?"

Kate groaned and ducked behind the cereal box so the boy—yes, he *was* a boy—couldn't see her beet-red face. No wonder her mother left as soon as she was old enough: Kate's grandmother was seriously unbelievable.

And this, *this* was the only person who could give her answers about her heritage? Help her fill in the missing pieces of why she was so different, so unusual? What was Mom thinking? This woman was *nuts*!

"Grandma. Stop. Looking. At. Him."

"Why? If you didn't want me to look, you shouldn't have asked me to look at him." Grandma plucked the cereal box out of Kate's hand and put it back on the shelf. "You don't want to eat that. It'll make your teeth rot."

Having lost her shelter, Kate had no choice but to face the boy. Sure, she could have dived behind Grandma, but that really was a bit childish.

Kate's face reddened even more.

Hiding behind a cereal box, however, was not.

The boy, she noticed—and again, *boy* was a relative term here—had his own cereal box in hand. But unlike Kate, he wasn't pretending like Kate was.

Nope. He was still staring right at her. Not hiding it one bit. Not a one.

The boy smiled. The freckles on his cheeks stood out even more, and his eyes were so very gray.

Kate spun around. She didn't smile back.

He was probably laughing at Grandma. As far as Kate was concerned, everyone laughed at Grandma. How could they not? No one wore brightly colored floral dresses, especially when there was snow on the ground. Spring, her mother said, didn't come to the north very often and when it did, it was often late and still cold. Here they were, even a few days into June, and Kate still felt like she needed a sweater standing in full sunlight.

Lighthome was the place her mother had run away from the second she could, really not much older than Kate, and hadn't looked back. Until this week. Or, really, until they'd gone hiking in Washington, at Mount Rainier, and Kate had a strange, not-fun experience involving shadows and mists that were trying really, really hard to eat her.

And the girl Kate had found, and brought home: Alice.

Kate closed her eyes, fighting really hard to *not* remember. It had been her...strangeness...that had found Alice and gotten them back safely again. Kate had thought she'd come to terms with, you know, being different. Weird. But school and a former best friend pretty much refused to let that newfound belief stay safe, and she had found herself hiding again.

What if...what if that the shadowy mist world hadn't actually been real? Hadn't actually happened?

Part of her, well, it was okay with believing that.

Her mom, though, had made a promise and she wasn't about to let Kate live in Pretendville. She'd reached out to Grandma, a woman Kate had never met, and so...here they were. A place with a single grocery store, no traffic lights, and signs strung up along the roads that said "Moose Crossing."

To say the least, this place (and Grandma) were *not* what Kate had expected.

What a way to celebrate her birthday, all seventeen years of being weird.

Grandma was currently putting back all the cereal boxes back, and Kate huffed and snagged the last one before the old hag found its proper place in the aisle.

"Honestly, Kate, there's nothing but sugar in that box. What you need is a nice whole meal with eggs, vegetables, some good uncured bacon. I've still got the pig Earl helped me slaughter last fall. That, dear, is a real breakfast. Not this."

Grandma poked the box, but Kate wouldn't let go.

"I like the sugar." Kate held the cereal out like a shield.

If she'd known grocery shopping was going to be a nightmare, she never would have come. And to think that boy over there watched the whole damn thing. No wonder her mother had given her *that* look right before Kate had dashed to the car for a short grocery expedition.

And, the boy had probably seen Kate riding in that monster of a truck, too, because really that was just her luck these days.

Kate muffled a groan behind her hand. Just fantastic. Trip over, birthday over, she was just ready to go home.

Grandma sighed, but merely gestured for Kate to put the cereal back in the rickety cart. Only a week, Kate repeated to herself. A week. Then they could leave, go back to her weird, miserable life, and then she'd never have to see her grandmother again or this tiny town with the strange boy...who was *still* staring at her!

Grandma picked up her shawl, shook it as if it'd actually do some good, then peered around Kate.

"Oh, that's the Sky boy, James. I think he likes you; hasn't been able to take his eyes off you since we walked in."

She knew it. He'd seen the behemoth.

"Would you like me to introduce you?" Grandma asked.

"No! I mean, no thank you." The fewer people she met, the easier it would be to forget this place.

Still, she couldn't help sneaking another glance. This time, his smile was accompanied by a small wave. God. She'd never live this down. But then the boy, James, put the cereal back, turning just slightly. Enough for her to see.

Kate's breath caught. Her fingers tightened on the cart.

His ears. They were like hers.

Grandma tried to move the cart and when she couldn't 'cause Kate was still standing in the way, harrumphed at Kate

"Ah, I *see*. A good lad. You'd like him. Might have a few things in common, you know, between you two."

No. They didn't. Couldn't.

Kate lifted her hand. She didn't want to; couldn't stop herself. She brushed back her sandy-blond hair and touched her ear, fingers trailing upwards towards the tip, and froze. She closed her eyes, felt the slight tip. Different from the usual nicely curved ears, the tiniest marker that she was different.

Tiny, but gigantic at the same time. A difference everyone seemed to notice. Like her former friends at school and everyone else she'd ever met. Especially when she started overhearing conversations from a distance, which was not normal.

James had noticed. That was why he'd stared at her, but for a different reason.

Could he be like her? Truly?

Kate let her hand drop. Was this why her grandma had wanted to take her shopping? Had she known? Had she arranged it? Kate had no idea. She didn't know this woman. All she knew was what her mother told her, and that wasn't much. And what she did say over the years weren't nice, either. Which Kate was seeing firsthand for herself.

Grandma was hitting in that "crazy" territory for sure. Like, look at that truck!

Kate grabbed yet *another* Cap'n Crunch box from the shelf and tossed it into the cart. She glared at Grandma, daring her to say anything.

"What else is on your list?"

Grandma sighed and, with a small shake of her head, pulled out the cramped, handwritten list. Kate practically snatched it from her. She needed something to do; anything to get that boy and his ears out of her head.

Her mother was wrong. They shouldn't have come. There couldn't be answers here for Kate, just...just couldn't be! Just a town full of crazies and weirdoes.

Nothing at all like her.

The rest of their shopping was fairly uneventful. At least, all Kate had to do was ignore Grandma's ramblings. Now the old woman was going on about the foods she wanted to cook for Kate, from home-made apple pie to the roast duck for Kate's birthday dinner. A duck, apparently, Grandma had shot herself.

Kate's stomach swirled at the thought. God, she wanted to go home.

By the time they'd reached the checkout counter, Kate was sure she could survive. Five more minutes and they'd be out the door. Of course, there was the twenty-minute drive just to get to Grandma's house, but the thought of slamming her bedroom door and hiding in her room for the rest of the day improved Kate's mood. A glorious stack of books awaited her.

They just needed to get to the door.

Freedom was short-lived. As soon as the automatic doors zipped into view, James got in line ahead of them.

Grandma at once become friendly with James and the clerk,

someone scrawny with a fuzz of red on his chin, and went into a long, lamenting speech about the recent closure of Sunset Road. Or something else of that nonsense.

Kate, on the other hand, was glaring at the exit.

Her limbs tingled with temptation. She was quiet; she could make it. Grandma was distracted and when she finally glanced back, Kate would simply have vanished.

Her unusual and unwelcome, err...gifts were good for something. Like sneaking off. Except, when she took a step, James was there with that damned smile on his face again.

"You're Kate."

She wanted to smack him. Who did he think he was? He was ruining her chance to escape.

"So?" she asked. "Who are you?"

"James." He held out his hand.

She just stared at it.

Yes, it was silly. She knew that. She was also determined not to blush again. He was, unbelievably, so much more good looking up close, including short blond hair standing out every which way it wanted.

James shook his hand in front of her face, nearly smacking her in the nose.

She pushed him away. "Stop that."

"Well, it's polite to, you know, shake."

"Fine."

She shook. See? She was polite—when she wanted to be, which was not now, seeing as how she was stuck in Lighthome, which should *really* be named Middle-of-Nowhere, and when all she wanted was to go home and forget everything. Especially her being weird. And different.

James's smile didn't change. In fact, it got bigger.

"You are Kate!"

"Do I know you?"

"Nope, but your grandma likes to tell everyone about her granddaughter. I knew it was you."

"And not because I was trying to set your hair on fire with my super-mind powers?"

James's smile wobbled but he held it strong. Kate wouldn't have noticed if she wasn't so freakishly good at seeing details.

"Of course. That and your scowl."

He imitated her. It wasn't funny.

"Ha. Ha." She crossed her arms and moved up in line.

Grandma, unfortunately, took this as the perfect opportunity to introduce everyone properly, which involved more handshaking and a scowl, this time from Grandma, for Kate to stop scowling. So Kate played nice for the ten seconds before the clerk cleared his throat and James paid for his cereal box. Not that James was paying attention. He was still looking at her.

Of course, when he plucked the box off the counter, it gave Kate a full, fairly close-up view of his ears. This time she really and truly did blush, and immediately turned away.

She was right. They were like hers.

James raised his eyebrows in question. Again, she ignored him. At least, she'd thought she had ignored him, until she realized she was flattening her hair to cover her own ears.

That damn smile of his was back and he winked.

Winked!

Kate raised her foot, ready to stomp on his, when Grandma tossed a Snickers candy bar at her. She fumbled to catch it and by the time she recovered, Grandma was ringing up her groceries. Not to mention the poor clerk couldn't put a tomato into the bag without Grandma's careful direction.

James was safely out of Snicker-bar-throwing reach, and with a final wave and smirk, he disappeared out the door.

Good riddance. As far as Kate was concerned, the whole event had been a disaster. She would stay in her room the rest of the trip. She didn't care how many books her mother had promised her, Kate wasn't going to open the door a single crack.

The ride home in the red behemoth was noisy and painful. Grandma seemed to find every pothole and ditch on this side of the mountains. Didn't seem to mind at all, either, but Kate's teeth jarred and clacked together every time. It didn't help that she couldn't get James and his stupid smile out of her head.

It was stupid, and she'd never see him again.

"So? What did you think?" Grandma asked, glancing at Kate, all smiles and being casual.

Too casual. Kate was too good at sniffing out traps.

"About what? The town? The road?"

Her teeth cracked together again.

"Well, of course, you'd never been home before," Grandma said. She was all matter-of-fact, too. "It's quaint and it's home, at least for me. Not your mother. She never did care for Lighthome."

Or Grandma, but Kate didn't say that. That would be rude. Didn't make it any less true, though.

Kate shrugged. "It was okay."

"Spoken like a true teenager," Grandma mumbled. "Your mother said the same things when she was your age, right before she took off."

Kate glanced up. Could she be, possibly, maybe, getting some answers?

"My age? And what happened? Mom won't talk about it."

And neither, apparently, did Grandma.

"I can see why. Hard time it was, for her. And, well, you're as tall as she was anyway, just a year shy, though."

Grandma didn't meet Kate's eyes, suddenly very concerned about the bumpy road she'd been rodeo-ing on for the last ten minutes.

"Actually," Grandma said, "I wanted to know what you thought of James. You and he probably have a lot in common."

"We don't."

"How do you know?"

"How do you know we do?"

Kate's heart pounded and couldn't help the feeling, as much as she wanted to. She remembered his ears, remembered, too, the feel of hers as she traced the small tip. Just like his.

She felt her face heat and hated herself for it.

Grandma gave her a pointed look and Kate turned a way. Damn it. Her grandmother had *not* just looked at her ears.

"Your mother hasn't told you much about your heritage, and I respect her," Grandma said. "You're her child and it's her right. But there are some things that can't...well, can't stay buried. Specially when the greater world won't let you."

"What does that mean?"

"Your mom tried running. Didn't work out so well for her. Or you."

Kate dug her nails into her jeans. This time when Grandma found a nasty bump, she welcomed it.

"There's nothing special about me," Kate said. "I'm perfectly normal."

Grandma just nodded and didn't say anything the rest of the drive. In fact, it was the first time since Kate had walked into Grandma's shabby, brightly colored home that she'd stopped talking.

Even with the bumping and tossing truck, so loud it was about to shake her teeth loose, the silence nagged at her. Mostly because it was trying to draw her own thoughts into places where her thoughts had absolutely no business going.

A magical gift of her grandma's, at least, so claimed her mother. This was why her mother always stated they could not, and never would, visit Grandma. Nothing good would ever come of it.

And yet, here they were.

In this, Kate had to agree. The last thing she wanted was to think about James, his ears, or about the mist and shadow world that had nearly trapped her before she'd found the lost girl, Alice.

No! She was *normal*. A perfectly normal teenager on a required distant family vacation. Not a vacation. That would mean fun. No, this was a visit and nothing more.

Even if there was someone like James here.

By the time they got back to the homestead and Kate pulled back the gate, locking it behind the truck so the cows wouldn't get out, it was nearly dark. The air had a cold bite to it that Kate wasn't comfortable with. Nothing like their small place in Seattle. Plus, it reminded her too much of that *day*, of that hike in Mount Rainier.

Out here, though, there were stars. Back home there was the distant light of buildings and homes and the echo of honking cars and rumbling engines. Here, there were coyotes, and they sang every night.

Grandma turned off the behemoth and the engine died in triumph.

"By the way, I meant to tell you earlier. We're having company for dinner. Tomorrow."

Kate's hand stilled on the door handle. She didn't want to ask. She wanted to be left alone. Like that was going to happen.

Grandma waited, quiet and expectant. For the briefest moment, Kate lost herself in Grandma's eyes, distant and cold, yet something completely familiar. Something she almost ached for.

Almost.

"Tomorrow's my birthday," she said.

"Yes. All the more reason to invite guests over."

"I don't know anyone here."

And if she couldn't spend time with her few friends back home.... The truth was, she didn't have any. Not anymore, anyway. But the very last thing she wanted was to spend her birthday with strangers and distant relatives.

Grandma patted Kate's knee like she was a good dog. "It's important to make new friends."

She didn't like making new friends. Friends and she never seemed to work out.

"Who?" Kate asked.

"James. His mother, too, if she'll come."

Kate jumped out of the truck. The door slamming behind her was more than enough of a reply. For good measure she slammed the porch door as well, waking the two old Labrador Retrievers from their place on the porch swing. Her mother called from the kitchen and Kate caught a whiff of roasting chicken, something they never had at home, before she stomped up the rickety stairs. Loudly.

Of course, she had to hear about her rude behavior later at dinner. Her mother complained, to which Kate simply pushed around her unwanted mashed potatoes with her fork. At least her mom's attitude switched to Grandma when Grandma announced they'd be having guests over tomorrow. Her mom was *so* not happy about that.

They spent the rest of dinner glaring at each other, which was fine by Kate. Neither said anything when she left the table early or when she stomped back up the stairs.

One more week. Then it'd be over. She'd never come back to

Lighthome. And now that she was here, didn't blame her mom one bit for leaving.

Unfortunately, whatever silence holding back her mom and Grandma broke the minute Kate cleaned her plate and left. They didn't even try to be quiet.

Okay, that wasn't quite true.

Kate leaned against her bedroom door. Their voices were clear and distinct. They weren't yelling; in fact, they weren't even talking loudly. She shouldn't be able to hear them.

But, of course, she did.

She was normal. Perfectly normal.

Her mother, however, wasn't helping.

"What did you do?" Her mother snapped. "I brought her here on one condition—one condition—and who do you invite? I can't believe you did this."

"And I can't believe you haven't told her. Does she even know the stories? Does she even have some understanding of who she is?"

"Of course not," her mother said. "She's a regular child, a teenage girl, and I will not let you fill her mind with your fancies and magic faeries."

There was a sharp slap. Kate's eyes snapped opened. She heard the sound, echoing in her mind, heard it as her Grandma smacked her palm onto the table.

She knew, could hear the difference. Grandma hadn't smacked her mother, but the table. With her bare, open palm.

She shouldn't know that. Shouldn't be able to tell from listening through a closed door up a flight of stairs. What was wrong with her?

"Not faeries. Don't even insult them with the name. You should know better."

Kate heard the scrape of her mother's chair as she stood.

"I knew better than to come back," her mom said. "I shouldn't have, and I shouldn't have brought Kate."

"That's not what you said on the phone. Mount Rainier. Her falling into Niflheim. You think you can deny that? Deny that someone was after her?"

Kate's breath caught. She recognized the name; it was what her mom had said when Kate had come running out of that shadow world with Alice.

"You can no more fight the pull than she can," Grandma said. "You know—better than anyone else in our family, *you* know."

A door shut and the conversation died.

Kate breathed. She shouldn't have eavesdropped. She pulled her knees to her chest. Her grandmother was wrong. There was nothing strange about her. She wasn't different and what had happened in...in Niflheim...that wasn't real. She was just lost in the forest and it was scary with lots of mist and shadows. She'd gotten lucky and found Alice.

That was all.

RIGHT?

Still, Kate couldn't help but feel a slight ache in her chest, the same she'd felt earlier when she lost herself in Grandma's eyes.

She pressed a hand on her chest, forcing the feeling away.

It wasn't until later, after she'd turned off the lights and felt herself drifting to sleep, that she remembered it was something she's seen her mother do a thousand times: pressing a hand to her chest, a sorrowful, longing look in her eyes. And a sadness, one that ran so deep Kate could never see how far it went.

Some time in the night, the coyotes woke her.

Kate's eyes snapped open. No. Not coyotes.

A soft tap on the glass of her window. It came again, faster this time.

Kate scrambled up and peered into the dark. Her heart pounded and she barely heard the rap-tap of rocks.

Rocks? Was someone there?

She wrapped the quilt around her and crept to the window, body low. Not even the boards creaked under her weight. She tried not to think about it, tried not to remember how unnatural it was.

Another ping. Her fingers tightened on the quilt.

She had no weapon, although she could scream. Grandma had

more than enough guns downstairs to hold off a zombie apocalypse or something. At least Kate's ultra-quiet abilities meant whoever was outside her window wouldn't know she was awake, and if she needed to sneak away and get Grandma and her guns, she could.

Carefully, making sure the moonlight didn't reveal her, Kate peered over the ledge. Even with the silver of moon, it was still dark. She narrowed her eyes, letting them adjust to the mix of dark and light. Then she saw him.

James.

Kate sprang from her crouched position and nearly flung the windows open. "What do you think you're doing?"

James paused mid-throw and grinned at her. Grinned. How dare he!

"Good morning, Sunshine."

"What. Are. You. Doing. Here?"

Kate wasn't in the mood. First her Grandma, then her mother, and now this.

"You know what? I don't want to know. Forget it. Go away."

She closed the window, careful not to slam it and wake her mother. Thank God Kate's bedroom was on the other side of the house. There was a slight chance her mother wouldn't have heard.

"Come on, Kate." James's voice drifted to her.

He was whispering and still she heard him as if he were standing beside her.

"I didn't mean to wake you." He paused. "Okay, I did, but that was only because you wouldn't talk to me before."

Kate squeezed her eyes shut. This was why she didn't want to talk to him. Because he knew. Damn it, he knew she could still hear him.

"Just give me ten minutes," he said. "If you think I'm wasting your time or you don't like what I have to say, I'll go. Promise."

She didn't know him. She'd met him for five minutes at the grocery store. Except she remembered his ears, the slightly curved point, so like hers.

Kate couldn't help but remember the conversation between her mother and Grandma.

Faeries.

Ridiculous.

"Kate." It was James. He was still down there, waiting. "Aren't you curious?"

"No."

"Yes, you are."

Kate jumped, startled. He'd heard her?

She swallowed, unable to think straight. He had heard her. She peered through the window, but didn't open it.

"See? You're curious. Five minutes. That's all."

It was wrong and stupid and she should just go back to bed. After telling her mother about the boy tossing rocks at her window.

Kate tossed the quilt down and slipped on her slippers and a warm coat. Then she crept down the stairs.

It was harder than she'd expected. Her mother's hearing was good, but Kate had learned to gauge just how well since she was a little girl. Still. The dogs were a piece of cake, but there was Grandma to consider.

She made it outside without incident, or else they'd let her go and pretended they hadn't heard. It was easier to not think about that. Much easier to be mad at James; after all, he was the one who'd woken her up.

James didn't seem surprised when she rounded the corner. In fact, his lopsided grin grew wider. She grabbed his arm and dragged him away from the house.

"Hey! Watch the shirt. You don't need to be grabby."

"I'll grab whenever I want to," Kate growled.

When they were far enough from the house that Kate was sure her mother couldn't hear, she let go. They stood at the boundary, on the edge of the forest and Grandma's home.

The darkness didn't seem so frightening now even though the woods loomed before her. Somehow, being here with James (and being mad at James) made it much easier to deal with.

"Now." She spun and poked him in the chest. "What are you doing here? Why are you throwing rocks at my window? And how in the world did you get out here in the middle of the night?"

James threw up his hands in defense. "Hang on there! I thought you said you didn't want to talk to me."

Another poke. "You woke me up!"

"If I'd had any idea how rough you'd be, I'd have reconsidered."

"Well, then you shouldn't have come."

James smiled. "Yeah, I can see that. I should have known you'd be like your grandma."

Kate reeled back.

James took the opportunity to distance himself from Kate and her poking.

"My grandma? I'm nothing like her."

"Sure you are. Just because you don't know her doesn't mean you're not like her."

It was absurd. Ridiculous. "Fine. But you don't know me either."

Finally, James's smile wobbled. It didn't quite fall. Instead, it felt as if Kate had stumbled into something else, something deeper. Like the joke she'd made at the grocery store about mind-powers.

"I know you." James met her gaze. He didn't look away. "I've known you my whole life."

She wanted to look away. She wanted to laugh and toss his silly comments to the wind because they were silly. She didn't do any of that.

"Five minutes," Kate said. "Five minutes doesn't quite equal your whole life."

"It was more than five minutes."

The ache in her chest spread, reaching deeper than it ever had before. Kate stumbled back. She pressed a hand against the ache, but it didn't stop. It kept going, reaching for something she didn't want to find.

Deeper. Something her mother didn't want Kate to find.

"Kate. Relax. It's okay."

James was there, kneeling on the ground beside her.

Slowly, so she wouldn't run or scream or back away, he reached for her hand. His hands were warm. The ache lessened, not much, but enough where she could breathe, where she could see.

A cloud covered the moon, hiding what little light it had given off. Kate swallowed. She realized it didn't matter. She saw James perfectly fine and he saw her.

"Who are you?" she asked.

No. She shook her head. She didn't want to know. She tried to pull away, but James held her hand in a firm but gentle grip.

"It's okay," he murmured. "I really have known you my whole life, and I would never hurt you."

She believed him. Damn it, she believed both parts of what he said.

"How can you know me?"

He shrugged as if it wasn't a bid deal in the least. "Dreams. A feeling. We've walked through these woods a hundred times in a hundred different lifetimes. It's part of my gift. That's how I knew you."

"Gift?" A shiver caressed down Kate's spine.

James stroked her knuckles with his thumb. She stared at his fingers, and for a moment, neither of them could take their eyes away from their intertwined hands. Then he looked up.

James's eyes glowed in the night, so gray and beautiful her breath caught. Who was this guy?

"I thought you knew. I thought..." He looked away, though he didn't stop stroking her hand.

She had a hard time concentrating on his words.

"I thought that was why your grandma brought you to the store. I thought you knew."

"Well, I don't know."

Good feelings or not, she was getting a little annoyed the way everyone danced around the truth, whatever the hell the truth was.

"So why don't you just tell me?" she asked.

"I can't. I mean, I can't tell you."

"Is this some kind of joke?" Kate jerked her hands away. "You come here, wake me up in the middle of the night. This is like a bad romance or horror movie."

"No! That's not it at all. Unless, unless you think this is a romance?"

"Not very romantic."

She was determined not to blush. It wasn't her fault his hands had to be so rough and soft at the same time. And it wasn't her fault no boy had ever held her hands that way before.

She was just overwhelmed, was all.

"Look," Kate said. "This is crazy. You're wasting my time. You obviously have nothing special you want to show me so I'm just going to go back to bed and you are going to go home."

She'd have to see him tomorrow, but maybe she could pretend she was sick or something. Her mother wouldn't make her hang out with James, not if she knew Kate didn't like him.

Yes. That was exactly what she was going to do.

James, however, didn't seem to know what to do with her. He'd tucked his hands in his pockets and the boyish charm he'd laid on her was gone. Good. It was better this way.

"No. You can't. Please."

"Go home."

Kate turned. She didn't get far.

James darted in front of her. He was so fast. She'd blinked and he was suddenly there in front of her.

"How did you...?"

"Didn't you ever want to know why you were different?"

She shrugged, trying to act like it didn't matter, trying to pretend her heart wasn't beating as quickly as her breath. He was so close.

"I'm a teenager," Kate said. "We all think we're different."

"But you are."

This time she shoved him out of the way. He grabbed her hands even as she stumbled forward, locking her to him.

"What do you want from me?" she asked, voice breaking. "Why won't you leave me alone?"

"Because I can't. Because every time I sleep at night, I see you. Every night you're there, either you or someone like you. Didn't you want to know why you could hear things, things so quiet no one else could hear? Didn't you want to know why whenever you walked through a meadow, the world stopped? As if the animals there were waiting just for you?"

"Why won't you just tell me?" Kate was shaking now. She tried to pull away but James held tight. "Why won't you or my mom or Grandma just tell me? Forget this cryptic bullshit and tell me."

James pressed his head against hers. She didn't want to think about how his presence comforted her, how her shaking slowly subsided.

"Because you wouldn't believe the stories. Your mother made sure you didn't believe."

"Believe in what?"

She could barely get the words out and even as she did, they were so low, so quiet. He heard her, though. She knew he could.

"Believe in elves," he said.

Kate jerked her head up, nearly smashing James's forehead. He'd been ready for her shock, however, and safely pulled away.

"See?" His smile, no longer joyful, was sad. "You don't believe."

The porch light switched on and the door banged opened. "That's enough, Kate," her mother called. "Get inside."

Of course her mother knew. She'd probably heard the whole thing.

"Well," Kate said, "she was right. There's no such things as elves."

She stepped away and James let her. But his eyes pleaded with her to understand, to believe, to trust. She wanted to press her hand into her chest, to push the ache away until it never came back. She didn't, though.

"They're fairy tales," she said.

"They're real."

Kate shook her head. She'd given him his chance. Ache or no ache, she was going to bed and putting this whole mess behind her. That was exactly what her mother intended for her.

"Katherine Silver. Get in this house."

"I'm coming." She brushed past James. "Good night."

And because he looked so sad, because he'd stirred something she hadn't even known was there, she touched his shoulder. It was a light touch, but more intimate than she'd ever touched a boy before.

A shiver shot through her.

His eyes met hers. Held hers.

He changed before her...no...not quite changed, but adjusted. Shifted. His features shimmered, as if they weren't quite solid, but then James was back.

No. Not back. Different now. Older, sadder. Much, much taller. Long brown hair tied at the base of his neck and his eyes, so piercing in the night.

James lifted her hand to his lips. His kiss rocked through her, and she rocked back. Gasped.

A tiny smile quirked at his lips. "Good night, Kátheryn Silverstar. The journey may be long, but by the time you return, I shall still be here. Waiting."

Kate wrenched her hand free. She stumbled.

James grabbed her before she could fall. The long hair was gone, as well as the older features and the prominent, very pointed ears.

"Kate!" Her mother called, this time more with concern than anger.

Kate didn't care. She couldn't take her eyes off James.

"Who? What?"

James's worry changed to triumph. Joy, pure joy, brightened in his eyes. He carefully helped her to her feet.

"I told you already," he said. "We've met a hundred times."

That wasn't an answer. Not after what she'd just seen or what she felt.

She shoved him away from her. "I'm tired of playing games. Both of you!"

Kate rounded on her mother, who was racing down the stairs.

Her mother froze. "Katherine, don't believe anything this boy says. There is nothing wrong with you."

"At least I'm not the one lying through my teeth," James yelled. "She deserves the truth. It's her life. She deserves to understand why she's different."

"She's not different," her mother hissed. "She's not like you or your mother."

"Or you?" he shot back.

"Enough!" Kate jumped in between them, hands held out. "All I want is answers. No more lies. No more cryptic clues. I want the truth."

"I am your mother and you have no right, young lady, to speak to me this way."

"Fine." Kate put her hands on her hips. "Then tell me why I just saw James transform into an older man with long dark hair and pointed ears. Tell me why I can hear and see better than anyone else my age.

Explain to me what happened that day on the hike, when I came out with Alice and that, that place...*Niflheim*."

"Niflheim isn't real," her mom said. "It doesn't exist."

James stepped in. "It does and you know it. Someone sent it to capture her and she wasn't prepared. You *know* what could have happened and *you* couldn't go in and save her. Not from the shadow world."

Her mother, she went pale. Completely and totally white.

And Kate didn't care. Not anymore.

It was true, all of it. And in her heart, she'd known it. As much as she'd tried to deny it, tried to pretend it hadn't happened, that it wasn't her hearing that had found Alice and got them out again, she couldn't lie to herself. Not anymore.

Tears pricked at the corners of her eyes. She was confused and lost and here were the people who had the answers. Her *mother* had the answers.

"Tell me," Kate whispered, "why I make hardly a sound when I walk. Tell me, Mom, and I'll go inside."

Her mother didn't move. Eyes wide, she shook her head. "I will not, not ever tell you. I don't care how many times you ask or often your grandmother begs, I will not speak of them."

"Who?" Kate pleaded.

Her mother didn't answer.

James did.

"The elves. Our ancestors."

At the very word "elves," her mother huffed. Kate was prepared, ready for the lashing she knew was coming. It didn't matter that she didn't deserve it or that she deserved to know.

Her mother had, and always would be, completely irrational when it came to family and history. For the first time, Kate caught a glimpse of why her mother was this way, though she still didn't understand.

The porch door creaked open, then snapped closed again as Grandma joined them. Why not?

Apparently no one slept up here.

"You will not tell her." Grandma wrapped her hideous shawl around her shoulders. "You've made your point clear on this issue, but that doesn't change a thing. She deserves the truth, just as you did at her age."

"Just because you have stories," her mother said, "doesn't make those stories true."

"No." Grandma nodded. "But these are truth. You have seen the truth in them, just as James has and now, just as Kate has."

Kate stepped forward. She didn't want to, couldn't help but feel reluctance straight to her soul. Part of her didn't want to know. That part wanted to stand by her mother, to deny everything.

She took another step.

It would be a lie, though. Just like the life she was now living was somehow a lie. The choice was hers. They were watching her, waiting for an answer. Her choice.

Or was it really a choice?

It was more a matter of truth.

Kate glanced at James. Remembered the feel of his hands brushing her knuckles, remembered the shadow-man and his lips, so similar, so different. Could she live without knowing?

Try as she might, she couldn't forget that kiss and neither could her body. She remembered the rush of heat and then the sadness following close behind.

"You can't go back," her mother warned. "Once you know, it'll be with you forever."

Kate understood that. She looked at her mother and understood. "Was that why you ran away? Was that why we never came here?"

Her mother's lips pinched. "Yes. And after this, I will never come back. I will go back to Billings and wait for you, *wait* for you to change your mind, to realize you were wrong. But I will never allow this to be part of my life."

The words struck Kate. Hard. She staggered back, surprised at the ferocity in her mother, the need to deny so strong she'd deny Kate.

Grandma came forward, shawl dipping to reveal her purple-dotted nightgown. "Enough, Cian. She doesn't have to decide tonight."

Yes, she did. Kate felt it within herself, felt it within the air.

Certainty settled within her. All her life, it had always felt like they'd been running from something. Her mother, always so distant, distracted, and unhappy.

Kate took James's hand and he let her, though he said nothing. She tugged him forward, up towards her mother and then past her. Kate's focus was on her grandmother, the grandmother she'd never known, the grandmother her mother had tried so hard to deny.

The grandmother who could give her the truth.

What Kate did with the truth was for Kate to decide.

"Tell me," she said. "Who am I?"

HIDDEN IN SHADOW

An Elven Heritage Short Story

Kate crossed her arms, the pale pink sweater her mom had bought her rising up her forearms. The sweater barely pushed aside the chill that even now crept in from the early morning, seeping through the closed windows, under the door. Even in early June, at this northernmost tip of Montana, it was still really, really cold, and sweaters (she'd learned quickly) were a necessity.

Even if they didn't happen to be actual, you know, good quality sweaters (and not just the cute kind).

Still, the sweater and the cold were the least of her concerns. Grandma, on the other hand...

Kate glared at her grandmother's back, and that god-awful shawl with too many tassels and fringes that draped from her shoulders. Grandma, who was bent over the stovetop, cooking sausages and doing her wonderful best to ignore Kate.

The sausages sizzled and one gave a small pop.

Kate willed her stomach not to grumble, even though the sausages happened to smell particularly good. As did those sliced heirloom tomatoes, the pineapple-yellow kind that Kate loved so much (which, come to think of it, how had Grandma known about *that*?).

Maybe her mom had mentioned it before she'd hightailed it out of the mountains, though Kate seriously doubted that.

But even with this...this amazing food that, okay, put her Cap'n Crunch cereal to shame, she was still annoyed—like, *really* annoyed. She'd come here for answers, willingly *chosen* to live with this old woman, a grandmother she'd never met in her life before a week ago. Hell, she'd given up the Internet, of all things, and for what?

All to learn one simple (or not-so-simple) truth: who she was.

Kate's heritage...it was a mystery—to her, anyway. Why she was so damn different than every person who walked the planet (okay, *most* people)?

She couldn't help it. She lifted her hand and traced the outline, the shape of her ear. Perfectly normal...except for that slight tip at the end. Hardly noticeable, unless, of course, you were looking. Unless, of course, you also noticed that she had incredibly good hearing, or the way she moved, silent and quiet, at least compared to most people.

All she wanted was answers.

And instead here she was, fighting a grumbling stomach because within two days of her mom packing up and hightailing it out of Lighthome, Montana, she'd learned nothing.

Absolutely nothing.

She'd at least gotten wise to Grandma's tactics. She wasn't eating a thing until she got answers.

"I want the truth," Kate said.

Grandma hummed to herself, acting as if she hadn't heard. Which Kate knew damn well that she had (crazy-good hearing apparently ran in the family), which only made her grumpier.

"Grandma."

"Such an impatient child. No wonder why your mother kept you from this place."

Kate's back straightened. "That's not why and you know it."

"Still." Grandma shrugged as she dished out a sausage for Kate and one for herself. "She was right, at least partly. All these years of keeping the truth from you? The truth isn't something to be taken lightly, or without caution."

The only thing her mother had been "right" about was warning

Kate that if she stayed, she'd regret it. Stayed here. With Grandma. Which, truthfully, she now did.

"Go get your plate. Breakfast is ready."

Kate did not move an inch. Instead, she dug her fingers harder into the soft fabric of her sweater.

If Grandma refused to give her answers, what was the point in staying?

"She was right to keep me away," Kate growled, "because she knew I'd want answers. Answers which I still haven't gotten."

"See? Impatience; that's your problem. Now eat up. Don't want your food to get cold."

Grandma didn't wait for Kate. She grabbed down two plates from the creaky cabinets, hinges as old and rusted as Grandma herself, and served them sausages and then a really, really good helping of sliced tomatoes to go with it.

And no, her mouth was so not watering. Not in the slightest.

Grandma sat down at the table, careful to keep it steady since one side was a bit unbalanced. She also didn't wait for Kate to sit down, and started digging in. As she did, Grandma tucked strands of her lengthy silver hair behind her slightly pointed ears, ears that were pointed like Kate and her mother's. The only other person Kate knew with ears like that was James. No one else.

She used to feel odd, as if she was different—slightly off from everyone else. Now, it annoyed her. She had been totally fine looking slightly different; in fact, was totally over how her last school experience had a former friend completely turn the whole school against her. Really, she could totally go back to that—could live with it, even.

What she wasn't okay with was Grandma keeping secrets.

Grandma's two Labrador Retrievers, Rocky and Jazz, were sitting nice and pretty beside Kate, a hopeful experience in their big brown eyes. Grandma scowled at them, then at Kate.

The dogs weren't dumb. They knew who slipped them small, yummy treats. Certainly not grumpy old Grandma.

It was a small victory, having the dogs favor her over Grandma (even if it was because of food), but it gave Kate the extra bravery she needed. Let's face it. She didn't want to know why she was different (couldn't she have just been born normal?)…but regardless of what she wanted, she had to know. She couldn't walk away from this, couldn't walk away like her mother had—like her mother now wanted Kate to do.

"You gonna eat?" Grandma asked.

"You gonna give me answers?"

She did, however, sit down. And…much to her disappointment, couldn't help her hands from going and cutting into the sausage, the juice and fat the slipping out, nice and clear and white. Damn, did it look good.

"It's been two days," Kate said. "You haven't given me a lot of reasons to stay."

"Yep. Only two days."

"We had a deal."

Kate had thought it simple and straightforward: she would stay with Grandma and, in return, Grandma would tell Kate the truth—the truth about heritage.

Only problem was Grandma wasn't exactly keeping her end of the deal.

Grandma paused mid-bite, green eyes sharp on Kate. "These matters can't be rushed. I told you in the beginning."

"You told me you'd tell me the truth. The only truth you've told me is you have bad knees, bad gas, and a bad temper during the winter," Kate shot back. "That's not a lot of incentive for me to stay."

"Do you want to go back to your mother? She'd be thrilled. Delighted. You can go now."

Grandma waved her fork at the door, sausage still speared, and the dogs followed with their sad faces. "Go and forget about learning anything of your heritage."

"Maybe I will. I'm certainly not getting any answers here. At least Mom has the Internet."

Disgusted and overwhelmed, Kate snatched her plate and tossed the sausage to the dogs. The dogs scrambled to reach the free food. Kate jumped over them and ran out the door.

To hell with Grandma.

She was tired of playing nice, tired of waiting—waiting for what, she had no idea.

The crisp Montana morning took her breath away, cooling some of her anger. Not the kind of early summer she was used to, even during their latest brief encounter in Seattle. Up here, in the high mountains, parked right next to Glacier National Park, it was still cold in the morning even though it was June.

Which, right now, suited her just fine.

Kate stormed into the forest. She'd never heard of it before, but that was one thing Grandma had been upfront and clear on the second Kate decided to stay: stay out of Alfeim Forest. Kate, of course, had ignored her. She'd gone trudging into the woods anyway. Sometimes daily. Always, though, it felt like someone was watching her.

Which, of course, only made her angrier right now.

A darkness. Or, more like a shadow. It seemed to follow her, floating from one tree to the next. Always out of sight, always hiding in the shadows.

Kate shivered and rubbed her arms.

Silent watcher or not, she hoped the walk would clear her head enough so Kate could at least have a civil dinner with Grandma. Still, it didn't change anything.

Kate had made a mistake. She should never have stayed.

She kicked a small rock and it bounced off a pine tree. Stories. She'd stayed for stories and Grandma couldn't even give her those.

Hooves crushed fallen needles and leaves. Far off, but getting closer. Kate knelt, reaching for a nearby stick. Her exceptional, freaky hearing was good for something.

Like people trying to sneak up on her.

Kate pivoted. Her hand tightened on the branch.

James rode on his horse, Eilan. For a brief moment, the James she'd known for the past two weeks, changed. Shifted.

Kate's breath caught. The older James had returned. Tall and elegant, every movement fluid and radiating grace. His pointed ears drew her attention once again, even as the light brightened.

The vision, as quickly as it had come, vanished.

Kate blinked as she tried to control her breathing, tried to recall what being normal felt like.

James sat straight and tall, his posture perfect even though he rode bareback. He was clearly the teenage boy with short blond hair sticking up every which way it wanted. Not the man from her vision.

Kate dropped the branch and straightened, her leg muscles wincing in sympathy. She had no idea how he could stand that.

"Well, it looks like I was right. You could use some cheering up," James said.

Even though he was still some distance away, he'd known she would hear. Kate, however, clamped her mouth shut. No need to point out their unusual differences.

And it certainly wasn't helping her already fantastic mood. Yeah, let's be reminded about the strange oddities Grandma refused to talk about.

Just what Kate needed.

James, however, simply grinned at her. She really hated that grin.

"What are you doing here?"

"A little bird told me you needed some company." Eilan slowed when they reached Kate, not even needing James's direction.

Kate glared at both of them. "I don't need anyone. Certainly not you."

She stomped deeper into Alfeim Forest, but this time she made as much noise as possible. That small defiance helped her feel more... normal. More human.

James, as was customary, completely ignored her. She heard him slide off Eilan and walk after her, Eilan following obediently behind.

At least James didn't try to speak with her. That was one thing he was good for. He knew when to keep his mouth shut and leave her alone. Though that didn't hold completely true, as he was still following her.

She really, really wanted to be alone.

Kate closed her eyes, wishing for James to disappear. Which didn't work.

She sighed, letting her shoulders relax, letting her mind drift. She tried to forget Grandma and James, forget why she'd even come here to the northernmost part of Montana.

It was strange, out here surrounded by trees. Here there was no sounds of cars driving past, only birdsong and the quiet clop of hooves.

Kate stepped over a fallen log without opening her eyes. She knew it was there, could sense its presence.

Another quirk of heritage, a heritage—and a quirk—her Grandma thought unnecessary to explain.

Kate's temper drained away and in its place she felt a distant ache. She wiped a tear with her sleeve, hiding it from James. She wasn't crying.

"Hey. Are you okay?"

"Yes." She made a point not to look at him. She didn't care if it was a dead giveaway. "Can you please go away now?"

"No. You need a friend."

It hurt, hearing him say that. A friend. Kate had had friends, back home where she lived with her mother in Seattle. Or had lived.

She imagined her mother was already packing their things and looking for the next place to drift to. Without Kate. A city, though. Always a city...or what counted for them here in Montana. Her mother mumbled something about Billings a few times.

That was her mom's choice, though.

"I don't need friends," Kate said.

"Liar."

So what? What did she care what he thought? "Look, I just want to be alone right now."

As usual, James ignored her. Sometimes she thought she was talking to herself. "Did you have another fight with your grandmother?"

Kate shrugged. When didn't she fight with Grandma?

James merely sighed. "What is it with your family? First your mother, now you. You don't seem to get along with your grandmother at all."

"It would be fine if she just told me the truth. Instead she keeps all these 'stories' and so-called truths to herself," Kate snapped. "I didn't turn my back on my mother just to let Grandma lie to me."

James and Eilan had caught up with Kate, and Eilan gave her hand a friendly nudge.

"You know, she might have her reasons." James lifted his hands in defense when Kate scowled at him. "Hey! I'm not saying her reasons are right, but maybe if you understood where she was coming from. Maybe she's scared."

"Scared? I'm the one who's not human."

"Sure you are. You're just...different."

Different.

"That doesn't even come close to how I feel right now."

"Okay. How do you feel right now?"

"Besides angry?"

"Yeah. I figured out anger, what else?" James had his cheery smile back on. An infectious smile.

Kate felt herself smiling in return, then quickly caught it and shoved it aside. James's smile widened.

Jerk.

"For starters," Kate said. "I'm scared. I'm confused and frustrated."

"Nothing new. Everyone in my class feels that way right now."

"Yeah, but I bet they can't see quite so well in the dark or easily listen to hushed voices through a closed door and down a flight of stairs," Kate countered.

"True. And neither can they talk to horses."

Kate froze. "Talk to horses? You can do that?"

James halted mid-step and gave her a sheepish look. "Ah, well, you can forget I said that."

"No way!" She darted in front of him. "You can talk to Eilan? Why didn't you tell me?"

Now he was keeping secrets. Just like everyone else. The thought hurt, a lot more than she would have expected.

"Not. Not exactly." He wouldn't meet her eyes.

"You mean Grandma told you not to tell me."

Her temper was back full force. The woods, once comforting, now felt like they were pressing in, like it was some trap and she'd walked right into it. Again.

"You're just like all of them," Kate spat. "I thought I could trust you."

"You can trust me. Come on, Kate, don't go. I meant what I said earlier about being your friend."

Kate glared at him. Eilan nudged James, pushing him forward a step. She met Eilan's dark eyes, sensing the intelligence there, hidden beneath the surface. Waiting. He could hear her. He understood.

Tears filled her eyes. She wasn't about to cry in front of them. Either of them.

"James Sky." Kate lifted her chin, willed herself to hold on a bit longer. To not cry now. "Stay away from me."

She didn't wait for his reply and ran deeper into the woods. This time she didn't fight the tears. The farther she ran, the more they came. Her tears wouldn't stop, so she didn't stop running.

Finally, out of breath and sides heaving, Kate collapsed against an aging ash tree. She didn't know where she was or how far she'd gone. She also really, really didn't care.

"Tomorrow," she aloud, "tomorrow I'm calling my mother. I've had it. I'm done with this, done with their lies. I'm going home."

"A true shame. We will be sorry to see you go." A voice echoed around her, so deep that it stole the rest of her breath.

Kate scrambled to her feet. She tripped over a gigantic root—how she tripped was anyone's guess, seeing how it came up to her chest.

She fell, her butt smacking the ground hard. She scanned the area, looking for the old man who'd spoken. She saw no one.

"Who's there?"

No answer.

Heart pounding, Kate pulled herself into a crouch. If she had to, she could run. What had she been thinking, coming out here by herself?

There were crazy people out here. People like her Grandma.

"I have a gun."

She didn't, but that was what her mother said she should say if she was alone. She was really alone now.

Kate peered into the dense forest, trying to distinguish between shadows and lurking shapes, shapes that could be a person intending her harm. She saw no one, but the hairs on the back of her neck stood.

She knew, without a doubt, someone was watching her.

"James? Is that you? I mean it. I don't like playing games."

"James?"

The voice was stronger now, closer. Kate strained, but couldn't pinpoint where the voice came from. It was all around her, like it resonated from the trees.

"I have not seen the lad today, though he should be along shortly enough."

Kate squeaked and whirled around. She'd heard him that time. Right behind her.

No one was there. Only the old—and extremely tall—ash tree. Kate peered into the branches, but spotted only the movement of birds.

James wasn't there, nor anyone else. The branches swayed again, but she didn't feel a breeze. What was going on?

"Who are you? Where are you?"

"Right in front of you, Little Eagle." A branch creaked, bending towards her as if bowing. Then just as slowly, it straightened again.

The tree had moved. It *moved.*

The world blurred and Kate sank to the ground. She didn't care how muddy her jeans got. She'd let Grandma yell later. Right now, she had to figure this out.

She was talking to a tree.

The tree had no face that she could see. In fact, other than a few swaying branches, it was just like any ordinary tree. Except, he was talking to her.

"A tree? I'm talking to a tree?"

"Why yes. Who else in the middle of Alfeim would you speak with?"

"Ah, I'm not sure. This is the first time, you know, I've spoken with an ash tree before."

The tree gave a large sigh as if a wind bowed its trunk. *"It is a great shame. I've forgotten how enjoyable it is to have someone to talk to."*

Kate stood and circled the tree. Yep. It was a true. No old man hid on the other side playing a trick on her.

She couldn't quite figure out if that was a good thing or a bad thing.

Holy crap. She was talking to a tree!

"Grandma, she, uh, forgot to mention this." Among other things. Like, a lot of other things.

"Yes, well, she's not one for sharing, which I don't think is quite right. I'm in need of company too, after all. Not right at all."

Kate had come back around, a little unsteady, though she told herself it was because she had a hard time moving in the mud. Her wobbly legs had nothing, nothing whatsoever, to do with the talking tree.

"Who are you? Do you have a name?"

"The last I can recall, I was called Yig. Yes, Yig shall do nicely. I have not needed a name in some time as few with the gift have visited me. Not even young James has the knack of it."

That's right, she remembered. Yig said he knew James. "How do you know James?"

"How could I not? Every time the boy rides through, he tramples the forest. Hasty, impatient boy. I think, though I'm unsure, all boys are like this."

"I suppose." Her legs still felt weak and since she and Yig weren't going anywhere, she climbed onto one of the three giant roots, the same one she'd tripped over.

"So, who are you exactly?"

Yig tilted his tall crown, as if getting a better look at her. *"I am myself. An ash tree, older than most, older than any I've yet to meet."*

"And there are others like you?"

The thought was a little disconcerting, especially as she'd had to use the ladies restroom in the bushes a few times. Kate tugged her knees closer to her chest, careful not to tip off the root and fall over.

At least she hadn't gone by this tree. Maybe he could give her a map of which bushes to avoid?

"Hmm...there are some, though most have taken root and changed, becoming like other trees in Alfeim. None are like me, though."

Like him? She wanted to ask why he was different, but thought that might be prying a little too much. Maybe Grandma would have heard of Yig?

"I myself was sleeping for some time, but then I felt a change in the wind. I didn't feel quite so sleepy and there were new footsteps in my woods."

He leaned closer, a small branch pointing at her. *"Perhaps it was you."*

"I haven't been here very long." She'd woken up this ancient tree? Kate didn't know how she thought about that.

She was still trying to adjust to the talking tree concept.

Yig sighed. Several leaves floated to the ground. *"And you'll be leaving. I wish you wouldn't. It has been so very long."*

To be fair, she now knew a talking tree; that was a tiny bit more incentive to stay.

"Couldn't you talk to someone else? You said there were others."

He stretched up his branches, reaching for the bright, warm sun. Every branch and joint seemed to creak and pop.

"Ash. There were others, but they've gone now."

Her mouth had gone dry. "Who were they?"

"The light ones."

The elves? The ones Grandma and James hinted at but wouldn't tell her about?

Somehow, Kate managed to take a deep breath and keep from jumping to her feet. She had to stay calm. If she pushed, he might not answer, and she needed answers.

"Who are the light ones?"

"Your kin, of course, though distant kin now."

Her kin. Not her human kin. Kate brushed the tips of her ears, unable to help herself. A thrill raced through her. This could be her chance.

She lowered her hand. For the first time, her ears didn't bring a feeling of loneliness, the knowledge that she was different. Instead, she felt anticipation.

"Would you—would you tell me about them?"

Yig watched her for several moments and Kate did her best not to fidget, to hold still and let him see how desperately she needed to know. And she did. She needed to understand who she was.

"Please."

"It is not my place, but you are too old by far to be without them. Yes, too old, and you've awoken me all on your own without knowing."

Kate inwardly groaned. Great. Another cryptic guide refusing to give her straight answers. What was with these people?

Err...now a tree.

"I asked my grandmother and she won't tell me anything. I even saw James...." Kate's breath caught. Part of her didn't want to remember, and the other part...

Kate blushed.

James had been older, but not just in age. Ancient and distant. The vision was brief, but it had been enough to show her something else was going on, something she didn't understand, but needed to.

Somehow, complaining to a tree felt good. He, at least, had to listen. There wasn't exactly anyone else he could talk to, and he couldn't slam the porch door and stalk around the house.

"Perhaps it is because she's afraid you're not ready."

"I am ready!" Kate leapt to her feet. "I'm tired of her and my mother keeping things from me and if you're going to do it, too, then I'll just leave."

"Peace, Little Eagle, it is merely a thought." He reached out a branch and it caught on her shirt.

Kate crossed her arms and glared. "Tell me why you keep calling me that. Tell me what that means."

Yig seemed to lick his lips, two giant clumps of moss pressing together. Was he irritated with her already?

"It means that you have come to teach. It is the way of the eagle, and the eagle sits quietly inside you."

Yig parted his mossy lips and harrumphed. *"Or perhaps not so quietly. But nonetheless, it is there."*

Kate highly doubted the teaching bit. Especially since the whole reason she'd stayed was so Grandma could teach *her*.

"Grandma said my ancestors were elves. Did you know them?"

He nodded. A small nest, empty of any eggs, dangled from his boughs, a few twigs holding it in place. The image looked so comical, so unreal. Kate couldn't help but touch his rough bark, running her hand down his trunk. He was real.

Grandma said the elves were real.

Hope stirred. So hard and fast, it nearly knocked her off Yig's root seat. "Will you tell? Please?"

"The light ones. This is the name they called themselves and they were the

ones to name the forest 'Alfeim'. A good name. They came from across the veil, traveling through the mists. I do not remember from where, only that it was not here, but they came and made Alfeim their home."

In the end, there was little to tell. He didn't remember much. He remembered their voices, like the softest bird songs, and how their presence had brightened the forest. They were fair, with hair the color of moon and sunlight and nightfall. All, he said, shone with light. They were tall with pointed ears, much more pointed than Kate's.

Like James. The James she'd seen in her vision.

"Are they still here?"

It was the one question Kate couldn't get her Grandma to answer, the one she needed to know. Not even James would tell her.

With a slow sadness, he shook his crown. *"A darkness came over the forest and their songs became silent. I have not seen a light one since. Though, it is difficult to say."*

He rested a branch on the place Kate had touched him. As if remembering. As if saddened.

"They have not walked among the trees but their presence still remains. Distant, faint, but here still. Even now."

Kate licked her lips. "Could they be people like me?"

"The light ones'," he said, *"touch on their human kin is faint. All of Alfeim can still feel the light ones, so something of them remains yet."*

"Could I find them? Maybe I could learn more if I do."

Yig pondered this and finally sighed. *"I do not know, Little Eagle. I believe they've gone. Something of them remains, but I do not believe they do."*

"Oh." Her shoulders slumped.

It would have been so much easier if she could have seen an elf for herself, ask him or her a few questions, pull on their ears and make sure they weren't glued on.

Talking trees, however, was a pretty good indication something was going on. Magic, even though she had never believed in magic.

"Well, if they're gone—and it sounds like they left a long time ago —where did I come from? Wouldn't their gift or whatever go away?" She gestured towards her ears. "Unless my ancestors inbred or something."

"Forest wind, no." Yig huffed. *"Nothing of the sort. Though you and your*

kind are nothing like those who came after the light ones, their human-light chil-dren, the gift of magic strong in them already. Not always true and different at times, but strong."

This wasn't helping her understand a thing. "So, you're saying I'm a descendant from a light one, an elf? I don't believe it. Elves aren't real. They don't exist."

"They don't anymore, but they used to." He leaned forward, patting her shoulder with his leaves. They scratched and stuck to her shirt, but he was trying to be nice so she stayed put. *"And even if they don't exist, you still do."*

"Yes, but I don't know who I am. That's why I'm asking." And he couldn't remember anything. Great. The one ancient tree she found had a long-term memory loss.

"I'm tired of being lied to and tired of cryptic answers. Can't you just please tell me?"

Yig leaned back and she felt a deep sadness within him. Now she'd upset him, too. Man, she was really on a roll.

Kate reached out and brushed his trunk. She didn't mean to hurt his feelings. And it wasn't his fault she was so damn frustrated.

"I'm sorry. I'm angry with Grandma. I'm angry with my mom for keeping all this from me."

"It is the way of your kind, and I easily forget. Perhaps...perhaps this is what you shall teach me, Little Eagle?"

He turned his large crown, looking past her. *"And here, the boy comes."*

James? Kate groaned. He couldn't take a hint. Why couldn't he leave her alone?

"Will you return to speak with me?"

"Yes, of course."

Kate peered through the trees and saw the distinct shape of Eilan heading towards them. Could James sense her? Was that one of his odd abilities?

If so, it wasn't one she liked. He always seemed to know where she was. Jerk.

Yig stretched again, this time it was more like a yawn. *"Then I will leave you to the boy. So much excitement, too much for one day. Now hold your promise. I'd like to see you at least once more before you leave."*

Kate turned away from James. Something about Yig, about his words, pulled inside her. She touched his rough bark again. The smell of ripe, sweet bananas drifted around her.

She closed her eyes, willing him to know she'd keep her promise. She would come back. She wanted to come back.

"Thank you," he murmured.

Kate jumped back. He'd heard her. "Yig?"

He was asleep. She could feel him slumbering, could feel the weighty breaths as he exhaled from the roots to the top of his crown. Asleep, but still there. She could feel him.

Kate knew, without a doubt, that if she were to come here years from now, if she decided to throw away this life and who she was, she'd still be able to find him. She could walk blindfolded and know exactly where he was.

Maybe she didn't need that tree map after all.

"Kate!" James slid off Eilan and ran towards her, not even caring that he'd simply dropped the reins.

Kate immediately pressed against the tree, just in case. She had no idea how well-trained Eilan was and she hoped he wouldn't run towards her like James.

She was fairly certain if she got to chose between a talking horse and a tree, she would pick the tree. A tree couldn't step on her toes.

James practically yanked her from her tree's safety and squeezed her against him. Tight.

"James. I can't breathe."

He didn't let go, though he did loosen his hold. "I'm sorry. I thought I'd lost you. I thought you'd run into the woods and got lost."

"Why would you think that?" She managed to wiggle one arm free, but James's grip was tighter than she'd expected. "Calm down. I didn't go that far."

His grip tightened. Only for an instant, but that was all she needed. He'd thought something had happened to her. He wouldn't have thought that. Not if he didn't have a reason.

Kate shoved him away. "What is it? What aren't you telling me?"

"No-nothing. I'm just happy to see you."

"No you're not. You're scared to death." Kate poked him in the chest. "You're pale, your eyes are dilated, and you've known me barely two weeks."

James made some kind of soothing motion at her, but it had the opposite effect. She wanted to dunk him and every person who'd lied to her in the nearest lake.

"I'll leave," Kate said. "I swear I'll leave right now if you don't tell me."

If she couldn't boss Grandma, couldn't make a tree remember, she was damn well going to bully James.

"It can be dangerous out here, for people like us."

She didn't buy it for an instant. "Not for you. You've been coming here for years, you said so yourself."

"Well, yes...."

"And you told me we're descendants from elves. I'm sorry, in my limited knowledge—very limited, thanks to you and Grandma—it seems like the forest would be our home."

"For some of us." He didn't meet her eyes. "Not everyone."

The hair on the back of her neck rose. She told herself it was the wind or maybe Yig waking up, though she knew he was fast asleep. "What do you mean?"

"You're not the first, you know." James dug a toe into the soft dirt. "Your mother didn't fit in, so she left. There have been others like her, and they left the area too. And they had families."

"What does that have to do with me?"

He shrugged, made a big show of patting Eilan and snatching the fallen reins. As if the horse was going to go somewhere. Yeah, right.

"Some of the families came back, you know, like you. They wanted to know who they were."

Just like her. Different. Afraid. Never quite sure why they were different.

Yes, she could imagine others coming back, even staying behind while their mothers continued their lives without them. Why? Because they needed to know, needed to understand.

"You still haven't answered my question. Why are these woods not safe?"

Part of her didn't want to know the answer, didn't want to admit she was deep in the forest and the only person she had for company was James, his horse, and a sleeping tree.

James shook his head, eyes pleading with her to let this go.

She wouldn't. No way in hell.

"Please don't make me say anything."

Kate stepped closer to the tree. She was now even with where Yig was rooted. Still, James said nothing, though his face paled.

Another step. She wasn't leaving without answers.

"Kate. Please. Let's just go back."

"Not until you're honest with me." Her eyes narrowed. "Fine."

Kate turned. She was done with these games. Anger drove her, made the fear diminish, though it was still there.

James was afraid, which meant somewhere within she should at least be wary. She wasn't. Right now she was pissed off.

Kate took off.

Eilan darted in front of her. Kate screamed, jumping back. She stumbled into Yig's trunk, scratching her elbow. James yelled for her. Kate kept screaming because Eilan kept coming closer.

"Kate. Warm winds, Little Eagle." It was Yig's voice, a small whisper in her mind. She felt the trunk warm as if he were reaching out, trying to comfort her. *"You are safe."*

Kate stopped screaming. James rushed over and pulled her into another hug.

"You can't, damn it, Kate! It's too dangerous." They both fell to the ground in a heap.

She was crying. Damn it. Why was she crying?

"Eilan!" James said something, spoke in a language Kate had never heard before. It was beautiful. He said only a single word, too fast for her to hear, but familiar.

Somehow.

Eilan calmed and Kate calmed. She felt so tired all of a sudden, tired and lost and ready to go home. She hugged Yig's trunk, pressed her cheek against the scratchy bark.

She wanted all of them to go away. Go away and leave her alone.

Her mother had been right. She should never have stayed here.

"Kate," James whispered. He tucked a strand of hair behind her ear, fingers slightly shaking.

"Why are you upset? You weren't the one who nearly got trampled by a half-mad horse."

Something flickered in his eyes, gone before Kate could even see what he was trying to hide. "Eilan's not half-mad and he didn't try to trample you. He wanted to stop you."

Kate slowly released Yig and winced when she felt the rough scratches. They stung something fierce. "Well, I wouldn't have fallen if it wasn't for him."

"You might have been lost if it wasn't for him."

She froze. Waited. James waited with her, worry for her disappearing to plain evasiveness. Maybe it was something in the water. Everyone in town seemed to have the knack whenever these strange stories came up.

James's shoulders fell. "You're right. I'm sorry. You wouldn't have run if I told you, and if you didn't run, you wouldn't have gotten hurt."

She crossed her arms over her chest and got comfortable. They weren't leaving until she was satisfied.

"I'll make a deal with you. Tell me about the forest and I promise not to go in by myself." She remembered her promise to Yig. "Not go past this tree by myself."

"Promise?"

She nodded. "If you promise not to sic your horse on me."

"He was only trying to protect you."

"Tell me about the forest and I won't ask why I keep seeing an older vision of you."

James's mouth dropped open.

"I also won't ask about the strange language you just spoke in." Today, anyway. "Yeah, I'm not that stupid. I noticed. So. You gonna tell me or do we have to do this again?"

She was fairly sure neither she, Eilan, James, or Yig wanted a repeat of her attack and subsequent screaming. In fact, she was fairly sure if there were any other talking trees, she'd woken them up. They probably wouldn't be very nice.

"Your grandma's gonna be pissed," James murmured.

They headed back to the house. James wouldn't say anything until he was sure they were leaving the forest.

"It's the forest." James scanned the nearby trees; what he was looking for she had no idea. "It's not safe for those who reject their heritage. Over the years, kids have gotten lost and were never found."

"Come on. That happens in every forest. People do stupid things. They go off trails, get stuck in a storm; they get lost and aren't prepared." Kate didn't see why this should mean she should be afraid, she or anyone else, for that matter, heritage or not.

He shook his head. "You don't understand. We don't get lost. *Ever.* If a hiker went missing, we could find them, even if they'd fallen into the deepest ravine. Kate. We could find them."

She couldn't help but think back to how this adventure all started: her mom's stupid instance on going hiking near Mount Rainier; the lost girl, Alice; the shadow world that had trapped them both...and how it had been Kate, and her hearing, that got them out again. That... and the overhead flapping of wings.

Her breath caught. Could all this really be true?

Of course, there was the talking tree to consider....

Eilan nudged her shoulder from behind and she merely batted him aside. Fear trickled in, but not because of the horse. Though he was much too close for her liking.

"You're saying people like us have a gift? They can find anyone in the forest?"

No wonder James always knew where she was. Great.

"That's right. Anyone, anywhere, any place. It's part of who we are, though some are better than others."

Her stomach tightened. If James could find her anywhere... She glanced backwards, in the direction she'd run. He'd been afraid. Afraid he couldn't find her.

"People who are lost, they really are lost. That's what you're saying?"

"Yeah. Lost. No trace, no sign, no body. And some of us are the best trackers in the world."

Kate rubbed her shoulders, trying to ward off the sudden chill. Eilan was there again and she scooted closer. He was big, tall, and scary, but right now he felt a hell of a lot safer than being alone. His large (very large) size comforted her.

She'd been alone up until she'd met Yig. Then, like a spoiled, unreasonable child, she'd nearly run deeper into the forest.

This wasn't any easier for James. He could barely look at her.

"I don't know why your grandma didn't tell you," he said. "Heck, I don't even know why your mother didn't warn you about the woods."

"She did." In fact, she'd warned Kate several times on the drive over, which of course meant Kate went and did it anyway.

"Yeah, well, if they'd told you the truth, you wouldn't have gone. It's dangerous, but you couldn't have known that." He scowled. "It shouldn't be dangerous, not for you and not for anyone with the heritage."

James told her more, but it wasn't very helpful. They had never seen what took the kids (and who "they" were, Kate couldn't get out of him). The kids simply went into the forest and never came out again. Sometimes, adults were lost, too.

"Most times, people are like your mother. If they survived until adulthood, they learned to stay away. They don't go into the woods." James kicked a small rock. It bounced hard off a tree but it didn't seem to cool his temper. "They may not believe, but they're not stupid, either."

Kate's steps slowed as they neared Grandma's house. She didn't want to go back, especially when James was actually telling her things.

She decided it was best to play fair and hoped if she told him about Yig, he'd keep telling her about their heritage. When Kate had finished her story, it took her a few moments to realize James wasn't following.

She and Eilan paused. James stood in the middle of the trail, mouth open like a fish, blinking at her as if she'd spouted horns or something.

"What's wrong?"

James tried to close his mouth, and made some kind of strangling noise.

"Huh," she mumbled to herself. "I guess Yig was right. Talking to him was a rare gift."

"You don't understand." James caught up with her. "Agh, it makes me so mad your mother didn't tell you anything. Listen. The last people who could talk with trees were the elves themselves, them and their nearest descendants, the first half-elves. But with...with Yig?"

Again, James swallowed. He still looked rather peaky. Maybe he wasn't feeling well?

"That's silly," she said. "So why could *I* talk with him?"

"Don't you understand who he is? A legend from the old tales, from many of them, in fact!"

She just looked at him.

"You don't know, do you?"

"I think we've been over that."

"He's, well, he's the World Tree. Yggdrasil. Roots and branches and all that connected to hundreds of worlds. You've never heard of him before? And yet...you could talk with him?"

She still just looked at him, this time as if she thought he was spinning one big-ass yarn.

The porch door opened, then slammed shut. Grandma stood there, hands on her hips, a slight bulge in her ugly fuchsia apron. Probably a gun.

"Because the kids of our line are special, that's why," Grandma snapped. "And what the hell do you think yer doing? Runnin' out in the woods by yourself. I know your mother told you better."

"Yeah, well, she also told me not to stay here with you. Remember?"

James waved at Grandma. "Good evening, Mrs. Silver."

"Don't 'good evening' me! You should have known better, letting her go off by herself."

James paled. "It wasn't her fault. She didn't know."

But of course, Grandma was determined to pin this on Kate.

Kate gritted her teeth, listening to the tirade, and suddenly realized where her mother got it from. Then she wondered if she got her temper from her mother—who must have put up with the same damn thing.

"Look. The only reason I ran out in the first place was because of you. And surprisingly, I managed to learn something."

Kate stepped forward, all her frustrations, all her pent-up anger rolling to the surface. Damn Grandma and her damn secrets. "James told me about the forest and the missing kids."

Grandma stilled. Her gaze didn't leave Kate. "Did he now? And did he tell you also what happened to your mother?"

"No."

He hadn't said anything about her mother. She wanted to look back, wanted to demand answers from James, but she didn't want him to see how it hurt.

Her mother? Had her mother seen the darkness?

"James," Grandma said, "I think it's past time for you to be getting on home. She won't be going out again. Not tonight, anyway."

Kate didn't hear him leave, barely even felt Eilan's tail as it slapped her shoulder on his way by. None of that mattered. "What happened to my mother?"

Grandma's lips pinched.

The phone rang, but neither moved. The ringing stopped, only to begin a moment later.

"You better get that." Grandma opened the porch door for Kate, shooing the two dogs outside. "It'll be your mother."

Kate literally had to bite her tongue to keep from asking. If Grandma knew, if she was right, it probably had to do with another of her heritage "gifts".

Sure enough, when Kate answered, her mother's shrill voice yelled out of the receiver. Kate held the phone as far from her as possible, which wasn't very far because Grandma had an ancient, corded phone.

At least it was a touch-tone.

A minute passed before her mother's shrill lowered to an acceptable level and Kate forced herself to answer. "Mother. I'm fine. Why are you calling?"

Kate watched as her Grandma kicked off her boots in the mudroom, then put down an old revolver on the kitchen table.

She didn't seem concerned about what had happened—or that Kate's mother was on the phone. Nope. It was back to work, scrubbing dishes and tossing the dogs whichever scraps she didn't want to save.

Grandma saved everything.

"You're not listening to me," her mother said.

"Sorry. I had a busy day."

There was a short pause, and Kate wondered if her mother was trying to figure out how to say whatever it was she wanted to say. They'd never been good at this, mostly because Kate wanted answers to things her mother didn't want to talk about.

Gee, like her heritage. That must also run in the family. She glared at Grandma.

"Why did you go into Alfeim?"

Kate sat up straight. Her mother knew. How?

"How many times have I told you? If you ever listened to me, for once in your life—"

"Mom. How did you know I was in the forest?"

Silence.

"If you want me to listen, you better start being honest with me. You and Grandma both. And if neither of you are going to tell me, fine. Then I'll ask Yig."

Another pause. From her mother, anyway.

A plate slipped from Grandma's fingers. The shatter echoed through the house, followed by Grandma's cursing.

Mom recovered first. "Yig. Who's he?"

"A tree. I met him this afternoon. He was rather nice, very polite. He'd like me to come back and visit with him. James told me he was called the World Tree. Know what that is? Plan on telling me, *Mom?*"

"Put your grandmother on the phone."

"Fine." Kate passed the phone over, stretching the cord as far as it would go.

Grandma took the phone, soapy hands and all. "Don't yell at me. You were the one who didn't tell her the danger. Well, of course I didn't know she could talk to trees. Did you? Is that why you never let her come here?"

Kate leaned against the kitchen counter, arms across her chest, and glared.

"It's not my place to tell her and it's not my story," Grandma snapped. "It's yours. No. You didn't prepare her. Light ones protect us, you never even told me you hadn't given her *any* education, let alone the proper one."

Light ones?

Kate's breath caught. That was the name Yig had given the elves.

Grandma paused, letting her mother speak, but she held a hand over the earpiece, providing just enough distance Kate couldn't hear a thing.

Damn. She pushed away from the counter. "This is getting old. Tell me what's going on or I'm leaving."

Grandma met her eyes and studied her. She gave a curt nod, then interrupted her mother and hung up. "It wasn't my place, but seeing how neglectful your mother's been, I suppose we'll have to amend that rule."

Grandma wiped her hands on a dish towel and tossed it into the sink. "I'd hoped she would least tell you about the forest and her...well, history."

"She told me to stay away."

"But not why."

Grandma's anger filtered away and for a brief moment, Kate saw her grandma, old and tired, though her spark burned bright and true. Still, she was old. She looked it right now.

Kate's stomach fluttered. She couldn't help but fear the answer, the answer she'd forced Grandma to give.

"I need to know. If there's any hope at all of...of this." Kate gestured to the house. "I need to understand."

"You do. It's just that...it's that your mother had said the same thing once."

One of the dogs sauntered over, as if sensing Grandma's sadness, and nudged her hand.

Grandma smiled and gave Jazz a friendly pat, though the sadness was still there. "Your mother needed to understand, when in truth understanding was the last thing she wanted. See, Alfeim has a way of knowing these things, even if I couldn't see the truth for myself. The forest, it knows and it acts. Your mother...I don't know how much James told you, but your mother is lucky to be alive."

Kate wanted to ask how, wanted to demand the answer. She held her tongue. This obviously wasn't easy for Grandma and whatever she was reliving, the memory wasn't easy, either. And the last thing she wanted was for Grandma to close up. And if she was anything like Kate's mother, she would.

Grandma gestured to the front porch and they went outside. The sun was no longer climbing in the sky and the world seemed to dim, bit by bit. Kate hardly noticed. She'd never realized how good her eyesight was until she'd come here, until she looked out into the dark forest.

Her chest tightened, but not in pain as it had done all her life. It had flared when any of her strange heritage gifts manifested herself, like a physical ache telling her something important was missing.

Now, she felt something different. A pull, perhaps? Not an acceptance, but there was something there.

"I know that look. You can feel Alfeim."

Grandma sat on the porch swing, her bones creaking. She really did look old. Nothing like the vibrant and well-aging woman Kate had first seen. She didn't like that, though she hadn't the faintest idea why. It wasn't as if she was starting to like her grandma or something. The woman was too infuriating for that.

"Did Mom feel the forest?"

After a moment, Grandma shook her head. "I don't believe so, though she said otherwise."

"And Alfeim knew?"

"It knew."

Kate sat on the bench. It rocked gently. "What's out there?"

"The trees, the birds, the earthworms." Grandma shrugged. "They are all individual beings, yet one and the same as well. They are the forest and in this forest, something of the old ones remains."

Grandma sighed. "When the elves lived here, their touch went deep into the land, so deep the land still remembers. It doesn't like being lied to."

Kate could easily relate. Being lied to sucked. "What happened to my mother?"

"She went into Alfeim, though only along the edge. Someone...well, he'd convinced her to try, to prove herself to me. Your mom, though, she wasn't a fool and didn't go deep. A fool nonetheless, though. Alfeim knew her heart, and she'd thought herself safe."

Grandma's sadness settled over her again. It was only Kate and Grandma and the memories.

As Grandma spoke, it was as if Kate were there, running alongside Grandma, into the storm searching for her daughter. Rain pelting every which way, pine needles slapping at her arms, her face. Lightning streaking and flaring across the deep black sky. Fear clutched at her, nearly dragging her under. The mud, so thick it nearly trapped her.

"By the time I arrived," Grandma said, "I don't know for sure... Alfeim wouldn't answer me and I couldn't sense it in that moment. Your mother stood there frozen, unable to move, staring at nothing and everything."

Kate leaned closer, desperately needing to know. "But you saw something."

"Her shadow. Your mother's shadow. It was there, it was angry, and it was coming for her. And I did something I never thought I'd do. I defied Alfeim. I wouldn't let the shadow take my daughter, regardless of whether or not she believed. And Alfeim...it let us go. Both of us."

Grandma rubbed her wrinkled, tired face. "But you see...it wasn't Alfeim that attacked, not exactly."

"But, you just said it was the forest?"

"You want simple, Kate, but our world, our stories, are anything but simple. Tell me, did you see a shadow following you today?"

"Yes."

Kate's heart hammered. The shadow had followed; even when she'd met Yig, she'd felt it near.

"I thought it was the forest," she said. "Was that what...was that what attacked Mom?"

"It is, but it is also more."

Grandma folded in on herself, as if losing more of her youth, becoming the old woman she hid so well.

"It was *your* shadow," she said finally. "The part of your spirit tied to their world. The part of you that is still tied to your great elven ancestors. Any descendant once connected to the elves by their bloodline carries that spirit. For some, that connection is weak; for others, it is stronger. And for a select few, well, let's just say they carry a bit more of the elves with them."

"More?"

"Souls reborn." Grandma waved a hand. "Not many, though, are blessed with *that* gift."

In that moment, Kate thought of James, of how his image would... change. Shift. How she would see someone else in him, both one and the same, but different.

"James," she whispered.

Kate knew darn well that Grandma heard, super-awesome hearing and all, but she kept quiet about it. Instead, Grandma focused on the shadow. Kate let her. For some reason, she didn't *want* to know the truth about James.

And why he was so connected to her.

"For those who don't believe," Grandma said, "like your mother, that spirit changes. Because of who we are, because of our heritage, how even now, thousands of years later, we're still connected to their magic, the forest changes that spirit. It becomes a shadow."

"And makes our shadows real?"

"Real enough to be angered. To pull us fully into that world, the world where all the stories are real and just as dangerous. The world of magic and elven descendants, the one that people like your mother *can't* accept."

Grandma closed her eyes, her forehead creased. "I knew the moment you and your mom came to Lighthome, the very moment you crossed into Alfeim."

"How?"

"Alfeim told me."

Kate tried to speak, but couldn't find her voice right away. She'd seen it, seen the forest. The very thing that had attacked her mother and nearly dragged her into its depth had simply...watched Kate.

"What did it tell you?" she asked.

"That my daughter had returned."

Grandma still had her eyes closed. The dogs had come back, sitting there with their best loving expressions. This time they weren't able to reach Grandma. For this, they couldn't comfort her.

Grandma wrapped her shawl tighter around her, knuckles white and wrinkled. She looked so old.

"But I knew it wasn't speaking of your mother."

LATER THAT NIGHT, Kate couldn't sleep. She huddled in her bed, covers drawn tight around her.

She half-wished James would throw rocks at her window. She needed the company. But she was also afraid of opening the window, of looking out into the darkness and meeting the gaze of the forest. A gaze that was on her, even now, watching her through the very same window.

The whole evening had shaken her to her core. And when Kate had asked about Yig, or Yggdrasil, as James had called him, Grandma had gone even more pale. (How that was possible, Kate hadn't a clue.)

Grandma's explanation had been simple…and yet, anything but simple.

"He…he must have come over with them. With the elves. Or maybe he was already here, his roots connecting our worlds through the veil. Which means…that those stories are true. How hadn't we known, after all these years?"

She shook her silvery head.

"And he spoke to you, of all people, Kate. The daughter of one who'd turned away from us and our heritage."

"Yes, but *who* is he?"

Grandma had then told her a little of Norse mythology, how the World Tree connected all worlds, from the one of the gods to some ice world and then of course, the world of men. She'd also mentioned that Yggdrasil's destruction had to do with the end of the world.

"Those, of course," Grandma went on, "*are* just stories. Or they were until you showed up and started talkin' to him. Truth is, we don't know much because the elves aren't around to ask, and what knowledge we did have was lost over the years—war and what-not, disagreements, you name it. But I tell you now, Kate, you keep your knowledge of Yggdrasil to yourself. It's safer for all that way."

The realization, about her shadow, about Yig, had shaken her as much as it had Grandma. And Grandma wasn't the sturdy, everlasting woman Kate had thought she was. Not a rock. That thought frightened Kate as much as Alfeim did.

She didn't want to be left alone, didn't want to be alone with all these questions and uncertainties.

Fear, however, had a strange effect on Kate. When the glowing light of her clock showed 2:00 A.M., another feeling took over.

Anger.

Why should she be scared? She hadn't done anything wrong. Hell, she'd come here to learn.

And this stupid forest had the nerve to watch her? To try and scare her?

No way. Kate wasn't gonna play.

She tossed the covers off her bed, pulled on warm socks, and stormed down the stairs. She paused long enough to grab her boots and jacket, and strode into the night.

This was her choice. Her acceptance.

When Kate reached the edge of Alfeim, when she felt the darkness within, the weight of the forest gazing at her, Kate glared right back. "I'm not my mother. Don't you dare treat me the way you treated her."

Kate took another step, then another. Now she was at the barrier itself. The boundary where her grandmother's land and the forest met.

The darkness pressed closer.

"I'm not my mother, but that doesn't mean I don't believe her. About you. About all this. I'm not believing any of this on faith."

A branch snapped to the right of her. She didn't look. Her heart hammered from fear and anger, both mixing until they were one and the same.

Kate took a deep breath. She might become lost like the others, but she wasn't about to live in fear, wondering when Alfeim would take her.

"I believe you're real. I believe you have a consciousness and that you can hear and understand me."

Something brushed the side of her face. The wind rolled through the trees, rushing past her, creating a wind tunnel so strong she stepped back. She felt something, or someone, all around her.

Kate didn't look. If she did, Alfeim would win. It would have her.

"What I don't know is if this life, this place is right for me. You might not be happy about it, but it wasn't right for my mother."

Kate crossed her arms. "Now. You can make your choice. You can either give me space and let me decide in my own time, or we can have this out right now. Either way, I'm tired and I'm going to bed."

Nothing stirred in front of her, though she still felt the presence... everywhere. All around her, and even, in some ways, inside of her.

This was her choice. Hers and hers alone.

Not her mother's, not Grandma's.

Hers.

Kate breathed in, lifted her chin, and faced Alfeim Forest. Except there was nothing there. She was alone, alone with Grandma's house before her, the dim porch light a shining beacon in the chill night.

Alfeim's weight, its presence, didn't leave her. It didn't stop her either, nor did it make itself known even as she turned around and trudged back to the house. It was watching her, though, as she opened the door and saw Grandma sitting on the stairs, both dogs pressed against her. Grandma's eyes were red and she clutched her quilt to her chest.

"I thought the forest had taken you."

"Not yet, anyway." Kate closed the door. "I said it could, but it didn't."

"Fool, fool child." Grandma closed her eyes. She was shaking, and though Kate wanted to reach out and tell her it was okay, she didn't.

This woman was still a stranger, grandmother or not.

Kate stayed where she was. "I thought it was more stupid to stay away. That's hard to do. It's kind of...big."

"Aye, it is at that. Used to be bigger, too, back in the before times when the elves were its caretakers."

Kate didn't move. "What was it like in those days?"

"It's hard to say. I wasn't alive, and those we could have asked are gone or have forgotten. Alfeim was wilder, happier, I think. The trees liked to talk and any traveler who'd listen would hear a marvelous story or two."

Kate thought back to Yig and wondered if he'd been one of those trees. She thought he might. He did like to talk.

"The stories," Grandma said, "say the trees used to sing. Every night you could hear the singing leaves and branches while the wind picked up the tune and carried it across the mountains. Some say it sounded like wind chimes."

"Have you heard it sing?"

Grandma blinked, as if realizing Kate was standing there and they were having one of those "must-not-speak-of" discussions. Kate thought it best to stay still. Hopefully Grandma would fall back into whatever mood she was in and tell her more.

"Nah," Grandma said. "I'd never heard the singing. Neither did my mother or grandmother. I told you, it was a long time ago. Alfeim has gotten quieter each year. Little by little, its falling asleep. Whatever the elves had done to wake the trees is fading. Or maybe it's the trees who are fading."

"And new trees," Kate whispered. "Young trees who may have never met the elves."

Trees that, in a way, were not much different than her. Born with strange or slightly unique gifts and yet having no concept or context for what it even meant.

Grandma stroked her chin and Kate relaxed. Grandma's hand was steady now. The danger had passed.

If Grandma wasn't worried about the forest, it meant Kate really didn't have anything to worry about. At least for now.

Later, after Kate had finally coaxed Grandma to bed—after promising she wasn't going into Alfeim—Kate lay in her bed. As she drifted to sleep, exhaustion and dreams taking hold, she thought, in the distance, she heard wind chimes.

HIDDEN IN FIRE

An Elven Heritage Short Story

HIDDEN IN FIRE

The thick layer of pine trees huddled so close together that the night's shadows seemed to blend from one to the other, never-ending, always continuing. A chill breeze rustled through the branches, the pine needles swaying and almost whispering, like a quiet song that you could almost hear, almost understand.

Or, maybe, that was just her.

Kate moved easily through Alfeim Forest. The fallen, dried-up leaves crunching under her tennis shoes as she walked. Not silent, not like her grandmother would be or even James if they were the ones sneaking through the forest at night.

Kate, though, Kate was an entirely different story.

She shivered, the pale pink sweater her mom had gotten her doing absolutely nothing to ward off the end-of-spring chill, a chill that didn't seem to want to let go regardless of the fact that they were straight-up hitting early July. Up here, in the northernmost tip of Montana, just a stone's throw from Glacier National Park (not that she'd been there yet, herself), spring was short and laughable, especially on the whole "warming up" factor. Summer, she'd been warned, was hot as hell. At least during the day. Night, though, night was its entirely own entity.

At least, from what she'd been told.

She hadn't had a whole bunch of experience with this weather thing in Montana. She'd been here only three weeks and already she was really, really out of her depth.

And quite possibly in big, big trouble.

It didn't matter how hard Kate looked, pleaded, or shouted, her shadow remained stubbornly hidden.

No shadow, no answers from Grandma, certainly not about her heritage.

She reached up, the gesture so automatic, she barely noticed. How she traced the edge of her ear, felt the slight tip...such a slight difference, but enough to set her apart from everyone else, everyone she'd ever met.

At least until coming to Lighthome. Until meeting her grandmother, and James.

Kate brushed strands of her long, dark blond hair over her ears—also an automatic gesture—and shivered.

Not because of the chill, that wasn't exactly bothering her much, but being out here, in the forest...still not sure what was going to happen. But at least the dim lighting wasn't a problem; not a big one, anyway. She didn't *need* to watch where she was going as she moved through the dark forest, didn't need to take care with each and every step like any normal person would in the middle of the night, how they'd be stumbling about totally blind and helpless in the middle of this big, dark, foreboding forest.

A forest that also had a bit of a temperament issue.

Kate slipped past hidden logs, paused long enough to push a pine branch out of her way. No, she no longer needed a flashlight or even the moon, so that must mean she was getting the hang of this. Maybe not like Grandma or James, but...she was making progress. Right?

She could see just fine—or close enough.

Every day her low-light vision—at least, that was what James called it—improved. It wasn't perfect, and maybe if it had been, she'd have spotted her damn shadow already and this sneaking out wouldn't be necessary.

Well, not like she'd actually stop sneaking out. She needed time away from her grandmother to think. To breathe. To figure out what the hell was wrong with her life.

Or more to the point, what the hell she was.

Kate still had no idea how she exactly felt about *that*. Of being the descendant from some strange, mythical, elf-like beings her grandmother was (mostly) keeping her lips zipped about. Which was why Kate needed to find her shadow—her spirit. It had been only a few days since her shadow (manifested via the not-very-happy-with-her forest) had nearly devoured Kate.

She'd won a small respite from the forest—Alfeim Forest, to be exact—and she wasn't about to push it too far.

All of which meant she needed to scour every pine tree, pine cone, and rock looking for her stubborn, and very uncooperative, shadow.

Maybe, just maybe, if she found her shadow, the part of her that was still tied to the long-gone elves, almost like a spirit...an elven spirit, according to Grandma, a piece of them that, even over all these generations, were still connected. And then maybe, once you found her elven spirit, she wouldn't feel quite so lost. Like maybe she would know what to do instead of just stumbling around, making all these mistakes.

She wasn't holding her breath—but she was determined to try.

Pine needles and scrunched-up leaves littered the small game trail. When she stepped there was no cracking or crunching sound. Just silence.

Creepy silence.

Maybe if a little luck dusted her way, she might even sneak back in the house without Grandma waking. Or, more specifically, if Grandma's ultrasonic special hearing didn't kick in and pull the old hag from whatever mythical dream she was having.

With her newly acknowledged gifts—not, she reminded herself, oddities that labeled her as "weird"—she spotted Grandma's house before passing the last tree cluster bordering Alfeim Forest.

Not like that was difficult, considering Grandma had turned on every porch light, gaslight, and lantern in Montana. The place lit up like a Christmas tree in mid-July. She might as well have put up a sign, "Kate—get your ass home now!"

Two months ago, when Kate's life had gone all topsy-turvy (with her nearly getting trapped and eaten by yet *another* forest), her mother had finally taken Kate to meet the grandmother she'd never seen or talked with before...and she then soon found herself living with said grandmother. Regardless, Kate had never been the type of girl who forced her mother to stay up late, watching the front door, fretting about what time it was or why Kate hadn't called. In truth, she needed actual friends to do that sort of thing and she'd only just turned seventeen, and being as weird as she was to everyone remotely close to her age, she hadn't exactly had a whole lot of opportunities for late nights, either.

But as far as Kate was concerned, she hadn't hit the "late" mark yet. Meaning it was before 2:00 AM.

Apparently, Grandma had other ideas.

Kate peeked through the shelter of pines and groaned. Maybe she'd be better off searching for her uncooperative and elusive shadow than going to bed.

Grandma lorded over the front porch, shotgun cocked, barrel out, waiting for Kate to return so she could shoot her ass.

Kate snorted. If she'd known what living with Grandma was like, she might have taken her mother up on the one-time, no-turning-around offer: leave with her and forget their silly little heritage.

Or stay and put up with Grandma.

At least her mother understood reason, whereas Grandma shot first and asked questions later.

"Quit sneakin' around there, Kate," Grandma growled. "And get yer ass back inside."

Of course she'd heard Kate—probably had know from a mile out that Kate was here.

"I will if you put the shotgun down."

She might have just met her grandmother only three weeks ago, but it hadn't taken long to realize just how trigger-happy her grandmother was.

Grandma frowned, her face easy for Kate to see from this distance. She could also make out her grandmother's slightly pointed ear as she tossed her gun—please God, let it not be loaded—onto the porch swing.

Adventures in living with an eighty-year-old crazy grandmother who also believed in elves, fairies, and whatever sort of mythical nonsense she could come up with.

Kate crept from the safety of her tree. Of course, if she hadn't met her grandmother, Kate wouldn't have met Yig, an ancient, talking ash tree who happened to like spending time with her.

Her shoulders slumped and she trudged the rest of the way. Definitely not the normal life she'd once dreamed of.

Grandma glared down at her, arms crossed, bright pink shawl wrapped around her as if she were naked underneath it or something. "Where the hell have you been? Is this how you treat your mother? Sneakin' off into the middle of the night?"

"No." She glared right back. "I didn't need to 'sneak' off when I lived with Mom."

Grandma's eyes did the furious-narrow thing and Kate could have sworn they flicked once to the shotgun.

"So you're startin' now? Is this something you learned from James? Trying to worry your old grandmother?"

"Yeah. Like you're old," Kate murmured.

Murmuring didn't matter much. She could have whispered the words, to the point where the breeze wouldn't have stirred, and her grandmother would still have heard.

"My tree rings are just fine," Grandma snapped. "I'm as old as any other old lady in the town."

Except those other old ladies couldn't swing a cane like Grandma. If Grandma used a cane, which she didn't.

Kate, however, took the diplomatic approach and said nothing. She merely crossed her arms and waited. If Grandma was as old as she claimed she was, then she'd be yawning any minute and it'd be off to bed.

Grandma didn't move. She leaned closer, as if knowing Kate's exact tactic, and Kate wondered if her mother had tried this back in the day. Anything was possible, especially considering her mom never talked about life here.

"What were you doin' out there?" Grandma nodded to the forest. "You know it's not safe."

She shrugged. "It's safe enough now. The forest isn't trying to eat me."

"You sure 'bout that?" Grandma spoke casually, almost taunting, but there was something underneath the words, something that made Kate step back.

James had told her she was safe. Her shadow—and the forest—had accepted her, had accepted her interest in her heritage. Had he lied?

"I was looking for my shadow."

"Your shadow. You went looking for your shadow. Tonight." Grandma's face paled. "You'd best get inside."

Kate paused, long enough to glance behind her. Nothing. No shadow, not even the moon's light. Nothing to explain why Grandma looked...so scared.

Best not to mention the previous nights. No point trying to unhinge her.

Grandma grabbed her gun and locked the door behind them. She even used the hundred-year-old, rusty deadbolt, then shooed Kate into the sitting room and then turned off all the lights... which, was weird.

Instead she headed straight for the fireplace.

"Grandma? What's going on?" Kate sat on the couch, though she had to scoot one of the old Labrador Retrievers, Jazz, over to make room. "What's wrong?"

"It's a good night for a fire, don't ya think?"

"Sure. I guess."

Since Kate had come to stay with her grandmother, she'd never seen the fireplace lit, even though there were always logs ready, and the small twigs she knew would help get the fire going. But as Grandma got to work, Kate's arms tingled.

It was a soft brush, the tiniest touch against her senses. She sat up straighter. A month ago, the feeling would have passed right over her. Not now. Not after everything she'd learned so far.

"Grandma?"

Grandma hunched over the fireplace, hands moving in the air. Kate didn't see a match or a lighter, not even a little gas knob in the brick to explain the sudden—and she did mean sudden—blaze of flame.

Kate jumped back and smacked into the sleeping Jazz. The fire roared up the chimney, flames stretching higher than she'd thought possible.

"Fires are good for these nights."

Grandma rose, her knees cracking. Besides her white hair and wrinkled face, there was no other signs of her age. Grandma blazed like the fire.

Kate blinked back tears and knew something was going on here. Too bad she had no idea what it was.

"Fires are good, because they help us see beyond the veil."

"The veil?"

"A boundary, if you will, separating our world and theirs..."

Grandma waved her hands towards the flame.

"What world?"

Grandma sighed and suddenly her youth, the light shining from her, dimmed. The older woman was back, though her shoulders drooped a bit more than they had when she'd waited on the porch, shotgun tucked neatly in her armpit.

"In truth, if the stories are true, the veil separates all worlds. Don't matter which you believe in, Norse or Irish mythology or the half-dozen others that got trampled on and beaten out through the long years. The veil is still one and the same. It keeps our world separated from the others. Spirit worlds, magic worlds and, important to our story: the world our elven ancestors came from. The world your mother ran away from."

Hope flared through Kate. "Tell me."

"That, dear, is part of the problem. I don't know how."

Grandma picked up her shotgun from where she'd laid it, cracked open the barrel and took out the two shells.

Holy shit. It *had* been loaded.

"Well, how about you starting at the beginning?"

After all, didn't all stories start there?

Grandma snorted. "Not even your tree friend could remember the beginning and he's old, much older than our ancestors. Yggdrasil." She snorted. "Never thought *he'd* show up on this side of the veil, but hey, just tells you we know a whole lot about nothin'."

"He prefers the name Yig."

Grandma snorted again, as if the thought were both funny and unbelievable. Not that Kate fully understood the big deal about her friend, this old, talking tree with his spotty memory.

"Anyway," Grandma said, "the forest itself might be young, you know, in terms of earth age and whatnot, but Alfeim—what it truly *is*—is not young."

Kate swallowed a snort of her own. Grandma *was* trying to be helpful here.

Right?

"You're gonna have to be more specific than that."

"Our ancestors weren't the only ones who crossed the veil. Alfeim, at least parts of it, well, it crossed with them. Maybe your pal Yig was one of them, or maybe it was already here. But definitely Alfeim."

"The forest? You're saying it's from another world."

And no, there was no hiding the sarcasm in her voice; it *was* just a tad bit unbelievable.

"And hence our little problem," Grandma said. "You think I, and all the rest of us, are crazy."

Grandma dropped the two shotgun shells in the pocket of her nightgown, then propped the gun against the wall. Still within easy reach, Kate noticed.

"Crazy or not, that's your call to make, but I warn you, your shadow, Katherine Silver, you must be careful of it. I don't know how else to explain to you. Yes, the shadow—and Alfeim Forest—have accepted you, but you haven't accepted them yet. Otherwise, well, it wouldn't be a shadow anymore."

She wanted to jump up and shake her grandmother until she told her everything. *Everything.*

"What about you? How did your parents tell you?"

Kate's words, anxious and fast, leapt from her mouth. She wanted to know, wanted to understand her family, the family her mother had refused to even acknowledge, let alone discuss.

"It's not so simple," Grandma said. "The world was different back then. My parents believed and, therefore, I believed. There was no debate, no disagreements."

Grandma waved her hand in the place where a TV would have stood, at least if this were a normal American household. Actually, there'd be at least three TVs.

"It was a different world back then, not like now. If my daddy was angry, he'd grab the nearest belt and I'd cry for all I was worth. If I were smart, I'd learn."

"Your dad hit you?"

"See?" Grandma pointed at Kate. "Probably never been spanked in yer life. No wonder you've got the issues you have now."

"I hardly see how my mother not spanking me has anything to do with my shadow."

"It has everything to do with it." Grandma sank into her rocking chair, the wood smooth from constant use. "I can't just prop my feet up, pour us some beer, and tell you the stories—the stories my parents shared with me. Stories my parents believed."

In truth, Kate could probably go for a beer right now. She might be underage, but these were desperate circumstances here. But she waited, pretending patience.

"Why not? Why can't you just tell me?"

"It don't work that way. Not if you're to believe. Not if you're to survive."

Grandma leaned closer, eyes piercing Kate. For a moment, Grandma's light had returned. It filled her eyes, her body, then faded.

Grandma had said it was a different world. Did she mean culture? Probably.

Kate glanced around the room, the stuffed deer trophies, the stack of fur blankets against the worst of winter's chill. It was a home that'd been in their family since forever—according to Grandma. It was the kind of home, Kate thought, where you could believe in fairy tales and legends.

The kind of world where elves were real and trees talked.

Kate didn't come from this world and somehow, that meant she couldn't see her shadow. "Did you have a shadow?"

Grandma shook her head. "My shadow and I were always one and the same. I accepted my spirit, my ancestors. Back then, we all did. It wasn't until later, until your mother's time, when our world shifted. We didn't see it at first, didn't recognize it for it was."

"And that's when the shadows appeared?"

"It's when we started losin' some kids, them disappearing into the forest." Grandma squeezed her eyes closed and it was several minutes before she opened them again.

Kate wanted to ask why, wanted to ask what memory caused her such pain.

"I lost your mother, even though she returned from the forest, even though the forest let her leave. I don't want to lose you."

Kate slid off the couch and touched her grandmother's knee. "If you tell me, then maybe —"

"I told your mother and look where it got me? 'Course, how was I supposed to know she'd hooked up with some magi. Damn people weren't even supposed to exist anymore."

Grandma clicked her mouth closed as if she'd said something she shouldn't have.

"Magi?"

"Oh, hell," Grandma cursed. "That, there, that was old age creepin' in and you took advantage."

Oh, no. She wasn't getting away that easily. "Who are the magi? Who did my mother meet?"

Grandma stood, shooing Kate away. "They're no good, that's who they are, and none are worse than the one your mother hooked up with. Our kind and theirs don't mix well. We'll get to those bastards in good time, but right now we need you to accept your shadow. It's best for you and this is the only way I can teach what you need."

Grandma grabbed Kate's arm and hauled her towards the fire. "Only one way to see if you've opened yerself enough."

That was how Kate found herself kneeling on the hard stone floor, staring at a very hot, and very close, fire. "How is this supposed to help me?"

Honestly, she couldn't help the sarcasm leaking from her. Different cultures, remember?

Grandma frowned, lips pinched in a tight line. Probably thinking whether or not she should spank Kate.

She didn't, which Kate thought was a bonus.

"The answer is here, in the fire." Grandma waved towards it, her spindly fingers dancing in time with the flames.

That wasn't very helpful. "Can you give me some more clues? Maybe a hint of what I should be looking for?"

"Yourself."

As far as advice went, looking for "herself" was pretty lame. And pretty useless.

Kate groaned, shifting her weight from one knee to the other. At this point, even her cheater pillow felt like a rock. And the fire was still just a fire; nothing at all special that she could see.

In truth, this was Kate's second fire, as she'd given up some time last night. She'd stared until her knees, her hands, and her brain had gone numb and mushy. But she tried. She really did. Even when Grandma sighed and told her it was useless and to go to bed, Kate had stayed.

She'd kept trying and kept failing, which was no different than how this second attempt was going.

Part of her had hoped that being tired would somehow trigger her sleeping magical abilities or something. Or at least make it so her conscious brain would take a hike.

When that failed, except for the falling-asleep part, Kate had stormed out the next day looking for advice, and since Grandma was her usual old and stubborn self (especially when Kate brought up the magi again), Kate went to the one person who could help.

Kate asked Yig.

If she was feeling fair and gracious—which she wasn't—Kate would admit Yig had given her some good advice. Okay, maybe it wasn't great advice, but he'd at least given her some direction.

"Your grandmother was correct. Fire is the easiest path to see between worlds."

Okay, that particular part wasn't very helpful.

Kate grabbed a log and shoved it on top of the shrinking fire. Immediately sparks crackled pink and blue colors. She had no idea why, other than the possibility that Grandma had sprinkled in some chemical to make it look like magic.

But that wasn't like Grandma's style. Sure, Grandma was evasive, but she wasn't deceptive—not like Kate's mother was.

"Focus." Yig's voice tickled Kate's memory as if he were there beside her, knowing she was indeed not focusing. *"You will never succeed, will never become one with your shadow, if you do not open your mind."*

Kate tossed a smaller twig into the fire. This one didn't spark like the log. She got what Yig was telling her. If Kate couldn't accept the possibility of magic, accept that she might possibly be a descendant from some ancient elf, then she might as well pack her bags and go home.

She wanted to change. She just didn't know how.

"Yes, you do." Kate growled.

Both Grandma and Yig had told her how. Time to buck up and give it a serious try.

Of course, this probably included her sarcastic thoughts about deep breaths and her visions of a white padded room.

At least she was alone, other than the two dogs snoring away in the fire's radiating warmth. It was as if that thought, her being completely alone, meant she could relax.

And for once, Kate didn't question it, and let her shoulders droop forward, let her breathing deepen. After a few minutes of turning off her mind, of thinking about nothing but breathing, she was surprised she actually felt good. Maybe Yig was onto something.

As Yig had instructed, Kate thought about the veil separating these two worlds. One world, her own, she understood, but this other one? She hadn't a clue. But that was part of the journey, she thought, this discovery. If she was starting on any journey, she'd have to start at the beginning.

Kate imagined herself opening the door. She took a deep breath and walked through, her feet stirring the small pile of leaves. The scent of pine and open air surrounded her, but she couldn't see the path, couldn't see where she was going.

Which left Kate with only two options. She could either go back or she could do the stupid thing and walk into the forest, by herself, in the pitch dark.

Clearly sunlight didn't apply to vision journeys or quests or whatever the heck this was. Kate hoped she was making the right (or at least not stupid) decision and strode into the creepy forest.

If she'd thought it was dark before, she was woefully mistaken. The light vanished and now she really didn't want to go forward.

This was a dream, nothing more. So why the hell was she suddenly so scared?

Amazingly, she didn't trip over anything. Her body, her senses, seemed to know when exactly to shift to the side, when to pick up her foot, and when to suddenly duck.

She scrambled over a boulder, feeling for grooves to stick her feet in, to pull herself over. And once she got to the top, after chipping her nails and scraping her hands, she had another problem. Somehow, she had to get down.

A rustle of feathers echoed in the darkness, as if a great bird had landed somewhere nearby in the trees. That sudden sway of pine needles as talons reached out and grabbed a branch, followed by a flap or two as the bird settled itself.

But no matter how hard Kate squinted, all she saw was the same darkness.

"I've come this far." And she jumped.

The soft earth cushioned her feet as she stumbled, and when she looked up, expecting to see darkness, found herself in a familiar grove.

Yig's grove.

Two rows of old pines lined the path, their branches bending and creaking as they shifted—no *gestured*—to the center. Giant wings flapped once, then twice.

She spun, squinting to see where the bird was, but saw nothing but trees and branches. And got the sudden sense that this bird was following her.

The closer Kate got, the more she realized something wasn't right. Not wrong exactly, but not right, either.

Yes, it was Yig with his giant, high, arching crown and his gnarled, twisted, and still beautiful trunk. The light shifted from muted gray to shimmering colors.

Yig's eyes, what Kate thought of as eyes, cracked open at her approach. The moss clumps lifted, revealing two large knobs. He looked...tired. Moreso than she remembered.

"Yig? Are you okay?"

His branches swayed more, as if stretching. *"Ah, Little Eagle. You've found your way to me."*

"Well, yeah. I mean, I knew the path." 'Course, she'd never tried walking in the pitch black before.

"You had known one way, but you did not know both ways."

"Both ways?" She held her breath. Realization of what she'd done—or might have done—filtered through her.

She wanted to scan the trees, the darker shadows, and search for her own shadow. She didn't.

Somehow, it didn't feel right. That if she searched, it wouldn't be right.

"There are always two paths, sometimes more, but always two." The twisted bark of his lip lowered. A smile. *"But yes, you found the way. You have entered the veil. And you now see me as I am. Not the truth, but closer to it."*

Kate slipped closer and sat on her favorite root. There were three like it, all giant and penetrating deep into the earth. This one, however, had the perfect indention for her butt.

"You look the same. I mean, you look more tired, but even that moss sticking out of your nose. Is the same."

Kate pointed, realized what she'd just said, and apologized. "I mean, I didn't..."

Yig chuckled. Yes, this ancient ash tree chuckled at her. Kate smiled back. Okay, it was a little funny, and he probably hadn't had someone point out his "nose" hairs in quite a few millennia.

If the elves even discussed this sort of thing, but she doubted it.

Yig's chuckle faded, and he lowered a branch and gently touched her arm. She didn't back away or flinch. For some reason, it comforted Kate.

"You still see me this way because you have not fully learned to let go," Yig

said. *"You've found your way, but this is only the start. To see me as I truly am, to see yourself and your grandmother as Truth, requires much more."*

"Well, shit. Coming this far was hard enough." And she wasn't sure how much more fire-staring her knees could handle.

"What is you wish for, Little Eagle? Why did you search the fire?"

"I wanted to find my shadow."

"But why?"

She didn't think "Grandma told me to" was the answer Yig was looking for.

This was the question Grandma hadn't asked Kate. Grandma hadn't asked why. Maybe she didn't want to know. Maybe she was afraid of the answer.

"Little Eagle?"

Kate dug her fingers into the dirt and squeezed. The earth was warm and soft, comforting. Real. She needed real right now; only real could give her that tiny bit of strength.

Enough strength to speak the truth.

"My shadow knows. It knows the truth about my heritage, about the forest...about me."

Kate glanced up at Yig, who'd bent closer, his crown looking like it'd topple onto her any minute. "I knew if I found my shadow, then I might learn the truth."

Yig's bushy, mossy eyebrows lifted. *"I see. And yes, your shadow does indeed know these truths."*

Kate released the dirt, ignoring the clumps under her fingernails. "It doesn't matter, though. I haven't seen my shadow and I'm back where I started."

"You are so sure?"

Her head snapped up. "What do you mean?"

"How do you think you found me if you did not have help? If you did not have a guide?"

Kate stumbled to her feet, her body suddenly not working the way it was supposed to. Was it true?

She searched the shadows, scanning the tree trunks, and didn't see anything....

A gentle flap of wings. A stationary flap, not the flying kind. Movement meant to draw her attention.

Afraid, anxious, and almost wanting to pee in her pants, Kate turned towards the sound. Whatever happened, whatever she saw, she'd be okay.

Kate's mouth went dry.

Yig called her "Little Eagle," but she'd had no idea he was telling her the truth. Telling her who she was.

What her spirit was.

There, perched on Yig's branches, was a bald eagle. Majestic white head, eyes that pierced through Kate. The eagle raised his wings outward and flapped once, twice.

Saying hello.

Grandma hadn't told Kate proper protocol upon meeting her spirit guide, so she bowed. "I'm really glad to finally meet you."

When she straightened, the eagle's eyes met hers. Something inside her shifted, clicked into place. Her vision cleared and the shadowy grove grew brighter and vibrant with colors and life.

The eagle raised his head and greeted her. His scream echoed through the forest, sharp and powerful, and completely beautiful.

Warmth rose in front of her face and sweat trickled down her neck and into her shirt. A fire.

She watched as Yig closed his eyes, watched as her eagle launched from his branch and flew off. She tried to follow, tried to see where he was going, but the forest faded.

No darkness this time, only the bright red of flames.

Kate opened her eyes and found herself back in Grandma's living room, the fire blazing hot.

"Ah, you're back."

Kate turned and saw Grandma in her rocking chair, knitting needles clicking as she wove together some hideous fuchsia yarn.

"Grandma?"

And out of all the questions Kate could ask, she picked the one her overloaded mind could handle:

"I didn't know you could knit."

"There are quite a few things this old lady can do, and quite a few not even your mother knows about."

Grandma cracked a smile, then chuckled, just as Yig had done. But unlike Yig, there was bit of a nervous tone to it and her face...it was a bit pale, even in the warm, orange-yellow light of the fire.

"Are you okay?"

Grandma put down her needles but stayed in her chair, rocking and back and forth, thinking, clearly, but her eyes never left Kate's. And the paleness in her face, well, that didn't change much either.

"Your journey went well."

"Yeah." Kate shifted and groaned. Her poor, abused knees.

"Happens, even to the young ones." And as if that was all the explanation Kate needed, Grandma went back to knitting. "Either way, it looks like you had a long walk. There's some dinner in the fridge. You can heat it up on the stove."

"Thanks." Kate stretched, reaching her arms over her head. "How long was I sitting there?"

"Awhile."

"You're not even going to ask what happened? Weren't you worried about me?"

Grandma closed her eyes. A shiver passed over her.

Finally she opened them and shook her head. "No, no, I'm not. Your vision quest is yours and it's none of my—or anyone else's—business. As to your second question..."

Grandma pointed at the front door with her needles. "I knew you were fine."

"Why?"

"Well, there's a rather good-sized bald eagle perched on our front tree."

Kate ran towards the door, ignoring her aching knees, and thrust open the screen door.

A bald eagle, just like she'd seen in Yig's grove, preened its feathers on the tallest branch. An eagle who'd clearly waited for Kate.

The eagle lowered its wing and turned towards her. Kate smiled, even as she heard the familiar, comforting scream.

She waved and noticed the dirt under her nails. It hadn't been a dream.

"What happened to you there," Grandma whispered, "it wasn't

what I expected. Don't think anyone in a hundred years and more would have expected. You found your shadow all right, and I think... more besides."

"Because of Yig?"

"Because of the veil, Kate, and the path you took to reach him."

Grandma placed a hand on her shoulder, the same place Yig had touched her. Her touch was warm, though, comforting. A touch that Kate knew, whatever happened, would always be there for her.

Unlike her mother.

"It's a start," Grandma said. "You're not there yet, but it's a start."

Grandma's worry, her fear, it was still clear as day in her eyes, but there was also something else...pride... something Kate wasn't used to seeing. Not in herself, certainly not from her mother.

She nodded, though, and felt that same pride swell within her chest. She'd done it. She'd found her shadow...and now, her elven spirit. Or, at least, a piece of it. There was still more to learn, still more to unlock and understand, but it all just felt right, like a lock slowly clicking open in her chest.

"And hopefully," Kate said, "one step closer to finding answers. Unless, of course, you want to make this easy and just tell me."

"Life ain't easy." Grandma patted her shoulder and her familiar, cranky grandmother was back. "Not even us elven-folk descendants. But you keep going and you'll find yourself some answers, maybe even a few you wouldn't want to find."

"It'd be the truth, though."

That was what mattered; that was all she ever wanted. The truth of who she was.

Just as in the grove beside the aging house, her eagle raised his wings—easily the same length as her arms—and disappeared into the night. His farewell cry echoed behind him, but she knew it wasn't farewell.

She smiled. One step closer to the truth, even if it meant traversing through fire vision quests and learning to speak eagle.

Where she went from here, Kate hadn't a clue, but she imagined her grandma had a few unhelpful and cryptic hints waiting for her.

At least Kate had found her spirit guide. She'd found herself.

HIDDEN IN FLIGHT

An Elven Heritage Short Story

HIDDEN IN FLIGHT

Kate did her best, her absolute best, not to slam the behemoth truck's door behind her.

The heavy metal of the door, all banged up and dented from God-knows-what (Grandma probably hitting a deer or two, or hell, maybe a moose). The red, slightly rusted and peeling paint seemed to slide off by the bucket-load. She dug her toes into the gravel ground of the grocery store parking lot, white tennis shoes no longer white but scuffed and dirty. The loose gravel shifted and gave way to her temper. And why gravel? Because here in Lighthome, Montana, they didn't exactly have a lot of money lying about for things like nicely paved, perfectly smooth roads. And why would they need them? It wasn't as if this was a hot spot for tourists, or hell, even visitors. In fact, this town, just like her grandmother, did absolutely everything possible to ensure that anyone who *happened* to stop on by wanted to leave.

Immediately.

The heat from the midday sun beat down on her, soaking through her shirt and making her sweat in seconds. Maybe she shouldn't have worn black after all. Maybe she should have actually listened to grandmother, too, about leaving the jeans at home.

And that was all she was supposed to do? Just listen to her grandmother? Take everything she said on faith and simply trust the old bat?

Kate dug her fingers into that hard, cool metal, doing her absolute best to not throw her own temper tantrum.

And would have totally succeeded, too, slinging her beat-up backpack over her shoulder, preparing to run away without damaging that monstrous beast of a truck...if Grandma hadn't opened her mouth.

Again.

"Don't you walk away from me. Kate!"

So, Kate slammed the door. Then, before Grandma got another word in, she stormed right into the small, closest-sized grocery store with its peeling-paint letters: Lighthome Groceries. Not as if she could avoid her grandmother for long, not when the store was the size of a thimble, but at least Kate had a few minutes of alone time, a few minutes to orientate herself and figure out what the hell she was going to do next.

She covered her slightly pointed ears with her long hair, hair that couldn't decide if some days it wanted to be blond and other days, a not-pretty version of it with all the dark it had going on. She darted in just as the sliding doors opened, patting hair over ears as she stepped over this threshold from private to very public. It was, in truth, a gesture as automatic as breathing...even though it *apparently* didn't matter, at least not here.

Here, in this small, tiny-ass town called Lighthome, parked next to Glacier National Park, in the furthermost tip of Montana, where Google Maps didn't even know the damn place existed...well, that didn't stop everyone here from knowing about *her*.

Including the cashier at the old-style checkout counter, who suddenly flushed and busied himself with rearranging the bills in the cash register.

At least Grandma had timed their weekly grocery trip perfectly so this place wasn't packed with the "rush hour" traffic. Of course, Kate easily picked up the distant conversations in the store...from the manager's whispered phone conversation (to someone important sounding named Aila) to those little old ladies gossiping about the latest—which, of course, was Kate.

All of which so didn't make her feel any better.

How was she supposed to know what she could and could *not* do?

This was totally new to her! She knew absolutely nothing about her heritage, who she was, where she came from, all because her stupid mom had refused—for Kate's *entire* life—to say anything, anything at all, about it.

And now here Kate was, holed up with a grandmother she'd only met three weeks ago, who got all mad when Kate made a mistake.

All this stupid elf-descendant stuff, stuff that her mom had willfully kept from her (and then dumped her here and ran off). All Kate wanted was the truth, except no one—including Grandma—would freakin' tell her!

So of *course* she made a silly, practically minor mistake.

It hadn't been her fault.

Kate swerved on the tile floor and stalked into the one aisle that gave her some amount of comfort, a tiny reminder of home and a normal life.

The cereal aisle.

Kate shoved her hands into her jeans and one finger poked out the hole she'd always thought was rather trendy. She passed the little old ladies, their eyes widening when they saw her, their conversation vanishing.

You'd think they'd seen a ghost. Or, to be truthfully, an elf descendant who'd made the mistake of crossing into the veil, some magical boundary thing separating their world from, apparently, this whole big universe of worlds.

And she'd done it. On her own. Without help or guidance.

Kate picked up speed.

Her eagle had been there, helping her. And there had been that face...just a glimpse, really, urging her to do this. In his comforting, safe voice, telling her to find answers. Find answers. Learn the truth.

The ladies, all wrinkles and hair curls of them, got so pale it looked like they might need a 911 call (as if this town even had an ambulance; Kate hadn't seen a hint of one yet!).

Maybe she wasn't being fair to their poor, beating hearts. Maybe they really *did* believe Kate was a ghost. After all, wasn't a local legend technically a ghost? At least, one from the past?

"What are you looking at?" she asked them.

If they said anything, Kate didn't hear because she stomped her boots, hoping to block out their words. Dodging locals, she decided, was not trendy at all. Maybe they could see her bad mood and that was why they paled as if they were ready to faint. Which would mean it had nothing, absolutely nothing to do with the local elf legends, even though (not by her choice) she happened to be part of them.

But even that wasn't entirely true. She'd had a choice. She could stay, learn who she was, or leave and never come back. Which was why she knew her mother was patiently waiting by the phone in whatever new city she decided to hide herself in (Billings, according to Grandma), expecting Kate's frantic call any minute, demanding that she come get her.

"I'm not leaving," Kate whispered. "Not until I have answers."

Answers Grandma was determined to keep from her. And hadn't she proved herself already? Facing down Alfeim Forest, which before had hated her and now tolerated her? Then there was her shadow—her spirit guide—who had finally decided to stop being a shadow.

You'd think that counted for something. You know, a few hints of her heritage here and there. Kate snorted. Not according to Grandma.

And going on her own like that, well, it wasn't like she'd *thought* it would actually *work*.

Even from deep in the store, over the gossiping ladies (whom Kate had now given even more to gossip about), over the clerk stocking the cereal boxes, Kate heard the distinct slam of her grandmother's truck door. If Grandma wanted to hassle it out in the middle of the store, Kate was more than happy to oblige. Not that Grandma would; not when it was about their "heritage".

She paused, one foot raised mid-stomp. Maybe that's what she should do. A good ol' public fight might jar her grandmother's stubbornness and give Kate some much-deserved answers.

Kate headed back up the cereal aisle, ignoring the "newest" marshmallow-limited edition to Lucky Charms, and felt someone tap her shoulder.

She spun, expecting to see her grandmother, who must have snuck up using her special gifts, except Grandma wasn't there. Kate was alone, with the exception of the clerk who fumbled with his cereal boxes when he noticed her looking at him.

"Was there someone…?"

The clerk practically jumped out of his skin, dropping a box of Golden Grahams, which split open and a sea of square honey cereal flooded the floor.

"Ah, sorry."

She would have helped since she'd clearly been the cause (though she hadn't actually done anything to frighten the boy), but he took off. All he needed was to raise his arms and scream. It'd make this a perfect day.

"Kate!" Grandma roared, her voice echoing from the front of the store.

Great, just great. Maybe her day would be perfect after all.

"Whatever." It was probably her imagination anyway. She turned.

A hand clamped down on her shoulder.

Kate didn't hesitate. She swung her backpack out, heavy books leading the charge, striking right where the guy would—

Be?

Her backpack carried her through the swing as she struck nothing but air. She skidded back on the tile, readjusting her grip.

She wasn't crazy. She was many things, even some descendant from an ancient elf or whatever, but she was not crazy.

Someone had touched her.

A ghost? Grandma hadn't said anything about a ghost.

Could it be her spirit guide? But no, Eagle wouldn't be here, not in a grocery store where nothing of the natural world existed.

Kate frowned. Was all this hocus-pocus making her jumpy?

"Be fair," she said aloud. "You believe in it too."

She held her backpack at the ready, expecting someone to materialize out of the air, but she remained alone—except for Grandma, who was heading this way.

Whatever she'd felt, whether someone had actually been there or whether it was her imagination taking her paranoia a giant step further, hardly mattered. Not when Grandma stormed down the aisle, her frayed pink shawl flapping behind her like a cape.

Definitely not Superman, or Wonder Woman, not with a wrinkled—and really pissed off—face like that.

Damn it.

Grandma's eyes narrowed, white hair streaming behind her, revealing delicate pointed ears, ears just like Kate's. It was as if Grandma had a homing beacon on Kate, as if she knew exactly where to find her.

Apparently everyone did these days, which really pissed her off. Couldn't she be alone for a few freaking minutes?

Kate lowered her backpack, but didn't relax her stance. She'd swing again if that phantom hand decided to get friendly. She'd show him—or her—or whatever it was.

"What are you doing?"

Grandma flicked her gaze to Kate, taking in her backpack and posture as if Kate's intent was written on the wall or something.

The rebellious side of her ached to be unleashed, to tell Grandma it was none of her damn business and give the old woman the finger. Why should she tell Grandma anything when the hag refused to do the same?

Kate lifted her chin. Over the past month, she'd lived with Grandma long enough to know what would piss her off. An accomplishment she was sure her mother would be proud of.

"I fended off an invisible groping hand, if you must know."

Grandma's feet slid on the tile as she halted—or attempted to halt. Her flapping shawl died for a moment, a deflated, sad look.

"I don't have time for smart-ass comments, Kate. And that's not something to make fun of."

"I'm not making fun. I'm telling the truth, unlike you."

The best way to get to Grandma was tell her the damn truth and storm away. Of course, the reason that bothered Grandma was because there was a high chance—Kate had figured—of her actually being in danger.

A danger Grandma didn't feel the need of informing Kate about, so the hell with her. She'd take her chances with the mysterious danger, so long as she got her answers.

And the last few times somehow turned out in her favor.

If you counted the scary shadowy forest that would have eaten her if she wasn't careful.

Careful was for weenies, anyway, and Kate was done playing by Grandma's rules.

"I mean it, Kate." Grandma scanned the cereal aisle, fists clenching her shawl she as spun, looking for...danger?

Impossible, there was nothing here except cereal boxes. Okay, maybe that was a danger, since they were clearly calling Kate's name and she'd finished the last box yesterday. Grandma hadn't been impressed with Kate's love of cereal, but, who knew, old dogs could learn new tricks.

Or, at least, pick the right battles.

"What happened? Tell me everything."

Okay, now Grandma was acting weird—weirder than normal and that was hard to believe.

"What are you doing?"

Grandma's hand whipped out and grabbed Kate's arm. She yanked Kate closer to her, but Grandma didn't take her eyes off the cereal. "I'm not playing. What the hell happened?"

She tried to quell the sudden shiver zipping up her spine. Fear and Grandma didn't go together, like water and oil or something like that. Grandma didn't get scared. She was a tough-as-nails old lady, the kind of lady who'd never spend her afternoons gossiping in the local grocery store.

Grandma shook her arm. "Now, Kate!"

"It was nothing. I just felt someone tap my shoulder, but it was my imagination. There was nothing there."

"Did it touch you?"

Grandma's face was inches from her. She tore her gaze from the cereal to glare at Kate.

"Did it touch you?"

Well, yeah. Didn't Kate just say it tapped her shoulder?

Grandma shook her again, harder this time.

"Hey." Kate shoved her arm away, not an easy task since Grandma had talons for fingers. "I just said it did."

For the briefest moment, Grandma's angry face paled, paled so much it matched her unruly hair. "We're leavin'."

"But we haven't even gone shopping and I'm out of cereal."

"You'll survive."

Grandma swiped for Kate again, but she pulled back. "I'm not going anywhere until you tell me what's going on."

"We don't have time for this."

Kate crossed her arms. She wasn't going anywhere, not without answers.

Grandma growled. It was the kind of sound nobody's regular sweet Grandma would make. She was positive Grandma had been a bear or something in her former life. Or maybe it was just Kate bringing out the best in her grandma.

"I'll tell you on the drive home."

"Not good enough. I deserve answers and if something invisible is gonna start paying attention to me"—Kate waved her hand at the air —"then I deserve to know so I can tell them to take a hike."

Kate heard the store doors sliding open and the shuffling of old, unsteady feet outside. Apparently Kate and Grandma being in the store—and mad—together, meant the customers were taking a hike themselves.

Grandma breathed through her nostrils, which practically flared red. "You will get in the truck. Now."

"Why?"

"It's not safe here."

Kate dug her toes into the floor. She wasn't going to budge, not without answers.

"It was safe last week," Kate said.

"You've changed since then."

She hadn't, at least not much.

Kate's eyes narrowed. "Because I found my spirit guide?"

"You found more than that, you silly little girl. You found Yig's grove, his *grove*." Grandma stressed the last word—which meant absolutely nothing to Kate. "Which was fine when you were on your spirit quest, but doing it *again*? And without telling me first?"

Kate blushed. At least, a little.

"He wanted me to visit him," she said.

"In person! Not trampling all over the magic-cursed veil like some fairy princess."

"And who's fault is that? It's not like you're actually telling me all your stupid rules and restrictions."

Sure, Yig was a nice, though rather old, ash tree who enjoyed Kate's company and conversation, who had actually *known* the elves when they'd walked Alfeim Forest...and quite possibly, had existed here before they'd left their previously magical world for this one. But this whole World Tree business? It still didn't mean much to Kate. Why would it? Her mom had kept everything from her, including every reference possible to that world. Of course, Kate *had* asked Yig all about this, but he had a spotty memory and could barely remember what their voices sounded like (wind chimes, apparently), let alone what they were doing back in those days. But when she saw him this last time, in the veil (apparently without the proper permission or magical shield), he had refused to tell her anything. Anything! And after all that, not to mention the shit she was in with Grandma, it had been a pretty worthless venture. One she wouldn't have done if not for that stupid dream. And wasn't a vision quest just another version of a dream? Was it not... okay to trust in dreams, especially ones in which she felt safe and comforted? As if she'd been held safe...loved and understood...everything she'd always wanted from her mom and never gotten.

Apparently not.

"I still don't see what the big deal is," Kate said.

"You stepped between worlds," Grandma said. "You opened the veil, you stepped on a path that anyone with half a brain, with even the *hint* of magic, could feel it."

Grandma leaned closer. "When you were using the fire, when you were on your spirit quest, you were *protected*, Kate. Don't you understand? You were shielded. Not anymore."

"Magic?" Kate straightened. "What about magic?"

This was the first time Grandma had said anything like that. Mysterious, cryptic, or just plain evasive was her usual response. Which meant Grandma was really scared about something. A "something" Kate was freakin' tired of guessing about.

She licked her lips. "Could magic...magic affect things like vision quests? And maybe...dreams?"

Grandma's eyes narrowed.

Damn, was that woman attuned to half-veiled lies.

"What about dreams?"

"Uh...nothing. Just, curious."

With how pissed Grandma was, this was clearly not the right time to bring up the dream incident(s).

"So," Kate said, "are you going to tell me? About the magic? Or do we need to play twenty questions in the middle of the grocery store, driving out the last of their customers?"

"I'll tell you in the truck."

Kate shook her head. Not good enough.

Grandma's mouth pressed into a thin, wrinkled line. "If there's any magi near, they'll hear. Get in the truck and we'll—"

"Magi? There's a magi here?"

Grandma had only mentioned the magi once before—to be clear, "let slip" was the more appropriate term. Kate had been too distracted searching for her shadow, and by the time she'd survived the vision quest, with her shadow/spirit guide in tow, Grandma had clamped up like a stubborn, old clam.

All she knew was that her mother had gotten involved with a magi, someone Grandma hadn't thought existed anymore, which Kate found rather silly considering what Grandma was descended from.

"What does a magi have to do with this?" Kate asked. "And what the heck *is* a magi?"

Unbelievable. Grandma's mouth tightened even further, until her lips practically disappeared beneath the wrinkles. It was also a look, a stubborn look, that Kate had learned within hours of meeting her grandmother: this conversation had just hit a stone wall and no amount of shoving, pushing, or beating her hands bloody would make Grandma spill the truth.

"Fine." Kate said. "You can keep your stupid secrets, but if you're not going to tell me, then I'm going to find someone who will."

She didn't wait for a reply, didn't need to wait. Grandma had made her position very clear to Kate. So, Kate took off. She ran out the front doors, which barely slid open in time for her to burst through.

Main Street involved a long street and stop signs. No traffic lights needed, not in the town with a population of about four. She thought of James, but he wouldn't be of much help either. Not after the talking-to Grandma gave him yesterday. (Grandma had learned that it was James who had, mistakenly, let slip that, back in the day, elves had zero issue walking the veil and they did it all the time.) And it wasn't as if Kate had *meant* to get caught. No, seriously, she could still feel Grandma clamping down so hard on her arm and pulling her right out of that misty but comfortable-feeling world. It hadn't felt like that scary place, back near Mount Rainier (which had started her on this stupid path to begin with), and *that* place had wanted nothing more than to suck the life right out of her. This place, this veil...it felt like home. Just like Alfeim Forest did (at times).

You know, like magic.

Every stinking bit of it she since she'd accepted (albeit reluctantly) that she was different...and most likely a very long-off descendant of a dead elf.

Besides all that, she *had* promised Yig she'd visit him, and apparently for a tree he was pretty good at telling time.

Kate snorted. To think she had a tree shaking its branches at her for being tardy.

Not once in her former life, the life of a normal girl (at least as normal as Kate's had ever been, which wasn't saying much), would she have believed it. She did now, though, and that was something. She'd come a long way.

Kate's feet pounded on the cracked sidewalk as she ran. Heart thumping, and for once, not in the least bit winded. She wanted answers, and maybe if Grandma wouldn't spill, this magi would instead? Except...did she really want to find one, anyway?

Grandma hadn't lied about how scared she was. She'd been terrified in the cereal aisle, no mistake about it.

Kate picked up speed, arms pumping. Her hair slapping her face, back and forth.

Well, if Grandma was really scared, maybe she should have told Kate and then Kate could decide if there was a reason to be scared.

"Stupid adults," she growled. "Always keeping stuff from me."

Still...Kate slowed. She hadn't gone to far, but far enough where it would take Grandma some jogging to find her. And besides, if she started the behemoth, Kate would hear it from a mile away.

Alone at last, but a heck of a lot more pissed off than she'd been earlier. Didn't that just figure?

Her breath came out in short gasps, but still was nothing like the panting most "normal" people would be feeling about now. Again, one of Kate's special little gifts that had some story relevance and that Grandma had kept silent about.

The distant rumbling of car engines scratched against her thoughts, though there wasn't a moving car in sight. Even here, on the edge of a town that was mostly forest, she still heard the hustle and bustle of urban life, and for whatever reason, right now, that was just too much.

She needed quiet; she needed the forest to think...and maybe even the soft swaying branches as Yig slept the day away.

Except the real Yig, and his real grove (not the one in this veil that scared Grandma silly that Kate could actually cross), were too far away. But, there was on option....

Kate turned and headed into the park, a park that looked nothing like the city parks she was familiar with. Actually, it was more like Alfeim Forest with some stone walkways and a scattering of benches. It was as if the forest had chosen to grow in the middle of town just to prove a point—that here, in this world, the forest ruled and civilization was allowed to exist in its tiny corner, but that was all.

The minute Kate stepped beneath the creaking branches, civilization and its cars, its radios and loud neighbors, vanished. All she heard were the sounds of leaves and pine needles, the sounds of birds and creaking branches.

She released a breath she hadn't been aware of holding. Her shoulders relaxed and the tension she'd felt all morning disappeared.

This was why she stayed. This was why, after everything Grandma did and her annoying habits of keeping Kate in the dark, she stayed. Because no matter what city Kate's mother had dragged her to, no matter how close they lived to parks, Kate had never felt this before.

She'd never felt peace.

A small smile tugged on her lips. Home. This place felt like home.

"Took you long enough," a voice, male and deep, said behind her. "I was wondering when you'd get here."

Right next to her, actually.

Kate spun, gripping her backpack just as she'd done in the grocery store, and swung it as hard as she could. This time, she wasn't alone. This time her backpack arched, heavy and menacing, at the stranger.

But like last time, it only connected with air.

The stranger slipped behind her again. A glimpse of red from the corner of her eye. Fast and smooth, but with nothing like the grace she'd seen from James as he moved through the forest.

Kate leapt away. She had no weapons and while her backpack was clearly not effective, it was distracting. It was also a great way to keep space between her and creepy voice. She swung yet again, though this time with less force, turned, ready to run—

When a hand clamped down on her shoulder. Hard.

Kate jerked back, smacked as hard as she could at the hand holding her, but he held on, pinning her there.

His mouth pressed against her ear. "Don't scream. If you do, you'll never know the truth."

Somehow, she froze, and her scream, ready to yell on out to Grandma, froze with her. Her heart pounded and her legs shook.

Grandma, she realized, had been right. Kate *was* in danger, but not from this man. The danger came from herself and all the stupid, childish decisions she'd made since she told her mother to go home.

She desperately wanted the truth.

"Good," he whispered. He didn't let go. "You're smart, but not as smart as your mother."

Kate's breath whooshed out of her. Her mother? But she refused to say anything. She wanted answers but there was no way in hell she was giving this asshole more power over her. And if his grip was any indica-tion, he was already a lot bigger than she was.

"Let me go," she said.

The man chuckled. "Maybe you are as smart as her, but let's not be hasty, shall we?"

He stepped back, but his grip dug into Kate's shirt, preventing her from pulling too far. He allowed her to turn, though, and she really wished he hadn't.

Kate's fingers tightened on her bag. She should have listened to Grandma, should have gotten in the truck and forgotten about the invisible touch. If she had, she'd still be safe in her ignorance.

Maybe not safe, but content. In bliss.

The man smiled. A strand of blond hair brushed the length of his cheek, hair that had a striking resemblance to hers. As did that facial structure and those eyes, dark brown and dangerous.

The face from her dreams. The same dreams that had urged her to seek out Yig, to ask more about the elves, the light ones, and any stories he still remembered. Yig who, normally so talkative, refused to speak of them.

Now, she knew. Now she understood what Grandma had wanted to keep from her.

Her father.

Kate's chin jerked up. "What the hell do you want?"

His smile didn't falter, but it lost some of its charm. "I'd think that was fairly obvious."

"And I'd think my swinging my bag at you—four times now—was pretty obvious as well."

"I am called Severi. And while you call me a stranger, I can see by your eyes you know I'm not."

His fingers only dug in harder. A little more and he might actually tear the fabric, meaning she'd get the chance she needed.

"Just because you're the guy who fathered me," Kate spat, "doesn't make you my father."

He tilted his head back and laughed. It was nothing like the merry laughter she'd heard from James, the way his voice tugged at her, wanting her to come closer.

This was the opposite. This felt wrong.

Her mother must have been freakin' crazy to sleep with this guy!

She needed to get away—once she was safe, that's when she'd freak out about meeting her...father. Oh, no. She had to stop that right now. This was the kind of guy who'd sense fear, could probably taste it on his lips.

"I take it back. You're nothing like your mother."

He chuckled and for the briefest moment, Kate glimpsed the man who'd probably charmed her mother. Except he wasn't trying to charm Kate; if anything, he was trying to kidnap her.

Which was so not happening.

"What do you want?"

He shook his head. "Now that sounds more like your grandmother; a shame, really. I'd hoped you had acquired some of your mother's more endearing characteristics."

Kate could care less about that; what she wanted was to get the hell away from this guy. If only she knew how to pull that off.

"If you don't let me go, I will scream."

He gazed at her, curious. "Would you truly do such a thing? Especially when I have all the answers, everything you've been searching for?"

Temptation, stronger than Kate had thought possible, wound through her. It knotted her stomach, held her there, trapped by both his gaze and by her own desires.

She wanted to know, oh, how she wanted to know who she was— what she was. This man—her father—could give it all to her.

Kate swallowed, wondered if this was what had trapped her mother and not his charm. His promise of answers.

"At what cost?"

That was all she could force from herself, all she could push pass the temptation, the yearning.

"It's not free," she said. "What you're offering..."

She sucked in another breath. It became harder and harder to talk. He leaned in, eyes holding hers.

This, she knew, was his gift. The temptation. Remembered, so clearly from her dreams.

Tears pricked the corner of her eyes. Why hadn't Grandma warned her?

"Come now, Kate. Are you always like this? I thought you wanted the truth. I thought you wanted to know why you were drawn to this place." His breath brushed her cheek. "I thought you wanted to understand your dreams, why you saw visions of James as something—as someone more. Greater."

James.

Kate forced her eyes closed and thought of her friend. The boy who'd told her his secret, and in turn, who'd allowed Kate to glimpse who she was. The boy who wanted to protect her.

Kate remembered Grandma, the shotgun on her hip last night, grumbling at Kate for keeping her up yet again and worrying until she'd come home.

Home.

Kate yanked her thoughts away from this man, from his temptations. "I don't know who the hell you think you are—"

"We've already revealed that secret. I'm your father."

"But that doesn't give you the right—"

Kate kicked out with her foot. He shifted his groin away from her, but that wasn't her target. Her target had been a much more incapacitating area of the body.

She slammed her boot into his knee. Felt the crushing of cartilage and heard her father scream.

Her father—no, the stranger—loosened his hold and Kate ripped herself free. He fell to the ground, cradling his injured knee to his chest.

"I could have told you everything." With a feeble hand, he reached for her.

Kate backed away. "No. You'd tell me what you wanted to, and nothing more."

Wind blew through the park. Leaves picked up from the tiny pathway, swirled around them. Several pelted her father's reaching hand, crushing on impact.

Even this slip of a forest knew who this man was, knew Kate had to escape. She spun, expecting to see the park's entrance, but she found nothing but darkness.

Kate's grip tightened on her bag. She'd faced this darkness before in her vision quest, but this was no vision quest. It was a trap her father had created for her.

He chuckled and slowly pushed to his feet, careful to favor his leg. "You think I'd let you escape so easily? That after all this time, I'd let you go?"

Kate stepped back. Cold and darkness seeped through her arms. "Why? What you do want with me?"

"Your gift is unique, Kate."

He stumbled closer. Kate held her ground. She wouldn't show fear; she'd never allow him the satisfaction.

"Your mother," he said, "she had the gift as well. But she was weak and afraid of Alfeim. You, though, you're not afraid."

Another step.

She'd have to run soon; regardless of where the trap led her, she couldn't stay here. He'd taunt her with the truth, tempt her. She couldn't let that happen.

"I don't have any gift, and neither does my mother."

The smile he gave her, charming and full of promise, tugged at Kate. This, she knew, was how her mother had become trapped. Someone who was afraid of what she was, of the stories Grandma had raised her on, and here this man was, offering promises.

Kate knew without a doubt the promise he'd offered her mother was an escape. "You told her you could make all this go away, didn't you? You used her for whatever—whatever twisted reason you wanted her for."

"I did, and I got more than I expected."

Kate's chest heated at the look he gave her. It didn't take a big guess to figure out what he'd gotten—which made sense considering how her mother had avoided men for as long as Kate could remember.

No fear, she reminded herself. The man came closer, and Kate pressed further into the darkness. His smile only grew.

Let him smile. She'd find some way out of here and, maybe, she'd find out what happened to her mother.

And maybe, why he wanted Kate.

But if he took another step closer, she'd kick out his other knee.

"It looks like you failed," she said. "Alfeim Forest nearly killed her."

Before Kate blinked, his smile shifted from charming to sinister. She shivered at his gaze, at the intent look in his eyes, the blinding anger. For a moment, it looked like he'd forgotten who Kate was, as if he were looking at her mother.

"She was weak. Even after everything I did, she couldn't accept Alfeim. Which made her useless to me, utterly useless. How could she cross the veil, how could open the damn gate if she was afraid?"

"A gate?" Kate's breath misted white. She barely felt her lips.

"Yes, my daughter. A gate to those who guard the forest, those who came here and changed the forest into something more."

He limped forward and extended his hand to her, palm up. "Don't you want to meet the guardians? Don't you want to meet those who you descended from?"

The elves.

"They're gone," Kate whispered.

That's what Yig had told her: the elves had vanished long ago.

"You're lying," she said, stronger this time.

He didn't drop his hand. "They are still here, waiting, though out of reach from even my magic. But not you. They could hear you if you called."

Kate shivered, but it was more than her own fear. It was the darkness and the cold as it seeped into her, as it headed for her soul. She had to leave soon. She didn't have the power to fight this; not when she didn't have a clue what she was doing.

Not when he was offering her everything she wanted—the truth of who she was.

She shook her head. She wouldn't do it—she wouldn't give in.

"Kate," he snarled. "I will offer this to you once and once only, just as I did your mother."

Out of the corner of her eye, she glimpsed a great bird lifting off a nearby branch, its brilliant white head a beacon in the darkened park. Her soul lifted. Hope flared through her.

Her spirit guide, leading her home.

Eagle screamed. The darkness shimmered.

Kate glimpsed a strand of trees and the barest hint of sunlight. Her father jerked back, his eyes wide as he realized the spell was breaking.

"Well, I'm not my mother." Kate lifted her chin. "And you can take your promises shove and them up your ass. I'll find my own answers."

She fled into the darkness. She ignored his cursing, ignored the cold as it pulled at her, yanking the heat from her soul, trying to slow her down. The darkness couldn't catch her and neither could he with a busted knee.

Kate ran after her spirit guide, Eagle, soaring above her. Whenever she stumbled or the darkness clouded her vision, Eagle screamed. She followed her guide, followed it until she burst through the last of the spell.

Sunlight pierced her eyes, blinded her.

Kate hunched over, gasping for air. She let her backpack slide to the ground and braced herself with her knees. It felt as if she'd run a marathon, not a few feet.

Maybe she had.

Kate blinked at the sky, squinting for any sign of her guide. Eagle had vanished with the darkness, but the old lady in front of her and that hideous pink shawl did not.

"Grandma?"

For a moment, Grandma didn't move. Her mouth moved, but no sound came out, and her hands shook as she hiked up her shawl onto her shoulder. Finally, she swooped Kate up into the tightest hug.

Damn, she had no idea her grandmother was this strong.

"Grandma, I can't...I can't breathe."

"I thought I'd lost you. I thought you'd go with him too."

Grandma didn't let go, but her hold loosened.

Kate breathed in a noseful of shawl, of the deep earthy tones of her grandmother surrounding her. Actually, it comforted her, helped to push away the last of the cold, the last traces of darkness.

"It's okay." Kate stroked her grandmother's back, which continued to shake as if she'd been the one trapped in darkness and cold. "I told him no."

Grandma pulled back. Her face was still pale and she looked like any normal, frail old lady. It wasn't a look Kate liked to see, not on her grandmother, not on a woman this strong—and stubborn.

"Severi. He's not one to take no for answer."

"Yeah, I kinda noticed."

"I'm...I'm sorry. I should have told you." Grandma squeezed her eyes closed. "I didn't know if you would run right to him, looking for answers. Like your mother. But I should have known...when you mentioned the dream...damn it, I *should* have."

The truth was, Kate had wanted to go to him. Oh, the temptation had been there, had pulled at her. If she hadn't found her spirit guide, if she'd met Severi only a week earlier, the outcome might have been different.

Kate glanced behind her, stared into the park that had both been a trap and a savior. It had called to her spirit guide, had helped her when she'd needed it. Her father was nowhere to be seen. The pathway was empty, the same as when Kate first ran into the park.

"I'm not my mother," Kate whispered. She didn't know if she spoke to her grandmother, to her father wherever he was, or to herself.

She wasn't her mother, but she would find answers. Even if it was one step at a time, one tiny clue at a time.

Her father. She'd always wondered who he was, had always gotten angry when her mother's mouth pinched and she refused to answer. Now, Kate understood why.

Her mother had been lied to, deceived, and worse, probably that she was in love and that he loved her.

But...at least Kate knew who *she* was and she knew, beyond a doubt, that her grandmother loved her. And if Grandma was hesitant about revealing the truth, if she was afraid to tell Kate to much, Kate couldn't hold it against her. Not when Grandma had nearly lost Kate's mother, and not when she'd almost lost Kate (a few times at this point).

One thing was for sure, Lighthome was a hell of a lot more dangerous than she'd first thought. There were magi and magic, and a forest that, apparently, could be controlled by the forces of bad. Had her father, no, *Severi*, been the one to attack her a few months ago?

Could he have the power to pull her into that shadowy place her mom had called Niflheim?

Kate shivered.

She had no doubt, none, that he could have done it. And...probably had. Without that day, without her mom being forced to accept that Kate *was* like her and her grandmother, Kate would never have come to Lighthome. She would never have stepped foot in Alfeim...or met Yig.

Or, apparently, seen and crossed this veil separating worlds.

That was a scary enough thought, that a man she didn't know had been keeping such close tabs on her this whole time.

Kate squeezed Grandma's hand, tugging her away from the park. "Come on. I thought we came to town for errands? Besides, I'm out of cereal and you owe me a couple boxes."

Grandma's bushy eyebrows rose. At least her face didn't look quite as pale as her hair. Kate took that as a good sign.

"And how many boxes are a couple?"

"Oh, you know." Kate shrugged. "Five or six. I might lower that if traded."

"A trade?" Grandma let Kate lead her back in the direction of the grocery store. "You have something in mind?"

Kate smiled. Her father might not realize it, but in the end he had given Kate exactly what she wanted. She didn't need him, his promises, or his stupid magic.

She'd do just fine on her own.

Kate picked up the end of Grandma's shawl, which dragged on the cement. "How about a story or two? Along with a couple of pints of ice cream."

"I think I owe you more than a few stories. And certainly ice cream."

It was the best trade Kate could have asked for. And, it was about damn time.

"It's a deal."

HIDDEN IN SPIRIT

An Elven Heritage Short Story

HIDDEN IN SPIRIT

A comforting breeze picked up the strands of Kate's hair, the thin blond locks somehow tangling and knotting together even more, if that were possible. It teased against her cheeks, her nose, that very small tip of her ears. The way her ears curved up, just slightly, but enough. Enough of a difference to stand out in the crowd, to never be normal.

The only outward sign of her heritage.

The wind continued to pull and play, joyous, even, as it tickled her ears in just the right way. Her face burned red to keep from giggling, and the wind, warm and welcoming, kept on at it. As if...as if it understood the promise being made here, as Kate's fingers closed around her grandmother's hard, callused hand.

The midday sun beat down on her, heating her thin black shirt and going right on through her jeans.

If the heat bothered her grandmother, she sure as heck didn't show it. She stood there, heavy, mud-splattered boots braced on that cracked pavement. The hideous pink shawl of hers, which Grandma had wrapped round her shoulders and hips, though the darn thing never *never* stayed up. And somehow she didn't show an ounce of discomfort on her aged, wrinkled, and pretty determined face.

Which was really pretty unfair. Especially considering Kate was anti-everything when it came grace and composure, and well, you name it.

Though, at the moment, the sun's warmth felt *wonderful*.

Especially after the freezing chill of the forest, the part that existed right in the center of town, with its sagging park benches, the paint chipping, the wood in desperate need of paving.

The sun felt wonderful, and it really, really felt wonderful to be free.

Even though the whole town was, more or less, a ghost town at the moment. No sounds other than the distant cry of Kate's eagle intruded on them (she'd glimpsed his outstretched, huge-ass wingspan a moment ago, soaring overhead). No car horns or slamming doors, not even the clanging cow bell from Martha's Ice Cream Shoppe.

Except for a Styrofoam cup and brown, twisted tumbleweed, rolling on down the cracked pavement that was considered the main street of Lighthome, Montana, there was no other movement. No other sign of life. As if everyone was hiding indoors, as if they'd felt the dark presence coming, and even though it was gone, thanks to Kate, they'd decided staying indoors with the doors locked shut and windows snapped closed was the better part of valor.

Or maybe just some good ol' common sense.

She really, really didn't blame them.

Grandma's fingers tightened around Kate's, as if she knew exactly what Kate was thinking, before slowly shaking her hand...and sealing the promise.

Kate couldn't help it. She smiled.

Okay, it wasn't a big smile or anything, but for the first time since she'd arrived in this tiny, backward town of Lighthome, a place that neither GPS or Google knew existed, just a stone's throw from Glacier National Park, her life was finally looking up.

Even with her dad still being out there (the evil, dark presence everyone was—rightly so—hiding from). Turned out he was also a guy who, apparently, had no issue using his evil magic to kidnap his daughter, either.

And no, she'd never met him, or heck, even heard of him before today, but it was pretty darn clear why Mom had left *him* out of her life.

Really couldn't blame her about that, either.

Thankfully, though, in the short time Kate had been living with Grandma (could it really only be a few weeks?) and learning about the quirks and gifts of her heritage (who knew long-lost elven descendants were a thing?), she at least wasn't defenseless. Mostly. She had Eagle, her spirit guide and, well, to tell the truth, she had her own long-buried elven senses coming to the surface.

Which was just crazy, considering her mom had avoided all things forest and nature since, like, forever.

But finally, *finally* Kate was getting some answers. Grandma had just promised to tell her the truth, not tomorrow, not two weeks from now, but *now*.

Hot damn, did it feel good.

About damn time, too.

Kate let go of her grandmother's hand, stepped back, and looked at the park. The place her father had lured her to, where he had attempted to steal her away. Those trees, with their dark sweeping branches, trees that had both trapped her and then helped her escape.

For a brief moment, she felt his magic, as if it still lingered on her skin, or maybe in the forest itself. She felt the dark mist gathering again, felt the cold seep through her skin, steal away what warmth the sun had given her, and even now, felt his dark magic searching for her soul.

She shivered.

No, she told herself, she was safe now. Safe in the sunlight, safe with her grandmother. Thanks to Eagle, her spirit guide, she was safe.

Kate had fought her way out of that park, which, it would have been good to know, was actually an extension of Alfeim Forest, a whole other consciousness of trees and woods that had no issue holding grudges against elven descendants who had forsaken their heritage. Yeah, she found *that* one out the hard way, what with Grandma and her stupid need for "secrets."

The forest was both dangerous and comforting, which was a good thing to know (as in, if you weren't careful, the forest might eat you).

But even as they stood here, surrounded by the small town's dingy, old buildings, most with paint peeling round the corners, the cracked and split asphalt roads (probably from the herd of elk or bison that made this their main thruway or something), even with the bits of "modern" here, cars and buildings and whatnot, Alfeim Forest made itself known. *It* had allowed these puny humans to develop here, to build civilization in this spot. This same forest, or least the bad parts, the parts that hated who she was and who she was distantly related to (incredibly distant, mind you), had no issue giving her dear ol' dad the extra power he needed to lure Kate in and turn the trees against her.

Yes, he'd failed, but barely.

What he'd wanted her for exactly, Kate still didn't understand. Something about crossing the veil separating worlds and opening a gate to bring the elves back. Which was silly. She'd only just gotten her spirit guide. Crossing misty veils and into magical worlds? Opening weird gates?

Yeah, so not something she could do right now. If ever.

And yet, he'd been serious. Dead serious.

"I can still feel him, you know," Kate said.

Grandma's mouth pinched together. The wrinkles road-mapping about her face made her look even older, but no less strong. If she could whip out a shotgun right now—heck, one for each hand—and take out Kate's evil magi dad, Kate had no doubt that she would.

"Did he tell you why he wanted you?" Grandma asked.

"Yes. He wanted me to cross the veil, to open...a gate, I think. A gate to where the elves were locked away."

Grandma jerked back as if Kate had slapped her. She'd gone so pale that, for a moment, she looked every inch of the eighty years she was, and another hundred added onto it.

"Why?" Kate asked. "What does that mean?"

"It...it means no good. That he wants to finish the war we'd started with them all those long years ago."

"War?"

"The one between the elves and the magi. The one that caused the elves, and all magic, to disappear from this world completely. Light ones saves us." Grandma shuddered. She wrapped her shawl tighter around her body. "How could we have missed it, for all these years?"

To Kate, it sounded like the descendants had missed a lot. Her magi dad, his evil plan, hell, they hadn't even known the legendary World Tree, Yggdrasil, was rooted in the forest not that far from Grandma's house. It had taken Kate stumbling around to awaken him.

This did not inspire a lot of confidence in the people who ran this place. Or in Grandma.

"You could have warned me that he was out there, you know," Kate said.

"I know, I know. I was hopin'...prayin' that he was long gone. I think I was wrong, that we were *all* so very, very wrong."

Grandma's shoulders fell, causing her horrible pink shawl to slide, the end of it brushing the cement again. She bent, her back creaking as she pulled up her shawl.

Kate sighed. She might not particularly care for her grandmother, but she was at least trying. She wasn't hiding the truth, not the way Kate's mother had.

"Here, let me help." Kate wound up the shawl and secured it.

Grandma closed her eyes and despite her strength, she was *old*. It was easy to when she had a temper that would rival a pissed-off mountain lion.

"I meant to tell you about your father," Grandma said. "I did."

"I don't blame you," Kate said, "not wanting to talk about him. It sounds like he hurt Mom too."

"He did. She...she loved him."

Kate could easily understand that, what with his charm, his gift for swirling up your perfect desires; the man's very being had dripped temptations. Kate had nearly taken it herself, willing to work with him for the truth.

"Grandma, I need you to tell me about him."

Grandma's hands gripped Kate's wrist and tightened. "I don't know much, honestly. You'll not be surprised to know that your mom didn't talk about him much."

"How old was she?

"Eighteen. A year older than you. She was...wild, then. Uncontrollable. But, I guess that's normal for kids your age who decide to rebel. I don't blame her; I certainly didn't make it easy on her. She was frustrated. Frustrated living here, frustrated with our ways, our 'outdated beliefs in faery tales,' as she called it."

Grandma snorted. "Should have known someone would have come along, promised your mom a different life. It's what Cian so desperately wanted. Would have done anything to get away from me, get back at me for forcing this life on her. And that man, Severi? Should have known he was a magi, that he was up to no good, and more than just breakin' yer mom's heart."

Kate watched as Grandma struggled to speak, fear seeming to come up from within her, as if by speaking it was making it all real, and being real...was suddenly too much. Except it was real, and, it had happened. Otherwise Kate wouldn't be standing here, right now.

She reached out, touched her grandmother's arm.

Grandma gave her the smallest nod.

"He *was* a magi. Just didn't know he was the one and the same, this Severi that was courtin' your mom. He came out of nowhere, I tell you; not a sign of him crossing the forest. And your mom, she refused to tell me a damn thing about him, though I'd know when she'd been with him. Eyes lit up like a nightingale, a light that went right on glowing when she looked at me, then, then it turned to gloatin'."

Grandma went on to tell Kate how this courtship went on for several weeks and how she and others hunted for him everywhere—once they realized the danger he was.

"We knew he was around, lurking in the shadows, but no matter how much we hunted for him—and believe me, we did—that man kept himself hidden."

Grandma shook her head. "I guess he was just barely a man in those days. But I didn't see him myself. Only your mother. He pushed her that day, to go into the forest, to reclaim her shadow. Didn't matter to him that she didn't believe. That...I could have lost her forever."

"He said he wanted her to open the gate, but she couldn't."

"No, no she couldn't. And he didn't care about that none, either. A gate." Grandma shivered. "That terrible word...but now his purpose, his being here, makes much more sense. And more dangerous than I ever believed."

"Why?"

"Because he's a magi. Because he remembers enough that we all should be afraid."

"Does he know what happened? To the elves, I mean?"

"No one knows; not us, not the magi. Anyone who was there that day, during that battle, they died."

"But what is this gate exactly? For that matter, *who* are the magi?"

Grandma opened her mouth, actually about to answer for once, when Kate heard the clopping of hooves. Grandma, clearly, heard too. She gripped Kate's arm, as if ready to fling her safely behind her.

It was faint, but it was definitely a horse and he was riding hard... and getting closer.

Kate's heart beat as if she'd just come running out of the park, running from her father. This time, it wasn't in fear, but safety. Comfort...

And joy.

"James."

Grandma's head jerked towards her, eyes wide as she stared at Kate, but truthfully, Kate barely noticed. She was already turning, taking one step than another, towards the clopping hooves. Ironically, coming from the park itself. It was as if like she felt a flutter in her chest, wings beating, pulsing.

She didn't know how she knew it was James, just that she did.

Sure enough, James turned his sleek black horse, Eilan, from small hidden path in the park. Bent low over Eilan's back, riding bareback as usual. His short blond hair pressed flat against his head from the wind, the speed. This time his eyes narrowed when he saw her, determined. Even from here, even over the thundering hooves, she heard the distinct rise and fall of James's breath. Another quirk of her heritage.

Heard his fear and anger with each inhale.

She froze. That, she realized, was not just another heritage quirk. That was really, really weird. And she'd had more than enough weirdness for one day.

James slid Eilan to a stop and vaulted off. He sprang towards Kate and before she could squeak, he pressed her against his chest, holding her close.

"Kate," he breathed. "Thank the light ones you're all right."

"You, you knew?"

James gripped her, tight and close, as if she might disappear in a heartbeat. Then, just as quickly as he'd hugged her, he drew back, holding her at arms' length. His gray eyes, usually filled with laughter, held the same fear she'd sensed from his breathing.

James, the boy who'd helped her see and understand who she was, a descendant of some long-lost elven race. James, the boy who shared the same slightly pointed ears as herself.

And like the first time she'd seen him, his face shifted, changed. For a brief moment, from one second to the next, she saw the "other" James. The older James, tall with long sweeping hair. High, perfectly chiseled cheekbones—but it was his eyes that held hers. It was his eyes that didn't change.

Her stomach swirled as he leaned closer, his gaze so intense she felt it through every inch of her being.

This was the elven face of James.

Could...could he be one of the few Grandma had mentioned? An elven soul reborn in a descendant?

Kate's breath caught in her throat. James did not loosen his grip on her shoulders as if he knew what she was seeing, as if maybe he saw the same thing in her.

It was too much. She shook her head, shook it until the image reverted back and she was looking at the seventeen-year-old boy she'd met nearly a month ago.

"How?" Kate asked again. "How did you know?"

Grandma caught Eilan's reins and led the horse over. "The same way he's always known. The same way you knew he was coming."

Grandma rubbed Eilan's head with her wrinkled, callused hands. She didn't look at Kate. Or at James.

"I told you, sometimes the elves left parts of themselves behind. Parts of who they were, their passions, their love. A few times they even left themselves behind."

Grandma's hand dropped from Eilan, her shoulders bent again as if holding a greater weight than Kate could imagine.

"And sometimes those souls were reborn in their children and their children's children. Or, just reborn the one time."

"Is that…" Kate swallowed. She had to know. Had to ask. "Like James?"

"Yes. And…like you."

Kate started. "Excuse me? I'm sorry. The only soul I've got in here is mine."

Grandma just looked at her, eyes sad as if she was the one who'd gotten some pretty awful, life-altering news.

"No." Kate shook her head. Long hair slapped her face. "You're wrong. She's wrong, right, James?"

For a moment, she thought he'd look away, as if it was too painful to hold her gaze. He did, though, and his gray eyes never once left her brown ones. For the briefest moment, like a shimmering mirage, the elven soul was looking back at her.

He too, looked sadly at her.

"But…" Kate said. "But how? You're not you?"

"I am still me, but…it's not just me in here," James said.

"That's, that's not possible."

He smiled, and it was warm and still kind. Somehow. "Just like elves and magic don't exist, right?"

"Yeah…I guess so. This…is just, a little too much to take in."

Or, to believe in. She had an elf soul in her? Could they be wrong? Why had she never sensed or felt someone, you know, elf-like in her? Hell, she was a *terrible* elf descendant as it was, and they were telling her she had a soul cozied up right beside *hers*? No way. Impossible.

"I still feel like myself," she said.

"Other than seeing my elven soul?" he asked.

"Right. That."

Not to mention Yig. And crossing the veil. Then there was Eagle, who had helped her get away from her dad and the forest that was trying to trap her. Other than all *that*, she was totally herself.

Okay, so maybe she could get behind believing that she was way more different than she'd first thought.

"Is that what my dad was after? Was that why he wanted me?"

A stained paper cup from the nearby drive-through rolled in the empty street. Everything was empty, abandoned, as if the town and its people knew to stay in, to stay quiet and hidden. She didn't know if everyone who lived here knew about the elves and the magic that lived in the forest, but she bet they were smart enough to know something big was going down...and wanted desperately to stay away from the eyes and attention of its local mysterious and magical neighbors.

Kate wanted to hide too, to hide the way her mother always had, but she couldn't. She couldn't run from this, even if she wanted to.

She took James's hand, felt his strength pulsing into her. She wasn't alone in this. No matter what, she wouldn't have to face this—and her father—alone again.

"No one knows what happened to the elves," Grandma whispered. "No one knows why they suddenly vanished or why Alfeim became suddenly quiet."

Not even Yig, the ancient talking tree Kate had befriended, knew what had happened to the elves, to the *light ones*, as he called them. But someone knew, she realized, even if they weren't around anymore.

"The elves," Kate said. "They know what happened."

Grandma's face pinched as if she wanted to deny it, wanted to tell Kate the usual "I'll tell you later" line. This time, she didn't.

Instead, Grandma nodded. "From all the stories I've gathered, from all the secrets I hold in safekeeping, I don't believe anyone else—not even Alfeim—knows what happened. Only the elves, the ones who disappeared, know."

Kate shivered, the need to hide growing stronger every minute. She could feel the dark forest at her back, the untamed park where her father could still be hiding.

She stepped forward, but didn't let go of James's hand as she faced her grandmother. "Or the ones who stayed behind. Isn't that right? The ones who were reborn."

Like the one she now knew was living inside her. The one she shared a soul with.

"You can see past the veil, like all our kind," Grandma said. "But you are the first who's entered it...the day you found your spirit guide and Yggdrasil's grove. That was you, actually crossing in the veil."

Kate swallowed. She would have sunk to the ground if James wasn't there, holding her up, supporting her.

"Uh...sorry?"

"Your grandmother's right," James whispered. "I didn't need the same spirit quest like you. I never had a reason to even try. But you did, and without even knowing it existed or what you were doing."

"Can you? Can you enter the veil?"

She needed to know that she wasn't the only one; that she wasn't the only one who was different. Weird. To think she'd come this far, to find others like her, and she *still* managed to find a way to be different. It was surprising to know that she even still cared. Old habits were hard to break, huh? Maybe there was some truth to that saying.

James looked away. She needed him to be with her, to not be alone.

"You can't," she said.

"I-I can see it," he finally answered. "But I can't touch it. Something...something holds me back. I can't cross over, not like you."

Kate rocked back. Her father had needed her specifically. She was the only one who could enter this strange boundary, this veil between worlds...the very place the elves had come from, and then disappeared to?

She swallowed. The realization hitting hard into her gut. Only *she* could pass through the veil separating worlds.

"Can we go home now?" Kate pressed a hand to her stomach. "I think I'm going to throw up."

That, at least, got them moving. Even Eilan seemed pleased as pie to get away from the dark, scary park, his hooves practically dancing on the cracked pavement.

Yet the whole trip back home, jerking and bouncing in Grandma's behemoth of a truck, she couldn't help but wonder...did she really want these answers? Was it possible that some truth were better not knowing?

She thought of her mother, the horror in her face when Kate had decided to stay. Her mother, of all people, knew what could happen. And the damage it would leave behind in a soul.

She pressed a hand to her heart. Suddenly, it all made sense. How her mother was constantly on the move, unable to stay in any place for too long, whether a big urban city like Seattle, or the more rustic areas like Billings. But never far from Montana, as if she couldn't get away from Alfeim Forest. As if...as if it wouldn't let her.

And her mom had known. She could never escape.

And maybe, not Kate either.

The second they'd got back to Grandma's house, James quickly cared for Eilan, rubbing him down, leading him to the water trough-thing. Grandma had shooed Kate right inside and once James was in, she locked the rusty, hundred-year-old dead-bolt, and declared, very matter-of-fact, that it was time for answers.

After tea, of course.

Grandma disappeared into the ancient, still functional kitchen to make tea, leaving Kate alone. With James. Sitting right beside her. With Grandma's two dogs pressed against Kate's legs as if they needed to protect her, too.

Actually, all they did was trap her there just as surely as her father had trapped her in the forest. But again, this time it was with James.

She'd wanted answers and now she was going to get some. Too bad it was with James. Right there, beside her. James...who had an elven soul in him, just like she did. A soul that, she had no doubt, she shared a serious...connection with.

"Great, just great."

"What's that?" James turned his head, which somehow caused them to sink even lower into Grandma's couch.

"Nothing."

Then Kate did her best to think dark, evil thoughts of him in hopes that her blush would magically disappear. Of course, it didn't. She slouched into the worn-out sofa, trying to ignore the very warm and very real presence of James.

And the way his body seemed to lean in to hers.

Comforting and close.

It was the ratty old springs, that was all. It had nothing, absolutely nothing to do with James and how right he felt...like he *should* be pressed against her. Or the way his touch seemed to calm her.

James smiled. "I'm glad you're okay."

"Yeah, me too, because being trapped by a dark magi would have been loads of fun."

His smile dropped. "Kate. This is serious."

"I get that."

What she didn't get was this, this *thing* between them. Yes, there was some truth (scary truth, to be honest) about having an elven soul apparently living right alongside her own, but...still. There was more going on and that made her nervous. And since she didn't want to talk about it (because her stomach was absolutely not a swirling mass of fluttering butterflies), she chalked it up to their elven souls or whatever it was they had.

End of story. End of discussion.

"Look," she said. "I just don't want to talk about it."

"You can't hide from it. You can't just forget what happened."

"I'm not hiding." She never hid. Ever. "And believe me, I'll never *forget* what happened, either."

A creepy magical father just wasn't the kind of thing you forgot.

"Okay." He shrugged, which only made him press closer.

Her face heated.

The entire living room was littered with chairs (some with stuffing poking out), blankets and pillows (dog blankets and pillows), and perfectly reasonable, expansive floor space...even if a few of the old wooden floorboards were jutting out. Right now, she'd have picked the floor for the discussion—far from James—if Grandma hadn't practically thrown her onto the couch. Plus there were the two dogs who seemed perfectly content to lie on top of her feet like that.

"You sure you don't want to talk about it?" James asked.

"Yes."

He looked away. "You don't even want to know how I knew you were in trouble?"

Kate stifled a groan. There it was again. This *thing* between them, and she was doing her absolute best to ignore it.

Weird elven heritage, she could handle. Mysterious soul that might have some sort of attraction and/or past with James? Sorry. She was *so* not ready for that.

"I'm sorry," he said, "but I need to tell you. I need you to understand."

Then he went and took her hand. Kate jumped up from the couch. She tripped over the dogs, who didn't even lift their sleeping heads, while James was nearly eaten by the old couch cushions.

"Look," she said, in one big rush. "You don't need to tell me anything. You sensed me or something. I'm glad you came."

She was flailing and knew it. Where was her nosy grandmother when she needed her?

James got to his feet, which he also happened to do a thousand times more gracefully than Kate had. He must have more of the elf-gift in him, which meant *he* should be the one to deal with veil or whatever that thing was. Not her.

"I heard you," he said. "In my head. I heard you calling for me."

"I wasn't. I mean, I hadn't."

She hadn't called for him. Right?

Kate swallowed. Shit, had she called him?

She couldn't remember, but the way he looked at her, the way his gray eyes took her in as if she was going to disappear if he so much as blinked, as if he was terrified that she *would* go away...she knew, in that moment, that she *had* called him. Had asked for his help. She'd done it without ever realizing.

She'd called to him for help.

James reached for her. She stepped back, nearly tripping over one of those tilted-up floorboards.

"I don't want to know. It's too much." She shook her head. "I can't deal with you, too, and this, well, whatever this is between us."

James's held his hand out for a moment longer, then slowly lowered it. "You feel it too."

Silence stretched, swirled around them, waiting with a held breath. The only sound was the snoring dogs and the faint mumblings of Grandma taking her sweet time making tea.

Finally, knowing she had to give him an answer, Kate nodded.

"I can feel it."

He closed his eyes. "Thank the light ones. I didn't think, I mean, I wasn't sure if I was the only one."

"You're not."

Even if she didn't want to admit it, she could at least give him this. After all, he'd ridden in on his white steed (well, black steed), to rescue her.

They stood there like that, separated across the living room. He ran a hand through his short blond hair, nothing like the long silky hair she'd seen in her vision of him. If she concentrated, if she tried, she knew she could see it. Could see *him*.

Kate looked away.

"All right. Fine. So we have these elf souls in us? Is that what this is?"

She motioned between them, hoping like hell he would understand what she meant without actually having to say the word "attraction." That was just...too embarrassing. Especially since she didn't know if it was *her* feelings or the elf soul who, apparently, remembered him.

It was hard enough figuring out her own feelings, thanks very much.

"Yes and no," he said. "I don't understand it much myself."

"How could you not? I mean, you grew up here. I'm sure your mom didn't try to keep the truth from you."

Not the way hers had, anyway.

"You'd be surprised," he said. "My mom has pretty firm...opinions about elf souls. Especially mine. And, well, yours."

"Why? Is it dangerous?"

This time, he was the one who looked away, and she knew he was hiding something from her. Or something he wasn't telling.

"The thing is," he said, "there aren't a lot of people like us. You've got to be careful—you don't want to lose yourself to your elven soul—but you can't wall it off ,either. And don't be mad at your grandma; I don't think she even really understands."

Kate cocked an eyebrow. "Doesn't understand or isn't telling?"

She heard the old teakettle whistle and the next thing she knew, Grandma creaked open the kitchen door carrying a tray of steaming teacups and a small cup of cream. She set the tray down and gave Kate a long, hard look.

"Doesn't understand, I'm afraid. I don't know how your father knew you that had this gift, or that your mother had it, either. Hell, I only suspected you might be carrying an elven soul in there. How that man knew...it's not a question I'm happy to be askin'."

"Or exactly what he wants me for?" Kate crossed her arms. "Gee, this is *really* helpful. Thanks."

Grandma's eyes narrowed. "Act all sullen if you like, it's not going to change a thing."

Well, she'd tried. Maybe Grandma was telling the truth, and after what happened today in the park, Kate didn't think she'd lie about something like that.

"Look, I'm sorry," she said. "This...this is a lot to take in. So, my jerk dad knows I have this elven soul and he wants to use me to bring back the elves or whatever he wants to do." She looked at James. "Does he know about you?"

"I don't think so," James said. "But I've never met him. I've only heard rumors."

Grandma pursed her lips. "Until today, I hadn't sensed him in years. Ever since your mother packed her bags and left."

Which meant they were at a dead end. Great.

Or maybe there was something else, something they weren't seeing because to Grandma and James, this was a life they knew. They both knew the stories, they knew Alfeim Forest, about the the magi.

Except *she* didn't. And maybe, because she didn't know, she could see clearer than them, maybe see something they missed.

"I think you need to start at the beginning. About the elves, about the magi, and why someone like my dad would want to find them again."

Grandma nodded. She sat herself down on the sagging armchair and scooped up a cup of tea, and no, she didn't spill a drop.

"That's a good plan, Kate. And James, you should listen too, carefully. It might be old stories to you but, well, maybe something new pops up with this changing...development between you two."

And yes, she did nod at them.

Kate blushed, but James nodded, all solemn-like as well.

"The beginning, the beginning..." Grandma mumbled. "Well, like I told you, you've got the elves in Norse mythology, but the truth is they ain't go much to say. Can't, really. Not that it's their fault. The problem is the light ones weren't living in their home of Alfeim. They were living here, in *our* Alfeim Forest. Or they were here."

"And something happened," Kate said.

"Yep. Something way back when, longer than the Norse gods remember, I reckon. They did something, conquered some world or whatnot, or had some big ol' fight with those ice giants—whatever that was, it screwed things up a bit. The veil, the one separating our world from every other damn world, it got real thin, thin enough that the elves crossed over. And not just them, either. With them came the magic. They brought magic into our world, a world without, and caused a hell of a lot of problems, I tell you. And some people living on our side of the line found they could *see* this magic. Use it, too."

"The magi," James said.

Grandma nodded. She took another sip of tea and licked her wrinkled lips.

"Aye, the magi. Now, once they could use magic, so could their kids. They had that little extra bit of somethin' in their souls, and they had their parents to teach 'em. But to elves, those magi, they were like moths drawn to a burnin' hot candle flame. Curious, they were, but the real flame? The real flame that caused all of them to leave their golden, shining halls and whatnot on their world?"

Grandma leaned in closer. Silver hair slipped down her shoulder.

"It was *our* world. A world just waiting to be touched, to be *shaped* by magic."

"I don't understand," Kate said. "It sounds like the elves coming here was a good thing. Right? I mean, they brought magic with them. Why are the magi are enemy?"

"The story gets a bit muddy here, and it's only because it's been so long and we don't exactly have either side 'round to ask what the hell went wrong. But I'll be honest, not all of them were good, and they certainly weren't all 'pure of heart' or any of that other bullshit."

James looked embarrassed. She had a feeling this was something his mom tended to leave out in the re-tellings. It only made Kate trust her grandmother more.

"Elves loved their magic, loved our world, loved it even better when their magic changed our world. Humans, for the most part, got in their way. Not a good thing, unless you've been touched by magic. Then, then those elves would want them badly. Sometimes as a trophy or as an object to keep."

"Or fall in love with?" Kate asked, a bit skeptical.

"How do you think we came to be breathing? I'm sure as hell no mystical, glorious elf!"

Grandma certainly had a point there.

"Okay, some fell in love," Kate said, "and others...got pissed off?"

"You bet. Pissed enough to mess with things that shouldn't be messed with. Magic. And a big ol' war started between the elves and the magi. The magi sought to destroy the elves for the evil and deaths they'd caused—I told you, they weren't the pure hearts popular media likes to make of 'em—and the elves fought back. They were led by their queen, who wanted to be more like the gods back home, I guess. As you can imagine, the magi weren't havin' none of that. A final battle was fought on Vetmaetr, or Samhain Eve, as you probably know."

Grandma took another sip.

Kate waited, heart pounding. "So, what happened?"

"Who the hell knows. The two sides fought. The magi cast some great spell to destroy the elves, but it got distorted somehow. The elves disappeared and the magic, well, it disappeared with them. Both elves and magic vanished beyond the veil and not a soul as seen 'em, or felt 'em, since. Not even your friend, Yggdrasil."

James slipped beside Kate, so quietly not even she heard him, but when his hand gently touched her shoulder, heat soared through her. Heat and something else. Longing?

Grandma's eyes widened at this, and the tiniest hint of understanding passed across her face, then was gone again.

But Kate didn't pull away from James. Instead, she turned until she was facing him. He was so close. Even if her eyes were closed, if her ears were plugged, she could have sensed him.

Would have known that he was there.

It was that feeling, that knowing, which gave her the courage to ask the one question she didn't want to know, the one question that sent a terrifying chill through her soul.

"All this still leaves one really, really big question," Kate said. "Why does a magi want to bring back the elves?"

That, she knew, was the answer they were looking for. Figure that out and they were one step closer to understanding her dad. One step closer to knowing what he wanted with Kate and this whole "open gate" thing.

James lifted her chin, his warm touch warring with the ice trying to engulf her soul. His image shifted again, changed to the elf hidden away within James, the one he shared his soul with.

"He wants revenge," he said.

When James spoke, his voice was deeper. It rolled through her, heating the ice until she was completely free from the cold. Instead, it left behind something else, left behind her heat, her intensity. She felt the barest touch of longing. The need for his touch, to be close to him. She could barely breathe as the feeling came on so quickly, so suddenly.

She didn't run away, though. This was one person, she knew, she could never run away from.

Kate raised her hand. Her fingers curled around his.

"Why?"

She hardly recognized her own voice, lighter and sweeter than she remembered, but she also knew it was her voice. It was a part of her even though it was different.

"Why does he want revenge?" she asked.

"We put their magic to sleep, Kátheryn. We put them to sleep, just as they put Alfeim to sleep and locked us away."

She closed her eyes, trying to draw up her memories, but they were beyond her. She had no knowledge of what he spoke about, only that she knew he was right. When she opened her eyes again, James was back to his usual self, but Kate still felt the other beside her, the elf who had once been called Kátheryn.

James blinked, and the movement seemed to bring Kate back even as the heat from their hands dimmed. It didn't disappear, but it lightened. Became normal again.

"Revenge," James said again. "Your dad wants revenge."

Grandma sank further into the armchair, as if her whole body was collapsing inward. "Bless the light ones and all our rotting luck."

Grandma's curse brought Kate back to herself. Of course, it wasn't much of a curse, but it did sound like her grandmother and not some ancient elf who was talking out of her mouth.

Kate stifled a shiver. Maybe her mother was right about staying far away and never coming back. This place was really screwed up.

Grandma shot to her feet so suddenly it was as if she'd just shed her old lady skin and was ready to kick butt. Now Kate was the one who felt like sagging on the couch and taking a nap. Every inch of her, from her feet to her fingertips, was exhausted.

"Grandma?" she managed. "What are you talking about?"

"We've got work to do. Lots of work and lots of explaining if we're going to catch you up on all this."

Kate's vision swirled.

James's steadied her and she rested against his solid, very real frame.

Right now, she needed real. She needed grounding. At least until the next big surprise came along, and she really hoped there weren't anymore. She had no idea how much more she could take.

But then again, sharing your soul with an elf was a tough one to top.

"And there's only one logical way to do it." Grandma slapped her hands together. "Even if those hermits are gonna have my head for it, to hell with 'em. I'm calling a Gathering."

James stiffened and Kate nearly ended up on the ground.

"A Gathering?" he asked. "You can't be serious."

"Damn straight I am, boy. And for the light ones' sake, don't drop her."

Grandma rushed over, grabbing Kate's arm while James held her other one.

"What?" Kate mumbled. "But why? What's a Gathering?"

Now her head was really spinning. Apparently she had two grandmothers instead of one.

"Well," both Grandmas said, "your dad and the magi are out for revenge and right now, you're the only one who can give it to him by openin' up that gate and finishing the war."

"Sure. Okay. Sucks to be me, right?"

She sure as hell thought it did, but Grandma ignored her.

"James and I can protect you," Grandma said, "but that's not going to be good enough. Kate, are you listening to me?"

She was trying. Honest.

"You need to learn how to protect yourself." Her grandmother (actually, there were still two) smiled as if she'd just had the greatest idea in the world. "And for that, we're going to need some help."

"Help?" James snorted. "You mean you need approval from the Gathering, and you *know* how they are with change. And crossing the veil? Walking it? You're nuts."

"Crazy, more like."

"Approval?" Kate asked. "Why would I need approval?"

This time, it was Grandma who looked away. "Well, not anyone can just go walking the veil all willy-nilly like. It was outlawed when the elves vanished. No one knows why, just that it's not allowed."

"And dangerous?" Kate said.

She felt it from James, his rising denial, his anger. Worry.

And Kate knew it didn't matter. She needed to do this. She would stand on her own two feet. She would protect herself.

Kate leaned into James, but kept her eyes closed so she wouldn't see the other him. Right now, she wasn't sure she could handle it, not with what she needed to say. If she saw him, saw that intense, soul-searing gaze, she had no idea if she could go through with this.

Kate squeezed her eyes closed, pushing away the fear that wanted to lodge in her throat, to keep her from moving forward.

"It's okay. I wanted answers, remember? I guess I got what I asked for."

More than she'd asked for. And somehow, she would see this through to the end.

James took her hand and squeezed.

At least this time, even if she was different than most girls, she wasn't alone. And never would be again.

HIDDEN IN DESIRE

An Elven Heritage Short Story

HIDDEN IN DESIRE

Kate eyed the overflowing hiking backpack and the beat-up, dented pot tied by a string. The whole thing had to weigh at least fifty pounds, not counting the mud still caked on it. In fact, it looked as if it had gone to war and back; even the stitching holding it together looked about ready to burst if you so much as breathed on it. And Kate, who'd never been camping in her life, who'd barely gone on short little nature walks, was supposed to use it?

(And have it not fail utterly in her care?)

And all the while, Grandma stood there, grin plastered on her wrinkled, leathery face, silver hair also tied back by a string (probably the matching sister string the pot was currently using). She kept nodding and tapping her boots on the uneven floor of her home, as if she was simply pleased as pie with herself.

Or the fact that she'd won the argument about going on this stupid trip in the first place.

But if there was one thing Kate was, it was persistent. And stubborn. Really, really stubborn.

She crossed her arms and gave Grandma her most deadpan stare ever.

"You've got to be kidding me."

Grandma snorted as she hefted up her own backpack, which bulged about as much as Kate's, and gave Kate her most level-headed stare back.

"You've known me almost six weeks. Since when have I ever 'kidded' you?"

Nope. No way was she budging.

Kate planted her feet firmly on the uneven, rickety floorboards. Her hiking boots, barely broken in, still managed to pinch her toes just while she was *standing* there. And she was supposed to move in these? Scramble over rocks and rotting logs and all manner of icky things?

Grandma was crazy!

Kate shifted, trying to relieve the squishing-toes feeling. They were a recent addition to Kate's ensemble after Grandma had practically thrown her tennis shoes out the window. She'd tried the same with Kate's jeans, as slim-fitting as they were, and those had not been met with approval either. Or the pale pink sweater, which, Grandma had declared, would be ripped by briars and pine needles and whatever else was out there before the first day was out.

Kate, though, had held firm on the sweater bit. Everything else, though, had been like running headfirst into a brick wall of determination that was Grandma.

"You're right," Kate declared. "*You* were born without a sense of humor. Not a funny bone in your body, but that doesn't excuse this."

Grandma snorted. "You gotta problem with camping?"

"I don't *do* camping. Ever."

This only caused Grandma to snort again, but because she tried to laugh at the same time, it came out like a cross between a wheezing pig and a vomiting dog.

"You've got damn elven-blood in your veins, girl! Of course you like camping."

Kate snapped her hands to her waist. She was *so* not having this conversation.

"This is stupid. Why do I have to go? And why do we have to back-pack? What's wrong with cars and motor homes? Or hell, what's wrong with running water?"

Grandma's smile vanished. "I thought you wanted to know who you were."

"I do."

And she did, so long as it involved her not leaving the luxuries of the twenty-first century. Even if Lighthome, Montana—not kidding, population of like ten, parked at the northernmost tip, right next to Glacier National Park (a town which, by the way, GPS nor Google even knew existed)—was, however, technically a town. With flushing toilets.

In most places, anyway.

"It don't work that way, Kate. If you want the truth, you're gonna have to work for it."

Oh, no. There was no way Grandma was going to pull that bullshit card on her.

"Oh, really? And what have I been *doing* for the last six weeks if not 'working for it,' huh?"

Like finding her spirit guide and walking the veil (some mystical misty place that was supposedly like a crossroads between worlds). Not to mention there was meeting up with Severi. Her dad. A real ass of a guy who had lied to and tricked her mom, tried to do the same to Kate...and then kidnap her.

He'd failed (barely) and now here Kate was, ready to go tromping through a forest with, literally, the clothes on her back. All so she could, maybe, learn what she was doing with her apparently inherited elven gifts and meet a bunch of other elven descendants who, judging by the heated phone conversations Grandma had been having for the past few days, were none to pleased about her.

Or the mess of things she'd (apparently) made.

Like...crossing the veil. Apparently that had kinda painted a big flashing sign to all the evil magi in the area (like her dad) saying, "Hey! New elf girl in town who just might get those long disappeared and their magic back to earth."

It hadn't been her fault.

Really.

Grandma, though, she wasn't budging. It was pretty clear where Kate got her stubbornness from.

"You"—Grandma poked Kate in the chest—"got lucky. And if you're gonna live to see next week or Samhain, you need training."

"Sam-what?"

Another poke.

"Not important now. First thing is convincing the others that they *do* want you on their side."

But Grandma kept poking as if that finger thing would drive home her point that Kate should really be serious. And be paying attention.

Except Kate *hated* being poked. It was exactly what her mother had always done.

Kate poked Grandma back.

Damn! That woman might be old but she had some serious muscles.

"Why do we need to go to this stupid Gathering, anyway?" Kate shot back. "Why can't you just train me, right here, and to hell what anyone else thinks? Besides. It's a house with a bathroom on each floor. Flushing toilets. Win-win for everyone."

Grandma's mouthed pinched in a tight line. "The Gathering."

Right. There went that "Gathering" thing again. Something Grandma—and James—had kept their lips zipped about. Kate didn't know much. Only that it was a bunch of locals—locals who had the similar quirky elven heritage like her—and they were supposed to protect her from bad magi like her dad, and probably big, scary things that went bump in the night. They also needed to *approve* Kate doing... well, whatever she'd already done.

Walking the veil. Something that was apparently really dangerous, had been outlawed since the elves disappeared (like, thousands of years ago). And these people were none to likely to like her. Or help her.

Which meant that it was a total waste of time, in her opinion.

To think that even here, when she was finally around people who were sorta like her and not some freak like she'd been growing up, always standing apart and different from the other kids...how she could move silently without meaning to, plus her exceptionally good hearing (not to mention that annoyingly slightly pointed tip of her ears).

And yet even here...she was still different. Like nothing she did mattered. She would always be different.

Lucky her, she apparently had a damn elven soul in her. Yep, sharing a soul right alongside hers. Not that Kate knew much about her elf soul (she'd been pretty much silent and worthless up to this point), but there was no denying it...especially when Kate saw James's elven soul.

One who, apparently, had the hots for Kate's.

This was turning out to be some huge, complicated mess. All she wanted was to stay here and watch some Netflix.

As if Grandma even *had* working Internet.

And truthfully, part of her didn't mind staying in Alfeim Forest, even if it meant no flushing toilets. It had...grown on her, had become a place where she felt calm and whole (for the first time in her life), but...backpacking? Spending the night (nights?) when she could literally feel the creepy trees watching her?

Because, hey, let's face it, not all the trees in Alfeim were on their side, as she'd only recently learned a week ago when her dad had nearly succeeded in kidnapping her. Sure, meeting Yig had been one thing. He was a nice talking tree with a real shitty memory, but the others? The ones that could, you know, be controlled by her dad?

No thanks.

"And what if I don't want to go?" Kate asked.

Because she didn't want to. She really, really didn't. And, she just had this sense, this feeling. Sure, she might learn more about who she was, and how she could control this "walking the veil" thing, but it also felt like she'd be opening something...something big.

Something that could never be undone.

Grandma sighed. She looked slightly older, but no less stubborn. Kate knew her negotiation was in jeopardy. If it even was a negotiation to begin with.

"Kate. You haven't got a choice. I'm sorry."

"Funny. You sure don't sound sorry."

"I am. I am, Kate, even if it don't look like it. Sometimes we're asked to do things that don't sit well with us, but we've got to nonetheless. What happened with your mom, her leaving, and now you. It's all been my fault and I'm trying my best to make it up to you."

Grandma reached over and gripped Kate's shoulders. "The least I can do is keep you safe out there, and that means learning the truth. And, accepting it, ugly bits and all. For that, I'm sorry."

Which was a really, really sucky speech on Grandma's part because she actually went and said all the stupid stuff she needed to say. Just like Kate *needed* to stay. She needed to learn the truth, learn who she was, learn about her heritage.

Her mom had wanted no part of this, had left Kate in complete ignorance, feeling like she was weird and different everywhere she went, no matter what she did or how hard she worked to fit in. Always different. Always out of place. And now, here she was, getting a crash course in all things elven.

Kate fingered her pink fleece sweater, the one her mom had given her before this trip to Lighthome. It was impractical and it'd be probably be the color of mud within an hour, but she also needed something of home with her. A reminder that she was someone else and not just some elf descendant (or the living vehicle of a long-gone elf soul). She wanted her mother.

Maybe it wasn't too late to back out, to call her mom and turn her back on who she was. Was it worth it? Worth...maybe dying for?

Because the dying part seemed to be a running theme of the past few weeks. That—and being kidnapped.

Grandma didn't move, didn't even show if the backpack weight bothered her. "You can change your mind, you know. You can go back, leave this life and never look back. None here would blame you. Not even me."

Kate let out a breath, felt the longing so very real in her chest. All she had to do was say yes.

"Your mother's waiting for your call, even now, knowin' her."

Kate looked away. She didn't want Grandma to know that was exactly what she'd been thinking. Except she'd never be able to forgive herself if she didn't see this through, if she didn't find the answers to the question that burned in her.

Running away from problems didn't change the fact that they were your problems. Her mom had taught her that.

Finally, Kate shook her head. The tip of her ponytail sliding over her shoulders.

"No. It's fine."

Grandma nodded. "You won't be alone. Remember that. You'll have me, and James. He'll be there too."

At the very mention of his name, Kate's stomach turned into a fluttering wing of butterflies. She tried to ignore the sudden wave of longing that crept down her spine. Especially since those weren't *her* feelings.

Well...she didn't think so, anyway.

"Oh?" Kate asked. "Cool. I mean, it's nice that I'll know someone there."

She did *not* look at her grandmother. She did not want to see the knowing look. Instead, Kate got on her backpack, somehow managed to stand up with all fifty pounds of it—and then, surprise, surprise, didn't fall over backwards.

Talk about progress.

Maybe this good Montana air was having an affect on her. Or maybe it was just the first time in her life she actually had to, you know, work or whatever. And in Grandma's house, long-lost elf living in her soul or not, Grandma made her work.

"We're burning daylight."

Grandma slapped her shoulder, which sent Kate lurching forward.

"Let's get this party started!"

She saw nothing to celebrate about, but Grandma, however, did. She opened the door for the two dogs, who jaunted outside, tails wagging. Kate heard her mumble something about a neighbor watching them while they were gone.

By the time Kate registered that comment—her heart nearly stopping—*how* freakin' long would they be gone?

Grandma had moved on.

Actually, the old hag had practically disappeared into Alfeim Forest, with its dark, spindly tree trunks that pressed against the boundary of Grandma's homestead. With no other choice, Kate cursed, grabbed her really cool cowboy hat with the neat deep brown eagle feather sticking out the strap (she'd insisted on Grandma buying it even though Grandma had only shaken her head at Kate's silliness).

She slapped on the hat, flattening down her ponytail, and jogged after Grandma.

Okay, she only jogged about two steps and then got winded.

What the hell had Gran packed?

Since running was clearly not an option, she settled in for a nice, brisk pace. This was actually a good thing because out of the corner of her eye, she glimpsed the giant spread of an eagle's wings. Its dark, molten-brown feathers stretched out as it disappeared into Alfeim Forest—ahead of both her and Grandma.

Eagle. Kate's spirit guide.

She smiled, catching only the barest hint of its white head, and then the eagle was gone.

Suddenly Alfeim, and this camping trip, didn't seem quite so scary. Well, those trees whose branches felt like they were reaching out and purposefully snagging on Kate's pink sweater were still creepy.

But she wasn't alone.

She had Grandma. She had her spirit guide.

Let her father try and get her now, because you know what? Kate was learning. And the more she learned, the more prepared she'd be when he tried to nab her again. She ignored the way her stomach clenched, ignored the tightening in her chest. She refused to be scared. She wouldn't.

Now if only her body would accept that fact and stop acting like it was scared.

Because she wasn't.

They hadn't gone far (or, Kate hadn't gone far—Grandma was a good half mile ahead of her) when her sensitive hearing picked out a slight shuffle on pine needles. Her head jerked up, fingers grasping the straps of her backpack. She turned, ready to kick out, to defend herself, but then a hand had been on her shoulder.

Completely freezing her.

That day in the park, when her dad had grabbed her, she hadn't been able to even scream or fight back. His magic had been that strong. Not this time. This time she screamed, good and loud. She ripped out the most piercing, high-squealed scream that would make girls in those slasher horror movies envious.

Only this time, it was James behind her. Not her dad.

She immediately cut the scream off and tried, very, very hard, to not to melt into a giant blushing puddle.

James grabbed her, yanking her behind him, towards safety. This was a little hard to do with her giant backpack and all, but boy, he was determined.

He spun, searching for danger. His hand darted into his jacket pocket, pulling out the most wicked looking dagger Kate had ever seen (complete with beautiful, flowing etched script on the blade).

But there was no one. No bogeyman. No dad coming to snatch her away.

Just James.

His defensive stance shifted. "Kate? Did I scared you?"

There was another shuffle of pine needles. Grandma.

"Oh, for Pete's sake, Kate," Grandma snapped. "I thought you were better than this."

Kate's face heated. Again.

And truly, it had *nothing* to do with James. Or how his hand still touched her.

"I'm, I'm sorry. I just..."

Just thought you were my crazy dad trying to kidnap me again. She, at least, managed to keep her mouth shut about *that*.

"Oh." This time it was James's turn to blush. "Right. Sorry. Didn't mean to sneak up on you."

He stashed the dagger away, the metal blade sliding against some kind of leather sheath. She squinted, trying to see where he even put that giant thing—and how he didn't skewer himself in the process.

He stepped back, letting her go.

This made Kate both happy and angry because really, it wasn't fair that he had this kind of weird affect on her. She was a teenager! She had enough problems of her own. She didn't *need* to deal with her elven-soul's issues, either. Even if those problems involved James, the very cute boy standing next to her. The very boy who was always running to her rescue.

Right.

She was shutting up about now.

That was when Kate noticed another woman standing beside Grandma. A woman wearing comfortable khaki pants. Not that the pants themselves looked comfortable. Okay, maybe they were better than the slim-fitted jeans Kate wore, but the woman looked comfortable in them. Just like she looked comfortable in the backpack. And the easy way she stood in the forest, as if she had nothing at all to fear from the creepy trees.

A woman, by the way, who was the one person Kate *hadn't* heard.

"Kate," James said, as he took her hand, "I'd like you to meet my mom. Aila."

Mom?

Kate blinked. Of course this was his mom. Same gray eyes, same tinge of blond hair, same everything. And while she'd never actually met his mother before, she'd instantly known they were related. But there was something more. Something she couldn't quite put her finger on.

James's mother smiled. And that smile looked just as comfortable as the rest of her, comfortable in a way Kate's mom had never been.

Why?

Simple. This woman had accepted who she was, had accepted her heritage. The very complete opposite of Kate's mom.

Her throat suddenly felt dry and, really, like she was suddenly very far out of her league.

"Hello, Katherine."

"It's Kate, actually."

And while James's mom might be smiling at her, acting as if she was pleased as pie to meet Kate, that smile didn't reach her eyes. A shadow hung there.

Worry? Fear?

Kate had no idea.

Still, Aila took Kate's hand in hers, her long fingers intertwining with Kate's. Power? Oh, yes, this woman had it in spades. It was like suddenly stepping out into the night and finding a hunter's moon, all golden and lit up with the barest touch of magic in its glow.

But there was nothing "bare" or little about this woman.

She glowed. Simply glowed.

And the woman who looked back at her? The woman who changed from one moment to the next, her features sharpening, reaching higher into the trees as if her power outstripped their existence. The woman who was now, very clearly, not smiling.

Guess this meant Kate and James weren't the only ones with elven souls, because Kate was very definitely looking at another elven soul. Too bad this elf wasn't pleased to see her.

Just her luck that soul happened to be James's *mom*.

"Uh, hi."

"She's exactly like you said, Emmaline." This, James's mother said to Grandma, not to Kate.

"She is."

"Emmaline?" Kate asked.

She couldn't help it. The word just about popped out of her mouth. She'd known Grandma all these weeks and she'd never known her first name. She was always just, just Grandma.

But Grandma hadn't moved. In fact, she didn't take her eyes off James's mom, instead acting as if Kate wasn't standing right there.

Kate *hated* that. Her mother did it all the time.

"And, what," Kate asked, "exactly, am I like?"

Aila's eyes swept over to Kate. Jesus. Even *that* was graceful.

"Someone," Aila answered, her voice wispy and mysterious voice, "who Alfeim Forest has waited a very long time for."

Her lips curved down as her eyes stayed on Kate. Searching. Studying.

It made Kate want to shiver.

Aila's image shifted back to the woman in the khakis. Her power, though, which Kate still felt pulsing through their *still* joined hands, didn't go away.

Her voice changed though, back to the kind some regular old mom would speak in. Not long-dead elves.

"I'm pleased to meet you, finally."

"Right. It's good to meet you too. I'm sorry you missed my birthday party."

Okay, Kate wasn't truly sorry, because she'd been busy dealing with the explosion happening in her life—meaning learning she was part elf.

"Yes. That was...unfortunate. On my part."

Uh-huh. Right.

Kate itched to pull away, to draw her own internal blinders over Aila's glow. Was this what James always felt when he hugged his mom? When he kissed her good night? (If boys even still did that anymore; she had no idea.)

Grandma, finally, came to Kate's rescue.

"Kate's learned a lot since then. Your son played a big part in that." She thumped Kate on the shoulder—

And because of that damn backpack, the thump caused Kate to sway, *finally* breaking Aila's grip.

"Yes," Aila said, "so I've heard."

Kate glanced at James from the corner of her eye. He had his hands tucked into his pockets, and he shifted from one foot to the next. Why was *he* nervous? He wasn't the one being stared down by the reborn elf soul.

"Aila's also the *laulaja*, the leader of the Gathering." Grandma's eyes flicked to Kate, warning her.

Like Kate needed the warning. For once, she didn't. For once, she knew when to keep her mouth shut and be polite. Because clearly, this big, bad, important woman (err...pseudo-elf) didn't like her. The question, though, was why—especially when James clearly liked her.

Which, of course, was only because of his elf soul and had absolutely nothing to do with Kate. As herself.

Not that she was bitter about it or anything.

"We should best get moving." Aila's smile was back, all motherly and caring again. No longer big, bad, and scary. "We have quite the distance to cover."

No problem. The sooner they got going, the sooner she got back to civilization and hand sanitizers.

Kate shifted her backpack, trying to adjust the weight (or make it go away) and utterly failing. "So, exactly how much distance are we covering? I mean, like how long until we get there?"

"Three days."

Kate, who was in the process of taking a step, nearly missed the ground. "Three days! As in—to get there?"

Aila did that motherly smile thing again, then with a grace Kate simply hated her for, slipped over a fallen log (nearly as big as Kate), and disappeared into the forest. James gave her another of his smiles, you know, the ones that made her stomach roll like a roller coaster's corkscrew, and followed after his mom.

Kate managed to catch up with Grandma before she disappeared, too. Not to mention she needed help getting over that log.

"Grandma," Kate hissed. "You packed my clothes."

"I did."

She'd done it only because Kate hadn't known the first thing about camping and backpacking and whatever, but there was one thing Kate *did* know—

"You only packed one change of underwear!"

* * *

JAMES, of course, had heard the underwear comment and hadn't stopped laughing about it. That's right. He took immense pleasure in reminding Kate about her underwear—something that made her blush every single damn time he mentioned it.

"Here's a good stream, Kate."

He skipped over the rocks, not even losing his balance when one wobbled, and made a sweeping gesture with his hands.

"Not too deep, good movement, perfect for washing underwear."

She attempted to rock-jump the way he did, and ended up with soaked socks and hiking boots. James grinned at her, looking nothing like his elf-version she sometimes saw, and everything like the seventeen-year-old he actually was.

"You're not a very good elf, are you?" he said. "Did your grandmother pack you a dry pair of socks or just the one?"

She stepped on his foot, or would have if he didn't have those stupid elven reflexes. This, of course, only made him laugh harder and made her hate him even more.

"You should be happy I even came on this stupid trip." She stomped past him, not caring how much damn noise she made.

This *was* a stupid trip.

A trip that involved them hiking through Alfeim Forest with no trail, no maps, and no GPS. Hell, Grandma and Aila didn't even use a stupid compass! As far as she was concerned, this trip had nothing to do with some secret Gathering of local half-elves and everything to do with making Kate look like an idiot. It wasn't *her* fault she didn't know how to be an elf. It wasn't as if she'd known she even had a smidgeon of it in her until she came out to this stupid place.

Mid-July in Montana wasn't exactly cool, like a nice, breezy walk on the beach. It was hot and pretty muggy, at least during the day. At night it was freakin' freezing, as if the wind had to blow extra hard from those tippy-top mountain peaks with glaciers or something. Even now, though, with the trees bending down giving them shade as they trudged over the not-trail, it was hot. And she was really, really sweaty.

Her T-shirt clung to her and she wiped a waterfall of sweat off her forehead. She'd shed her sweater long ago, tying it to her waist. At least Grandma had packed Kate's deodorant, otherwise *then* she'd say screw them and head back to civilization, whichever direction civilization (and running water) was.

Seriously, though, by the time she actually reached the Gathering, the only thing people would see was a girl covered in sweat, mud, and giant-sized red welts from mosquito bites. They'd take one look at her, see this as proof she wasn't really one of them so therefore shouldn't be trained, and be ousted on her ass.

"This is the worst summer vacation ever," she grumbled.

"Yeah, but you did choose to be here," James said.

Kate started—where the hell did he come from?—as he leaned over her shoulder. The jerk didn't even look winded, not like Kate who could barely keep herself upright and was sweating like a pig.

He was like his mom. Born for this stuff.

And not a dot of sweat on him. The jerk.

Kate was born for cable Internet and hot tubs with tutti-frutti bubble baths. Not that she'd had either since the trip to Grandma's house—but like James said, it *had* been her choice.

If only she'd known what she was getting into.

"Besides," James said as he came alongside her, sidestepping a prickly bush without even looking. "You know half the reason you stayed was because of me."

"As if."

She pivoted away from him, flicking her ponytail in his face. He certainly didn't need to know that he had been, in fact, a big reason of *why* she'd gotten the gumption to come in the first place. Nope. He certainly didn't need *that* added to his elven ego.

She headed towards Grandma and Aila, who chatted quietly by some log with two feet of moss growing on it. Aila's gaze rested on Kate. There was the tiniest crinkling around her eyes, but that was all. Still, it was enough for Kate to know that she'd heard good and well what she and James had said. And, that she disapproved.

Kate glanced away. For some reason, didn't want to look at Aila too long. Felt her heart kinda kick up an extra beat or two. Why did Aila freak her out? And hell, why didn't Aila like her? It wasn't as if Kate had exactly caused a whole lot of harm since she'd been up here (relatively speaking), but she wasn't the one pursuing things. James was. He kept bringing up their past lives, their bond, or whatever it was. So why wasn't his mom talking to *him* about it and leaving her alone?

"I'm glad you caught up," Aila said.

Ha. As if there was no condescending tone in *that* voice.

Grandma, always helpful and supportive, frowned at Kate's wet boots.

"You're gonna have to set them out to dry. Don't want you get blisters or any kind of fungus growing there."

"I'm sorry, what?" Kate asked. "Fun...fungus?"

And yes, her voice truly had just risen an octave.

"It's fine." James slid beside her, brushing her shoulders. "We can camp here, right? I mean, this is about where you wanted to stop anyway."

Stop? Here?

"I thought you said you didn't know where we were going?" she shot back at him.

Again, there was that half-grin and that little half-shrug.

Ohhhh, he *did* know more than he'd let on, the little liar! He even knew the damn route. The second she got him alone, she was going to kill him for keeping this a secret, torturing her every stupid step of the way, every stumble she'd taken.

But because Aila was watching, those gray eyes of hers like steel as she studied Kate, Kate managed to swallow her temper and nod.

"It sounds like a good idea too me. I am beat, after all."

Aila frowned, glanced at Grandma. "Of course. This is…new for you, after all. We'll camp here. James? Will you help me set the traps?"

"Traps?" asked Kate.

No one answered her. James did make little hand motions as if he were slitting his throat. Right. Hunting, for dinner. Or…she hoped he meant dinner and not actual traps because someone was after them. That'd be uncool because no one had actually mentioned that part of the camping trip (which wouldn't surprise her in the least).

Kate took a deep breath. Her stomach rumbled.

She wasn't at the Hilton with her mom anymore. She could do this. She would do this.

And she would absolutely not show Aila how in over her head she was.

Kate peeled off her backpack and let it thump onto a bed of pretty gnarly pine needles. She didn't care. Instead, she gave the biggest sigh of relief in her life. Every inch of her hurt. Every inch felt like it'd been rolled over by a boulder that had started at the top of a mountain, then causally just taken her right along with it.

Then there was all the damn mosquito bites.

She tried not to scratch but when you had a bite on just about *every* inch of your skin (how they gotten through her shirt, she had no idea), it was hard *not* to scratch.

"Here." Grandma held out a jar with some white, creamy stuff that smelled suspiciously like lard. "It'll help."

"Do I want to know what it is?"

"Nope."

Grandma grinned. It was the same grin she'd had plastered on her face since she'd started packing.

"At least one of us is having a good time." Kate scooped out a good dollop of the stuff and smothered it on her arms, neck, face.

And yes, she now smelled awful.

But at least she wasn't itching anymore. And heck, she wasn't a complete and total loss with this camping thing.

The clearing itself was rather flat with only a handful of rocks and sticks. The grass had a soft, almost spongy feel to it, so when she walked it felt like she really did have a cushion or a carpet under her (granted, one that had bits of wiggly bugs every so often, but she was even becoming less squeamish about that). Under Grandma's direction, she learned how to set up camp. They started with a fire—Kate dutifully gathering fallen wood (*only* fallen wood, Grandma stressed this)—and then ended with a trip to the stream to refill their water.

And as much as Kate missed her toilet with its convenient flushing, it really was beautiful here. She liked Alfeim Forest, liked how her muscles loosened, how she could breathe a little easier. Sure, the forest still had its creepy factor, or, really, certain trees that were twisted and dark with giant cankerous bulbs growing out of their limbs and trunks. *Those* her senses told her loud and clear to stay away from. But, it was more than that. It was like this place felt ancient, as if the forest sensed her and the others walking under its branches, the shrubs feeling their movement, the slight air of their passing. And it didn't know quite what to make of them.

Or, more specifically, of Kate.

By the small stream was no different. The freezing cool water came straight from the glaciers high up in the mountains, she guessed. Even the water seemed to almost flow briefly around her hand without a droplet touching her skin as if it, too, was surprised.

Grandma filled up their second inflatable water carrier and held it out for her. Kate took it.

"You are doing well, you know."

"Well, huh?" She placed the carrier on the ground alongside the first. "You mean I haven't killed myself yet or sprained an ankle."

"Something like that."

But Kate could tell Grandma was actually proud of her. Which... was weird. It wasn't something she was used to. Mom never looked at her in that way, with pride and confidence. She couldn't. She'd spent almost her whole life on the run from this place, from who she was.

Kate glanced away.

And truthfully, she wasn't feeling proud of herself or that Grandma should either. Sure, she was slowly figuring stuff out, learning to understand her heritage and all her crazy quirks. But she hadn't actually done anything. Not really. She just kept messing up, making too much noise, or walking too slow.

Or, telling all the evil magi that an elf descendant had gone and crossed the veil so they should all head into town and have an evil magi party.

As if sensing her thoughts, Grandma reached out and touched Kate's leg. Her jeans were so dirty, they didn't even look blue anymore, but the dirt didn't bother Grandma. She gave her a good pat anyway.

"I know it feels like Aila's being hard on you. She's got her reasons, but you've got to understand, Kate, the whole Gathering will be hard on you."

She sucked in a breath. Finally Grandma was talking about the Gathering, and what the heck she could expect.

Which was also frustrating that she still didn't *know* and again, she had that sense, the hairs-standing-up-on-her-neck sense, that something else was going on. Something she needed to be prepared for, not kept in the dark about.

"And that's supposed to make me feel better? I'm trying, and it's like no matter what I do, *someone* isn't happy with me. So, thanks a lot. I'm glad me 'trying' here means something to you people."

She even said the word "trying" in the same uppity, snooty voice Aila had been using all damn day. Only with her, of course.

"Kate. That wasn't what I meant."

"Bullshit."

Grandma sighed, shoulders drooping slightly. A strand of silver hair swayed along her jawline.

"I didn't mean that. And it's not your fault your mother ducked out of here, didn't teach you anything, didn't even tell you who you were. It's not your fault you're not trained."

"So then why does every word make it sound like it is?"

"Because we need you. It's dangerous. Your power...it's dangerous. Crossing the veil itself, who knows, whole worlds you could possibly open—and your father"—Grandma spat his name—"he's not far behind. And opening the gate?"

Grandma shuddered. "There's a reason the elves and magic were locked away. There's a reason the two were taken from this world. It's something only the gods know, but...and here's where the stickin' point is...not everyone agrees on what's to happen next. And not agreeing on a power as strong and game-changing as yours?"

"What do you mean?"

Grandma shook her head. "Just that it's dangerous for you. Sure as hell not a position I want my granddaughter in. Not in the slightest. But none of us seem to have a choice these days."

"Okay, fine," Kate said. "You're sorry. But you still dragged me out here because it's what I 'need,' and now it feels like I've failed before I was even given a chance to try."

"I know."

"Well, I'm not like you. Okay? I'm not ever going to be like you or James or Aila. Mom saw to that, and if you can't accept that, can't accept that I'm me, then why did you call this stupid Gathering in the first place? Because let's face it. I can't even be anything more than me. I'll never be some perfect elf descendant."

Not like James.

Not like Aila.

"You know what?" Kate said. "Just, just forget it."

She didn't wait for Grandma and simply took off running. She had no real direction in mind, just needed some distance, a chance to think.

A chance to let her guard down.

The pine trees passed in a blur. She followed the sound of water, fast-moving, unforgiving. Kinda like how her life felt. This time, the branches didn't reach out for her, didn't snag her as she went by. She didn't stop to think why.

Maybe she should have.

Maybe if she had, she would have stopped and run the other way.

But she didn't. And why should she? It wasn't as if she was alone.

High in the sky, beyond the trees and pine needle branches, in the heat of the sun and soaring on those tunnels of heat, was Eagle. She heard his scream, loud and clear and comforting, so she kept just on running.

She *needed* this.

She rounded a small bend, ducked beneath a low-hanging branch, feet taking her ever closer to the sounds of water. Rushing and angry, but also peaceful, and it eased her mind. She needed to move faster, smoother. She never once stepped on some sharp rock or twisted log that would cause her ankle to roll. Every step was sure. Every movement calm and graceful, just like her breathing, just like the sense she had slowly trickling through her whole being...

...that finally, she was home.

Eagle's cry was suddenly piercing and sharp. She reacted, barely thinking, just moving. Digging the toes of her boots into the loose, powdery dirt. It sprayed up into the air, stinging her eyes. She had a sudden glimpse as the trees parted, as she stumbled forward, of just how close the river was.

And the cliff she was about to run right off of.

She skidded forward, her momentum carrying her towards the giant, whitewater bubbling up beneath her. She grabbed for trees, rocks, anything.

There was nothing. She was going over.

A hand grabbed her arm.

Kate felt the sudden flare of power, as if it collided with her soul and there was some big push between them. And like that, as if it were magic, Kate stopped falling towards the cliff's edge...and the thunderous whitewater and spray and jagged rocks below.

Aila, who held on to Kate's arm, slowly shook her head. "It is a wonder, Kátheryn, you're still alive."

With the constant movement of water crashing below, the way it thundered against either side of the rock cliff, it was actually difficult to hear—even for Kate. But no mistake, Aila'd called Kate by her elven soul's name.

Again came that sense, that tugging in her gut. She felt herself still falling towards the cliff's edge even though both feet were planted firmly on the soft, dust-covered ground.

Falling ever closer...to what, though, she still didn't know.

Kate took a deep breath, hoping to steady her soul or something. "It's not like I'm trying to get myself killed."

"I wonder about that. I also wonder what it is you intend to do about my son."

"Do? I don't intend to do anything."

Okay, soul steadied. Now, now she was mad. Really mad.

Kate yanked her arm free and stepped away from the scary cliff. "In fact, the only thing I intend to do is find out what the hell's going on. I don't *intend* to do anything with your son."

Aila wiped away dirt from her pants, casual, as if, as if this was just a small little conversation in the woods. A conversation that was simply no big deal, not that Kate was steaming mad and seriously contemplating pushing the other woman into the river below.

James's mom or not, this woman was being a bitch.

"I have seen the way he looks at you."

Aila again wiped at dirt that Kate couldn't see at all, not once meeting her eyes. Could she be nervous? Was that why she was fidgeting? Impossible! Not this crazy-powerful woman who could probably squash Kate like a bug.

"I can't help that," Kate said.

"Yes, you can."

Aila gave up on the dirt and stepped closer to Kate.

Kate's natural reaction was to take another step back, but considering the edge of the cliff ended about there, it probably wasn't a very good idea.

Instead, she raised her chin. "And what? I'm just supposed to ask, 'Please, James, stop staring at me like I'm your long-lost girlfriend'?"

Aila's lips quirked up. "Something like that, though I would prefer a bit more subtlety. Actually, discouraging his affections would be more preferable."

Kate crossed her arms. First, she wasn't going to do a damn thing (mostly because she happened to *like* the way James looked at her)—but Aila didn't know that. And second, this was exactly the opportunity she needed. This was her chance to find out why Aila had it in for her.

"Why?" she asked. "Why do you care what James feels?"

"He's my son."

"Uh-huh. So you give the scary handshake to any girl he winks at in school?"

Aila's smile turned into a full-on scowl. "There *is* no other girl. There is only one girl. One. You. And I'm not about to let my son fall. I will not let him get sucked in by these elven souls, do you hear me?"

Aila stepped closer.

Kate nearly forgot about the cliff, but then Aila's hand was suddenly tangled in her sweat-soaked T-shirt and she had no idea if it was to keep her from falling back or to shake her silly.

Both, probably.

But Kate wasn't about to back down. Not now. Even if she *was* shaking and her nerves were shot, she wasn't about to let this woman win.

"Why?"

Because she *had* to know, had to know what Aila saw in James—and what she saw in Kate—that was so bad, so terrible it would make a woman like this angry.

Make a woman like Aila lose control.

"Why?" Kate asked. "Why would he fall?"

"Because it is so easy to forget. So easy to forget where one soul ends and the other begins."

Aila's face was so close, her breath hissed against Kate's cheek.

"And when that happens, when he forgets who he is, my son will be gone. I will not let that happen."

Kate released a breath she hadn't realized she'd been holding. "So, it's not me that's got you freaked? It's James and his soul?"

For a moment, Aila's eyes cleared. The crazy woman got pushed back and Kate glimpsed the mother underneath. The mother and her love—that was the reason she was confronting Kate. Something Kate wasn't sure even her own mother would do for her.

"No, Kate," Aila whispered. "You are dangerous, just like your mother. Dangerous because you can walk the veil, because you can reach out to the lost ones. Dangerous because you are untrained."

"Yeah. And who's fault is that, exactly? It sure as hell isn't mine."

Aila pulled back a little, but her hand was still snaked in Kate's shirt, stretching out the fabric. Good thing Grandma had insisted on packing some cheap shirts off the $5 rack and not any of Kate's good ones, otherwise she'd be pissed.

"My son cannot be allowed to follow his attraction, do you understand?"

"Not one bit."

Aila frowned and for the first time, Kate could see the hint of a regular mom trying to deal with a teenager (and not some epic graceful elf or something). Actually, Aila looked as if she wanted to smack Kate's head into a wall about now (if they weren't surrounded by nothing but trees and rocks). Maybe *that* was Kate's superpower? Maybe everyone was making too big deal about her walking the veil when in reality, her gift was just to drive people crazy.

Aila finally took a deep breath and stepped back, letting go of Kate and her shirt.

"If you encourage his attraction, James will lose himself to his elven soul. He will be gone. Forever. Is that what you want?"

"Of course not!"

She liked James. Maybe even a little more than she should (no way was she admitting that to his mom, though). What she didn't like was not knowing when those were her feelings or those of the strange elf inside her. It sure made the idea of going out with James a little weird since she wouldn't exactly know who she was dating—James or long-dead elf.

Behind her, Kate heard Eagle. Sharp and piercing. His voice echoed off the mountains, the rocks; seemed to echo within her heart.

She wasn't alone. Never would be again.

Even James had promised that as well.

She felt them both in that moment, their presence. And for a brief moment, Kate actually *saw* out of Eagle's eyes. Saw the world from so high up in the sky, and then, no, further still. A place of mist and shadows, a place where she could feel the faintest hint of magic, like a lingering smell the wind hadn't quite yet stolen away.

Eagle's view, but not of this world—of the veil.

Kate didn't fight it or deny it, not like she first would. Instead, she breathed in, letting her conscious sink deeper into Eagle's view. She stared into the veil, this separation between their world and all the others, this pathway, this between-place. Grandma, James, and Aila too (probably), could only see the veil. They'd never been able to cross over, to actually walk it.

Unlike Kate, who'd done so twice now.

From Eagle's eyes, she saw the river shift from white rapids to purple and blue. She saw Aila standing there, proud and strong, and in the next instant, hunched and afraid. Afraid of Kate.

No, not Aila...but the elf soul within her. That was who feared Kate, her and her elven soul. Feared her unwavering connection to James, one that had lasted for a millennia and more now, never ceasing, always there, steadfast and true.

Again came that sense. It spread through Kate's chest, warm and comforting, but still with that tinge of warning.

If she continued her path, she'd never be able to walk away again. Not like her mother had.

And then it was over.

Eagle's gaze fell away, just as quickly as it had come. She didn't know why Eagle had felt the need to show Kate the deeper truth; he must have known it was what she needed, to give her the confidence and surety of herself. Something that had been woefully lacking these days.

It had been enough, though. Enough for Kate to trust in herself again, as new and inept as she was at this elf-thing.

She took a step back (not literally—the big river was still behind her), and really looked at Aila. Yes, she'd seen the scary, powerful woman. Calm, collected, and even now in control. It was like she was one of those crazy moms who never lost her marbles and juggled three kids and worked full time (you know, the *super* moms). And Aila should have gone at least a *little* crazy with Kate.

She hadn't.

Okay, she'd gotten a bit crazy there, but not the regular, just-pissed-off-at-Kate crazy.

And that meant something. Just like Eagle's vision had meant something.

Aila had something to hide. Something she didn't want Kate…or anyone else knowing. Or maybe in this case, noticing.

"That's what happened to you, isn't it?" Kate asked. "You lost yourself to your elven soul."

Aila's back straightened. Her hand fell to her side. If Kate thought she was stone-faced before, that was nothing compared to this. She willed her other sight to click on or something, you know, like what had happened with Eagle. To reach back to her spirit guide and see through his eyes, to see what Aila was thinking or planning.

Nothing happened.

Figured.

Maybe she *did* need some more training in that. Or, just practice.

"No," Aila said. "It didn't happen to me. It happened to James's father."

"Oh."

No, that wasn't what Kate expected. The tactful thing would be to drop the subject, maybe just go back to the camp or get water or something. But no, not Kate.

She wasn't exactly good with tact. She was a teenager, after all, and didn't care much about things like tact and adults.

"Is there something up here about crazy dads?" she asked. "Something in the water?"

Any tact. At all.

Aila bit her bottom lip until it turned white and Kate figured she'd stepped over the line with that last comment. Oops. Or, maybe, *good*.

"There is a reason why the light ones are gone," Aila said. "There is a reason we have failed at all our attempts to reach them."

"Is that what *you* want? Grandma said everyone wants different things and that's gonna make this Gathering thing really hard."

"Of course it's what I want. You think I want to see our people fade away into nothing? This forest, our legacy, fade from *human* minds?"

Aila was shaking now.

At least Kate had managed to push the woman's buttons. Guess that meant she was telling the truth about not losing her soul to her elven half. Elves probably had the ultimate calm, Zen thing going on.

Kate stepped away from the cliff. No telling what a pissed-off mom would do to protect her son. Just to be safe.

"So... you've tried to reach them?"

Aila, for a moment, paled. Then immediately turned her back on Kate.

"We are done with this conversation. You will speak before the Gathering as planned; if they determine you are ready and if they believe you are true with your intentions, they may reveal some of this to you."

Unlikely. Especially with Aila at the head.

"And," Aila said, quite clearly, "you *will* stay away from my son."

Then she left Kate standing there, gliding into the forest as if she were a ghost or a forest nymph. In between one blink and the next, she vanished.

Kate knew she'd never be *that* good—either at being quiet or disappearing. And for some reason, it made her shake, made her feel lonely and realize just how out of her depth she was. Even with Eagle's help and Grandma's and everything she'd learned so far. She could never compete with *that*.

The backpacking was the easy part. Dealing with rules and a world she didn't know? Way harder.

Not to mention the James issue.

"So what am I going to do?"

Kate rubbed her arms, feeling colder than she had when they'd left at the butt-crack of dawn this morning. Or maybe Aila just took all the day's warmth just to prove a point to Kate...that she was out of her league and seriously screwed.

She sighed, figuring it was best to walk and think at the same time. She probably wouldn't come to any amazing revelations, unless her spirit guide decided to swoop in and help, but walking might clear her head. It was also about the only thing she had actually control over... putting one foot in front of the other.

Kate followed in the general direction Aila had disappeared and ducked between two trees that formed a vee. The path was clear enough. Not too much underbrush to snag at her jeans, not too much to distract her thoughts.

The trees didn't feel quite so scary and she wished she were back home, talking with Yig about this. He'd probably know what was going on. He was old, older than he remembered. He was, according to Grandma, the legendary World Tree with roots and branches in about every world in existence. It was cool that he'd decided to become her friend, and if anyone knew the hornets' nest Kate had just stomped all over, it was him.

Maybe...maybe if she walked the veil, she could find her way to his grove and ask him?

Of course, last time she did that, she'd painted a flashing neon sign to her dad showing where she was. Grandma (certainly Aila) would *not* be happy if Kate showed the magi exactly where they were.

She let her feet and the trees guide her back to camp, but try as she might, she couldn't stop thinking about James. She'd only just learned about their connection, that their elven souls had loved one another. Still did, actually.

She understood why his mom was freaked. Truthfully, she was a bit too.

"But I can't exactly make a decision without knowing why it's such a bad thing."

Vague warnings were one thing, but actually knowing what had happened to James's dad was another. And as if her thought had conjured him, James appeared out of the forest.

He leaned against a boulder nearly three times his size, head tilted back, a calm, relaxed smile on his face. His gray eyes so warm, so inviting. All she had to do was reach out and touch him, trail her fingers down his cheek.

He was real, and he was right there.

He always would be; he'd promised, after all.

And then she remembered the crazy-good hearing of all elven descendants. Had he heard the conversation between Kate and his mom?

She swallowed, feeling fear and embarrassment and something else colliding hard in her chest.

No, that was impossible. Even for James. He'd been too far, even for his hearing, especially with the water and rapids below the cliff.

Unless...unless that had been Aila's plan from the start. Waiting right there, waiting to talk with Kate in a place she knew James would overhear.

That thought unsettled her so much she lost her connection with the forest, and her body, apparently. She tripped over a small branch and stumbled—

Stumbled right into James's arms.

Warmth rolled through her, followed by ice, and then a sizzle that went absolutely against his mom's warning.

Stay away from her son.

Right.

Yeah, that *sooo* wasn't happening. Not when just looking at him made her want to lean in, to kiss him.

Kate looked up at him, tilting her head. He was close, so close. And his lips were right there.

Her vision wavered and she briefly glimpsed his elven soul. His long, dark hair tied back like always, those soft gray eyes as they gazed down at her.

Then, he grinned.

A grin that was nothing like an elf and everything like a teenage boy—who was now holding the girl he'd been picking on all day.

"Careful. I thought you would have found your forest legs by now."

"Come talk to me in another decade and I'll let you know."

His grin got wider. He also didn't let go of her. She felt herself pressing closer, feeling his warmth seeping into her skin, hiding the cold his mother had left.

It was his warmth that made her remember, made her pull back. No matter how much she wanted this, no matter how much she itched to lean in that last inch and touch her lips with his, she couldn't.

Not until she understood. Not until she knew exactly what was at stake.

"Thanks again. For that." Kate motioned her whole almost-falling. "And even for teasing me today. It helped take my mind off what we were doing and where we were going to."

"Sure."

James's smile dropped. "Do you want to tell me what's up?"

"Why? I mean, how do you know something's wrong?"

He shrugged. "I can sense it, I guess. For the past half hour or so."

"Sense it. Like with your soul... I mean, with *that* soul?"

"I don't know. Maybe."

Kate turned away. Then maybe his mom was right. Maybe it was easy to forget who you were and only remember who the elf had been. It wasn't a comforting thought. It was one that had worried her as soon as she learned her tie with James.

His arms wrapped around her. "See? Like this. I can feel it. Tell me, Kate. Please."

She took a deep breath. She didn't know anything about his dad, what had happened, or heck, if the guy was even around. But she had to start somewhere, before she lost herself to feelings that might not be hers.

She turned around in his arms. "Why doesn't your mom like me?"

"Not like you? Why would you think that?"

He was lying. Not only could she see it in his eyes, she *felt* it.

"You're lying. Why?"

His arms dropped away and it suddenly felt as if there was a giant gulf between them.

"She's just...worried, that's all. It's nothing. Everything will be fine."

Fine. There went that "fine" word again.

"Fine," Kate said. "You mean like things were 'fine' with your dad?"

James's eyes widened. She glimpsed hurt and pain and anger, then it was all gone, shuttered. He turned and she felt him closing off to her, shutting his emotions away so she couldn't see them, couldn't feel them.

"My father isn't us."

"James. I need to know. I need to understand."

Kate reached out, touched his shoulder, but James shrugged away.

"Understand?" he said, voice angry.

Anger. It wasn't something she'd heard from him before and it... well, it shocked her.

"Right," he said. "Now you're all ready to understand, ready to accept your heritage? Bullshit, Kate. I know you better than that. You don't care about any of this. You don't even know if you want to be part of this."

He might have been talking about the Gathering or the veil or heck, even their elven heritage. But she knew he wasn't.

He was talking about them.

About her and about him. About the connection between them.

And *that* wasn't fair.

Kate grabbed his sweater and yanked him towards her before he could dart away like his mom had, running away from this conversation. She wasn't going to let him.

"What I want to understand," she snapped, "is who I am. You know who you are, huh? Well, great for you, but I don't."

James's eyes narrowed. "Sorry for the inconvenience."

"Stuff it, James. I don't know who I am. I don't know if what I'm feeling is me or if it's the stupid elf in me. I don't know if the reason I'm here is because of you, because *I*—Kate—can't stop thinking about you, or if it's the damn elf! Okay?"

She wasn't done. She didn't care that his mouth dropped open or about the shocked look on his face.

She. Was. Not. Done.

"You, your mom, even my damn grandmother needs to get off my case. I'm trying."

She felt her tears filling her eyes, felt her throat constricting as she tried to breathe.

"I'm doing my best," she said, "but I will not, will absolutely not kiss you until I know it's *me* who wants to kiss you and not some stupid elf!"

James's mouth worked, opening and closing without anything actually coming out. Finally, he said, "You...you want to kiss me?"

Great. Now her face burned hot—a perfect match to her crying.

"Maybe," she mumbled.

"You do."

"Yes, but I just don't know...there's so much I don't know right now. Everyone's judging me for being someone I'm not or for not knowing something I should. I can't deal with it from you, too, okay?"

She wiped at her eyes, but by the second wipe, James was there. He held out a cloth handkerchief, but when Kate reached for it, he ignored her. Instead, he wiped her cheeks by himself.

"You're right," he said. "I'm sorry. I *am* pushing, but that's...that's just because I've been waiting for you, Kate. I've waited for you my whole life."

"That's what I'm talking about," she whispered.

He closed his eyes. Their breath mingled and Kate felt the power between them, felt Alfeim Forest tense and stir. She knew, without a doubt, that the forest could sense this connection between them, and maybe...maybe wanted them to reawaken?

Awaken.

Again there was that feeling, the swirling she felt standing above those white, thundering waters of the river.

Kate didn't know, couldn't tell where she was or even who she was anymore. Not as she felt this fluttering in her chest...her elven soul, Kátheryn, slowly reawakening.

Her throat had gone dry. She swallowed.

But she finally knew what she wanted. A chance to be herself. To get her feet under her. Regardless of her attraction to James, of how much she wanted him close, she couldn't.

"Maybe, maybe it's best if we just try being friends," Kate whispered. "And I don't mean that in the way most girls would say it, but I can't be with you until I know and I'll never know if—"

"If I don't stop pushing. You're right."

His hand lowered, but instead of backing away, he gently touched her cheek. She felt the sizzle between them, felt her pulse quicken, felt her desire roll and coil in her stomach. With just a touch, she nearly forgot everything she'd just told him, everything she'd just decided.

James saw it, too.

His fingers trailed down her cheek as he stepped away.

She felt the loss of his touch instantly, but she swallowed and forced her feet to remain grounded, to not go towards him, to not reach for him.

"Can we try it?" she asked. "Can we be friends?"

He nodded. "I'd like that. I'd like that a lot, actually, especially since...you're right. My mom's right. I don't want to lose you, not even to Kátheryn Silverstar."

Hearing James say her elven name again made her feel more... relaxed. At ease. It was a name to the feelings she felt, the feeling of otherness in her.

And it helped, in some small way; made her not feel so scared. Not quite so out of her league.

One step at a time. That was what she had to do. That was what she had to remember.

"You gonna ask me what my name is?" James asked.

Kate smiled, a little half smile that pulled at her lips. "Nope."

Why?

Simple. Because the very thought of hearing his name sent the deepest wave of longing through her body, something she felt straight to her soul. Both of her souls.

"No?" James asked, surprised. "Why not?"

"Because I think I'd like to find out on my own."

And that was what she wanted.

She wanted a chance to learn who she was, learn about the elves and what had happened to them, on her own. She'd learn who James was in her own time. The more time she had hopefully meant more separation between her and Kátheryn Silverstar. Because one thing Kate knew for sure, if what she felt for James was true, then there was no way in hell she would risk losing herself, and her feelings, to an elf.

Kate held out her hand. "Friends?"

James glanced between her and her hand, then with a grin that sent the Kate part of her tumbling, he shook her hand. "Friends."

He was worth it. Worth finding out the truth, worth discovering exactly what her feelings were. Worth risking further kidnappings and potential sudden death.

If Kate could survive this damn trip with one clean pair of under-wear, she could—and would—do this. Even if James's mom hated her.

HIDDEN IN MEMORY

An Elven Heritage Short Story

Every trudging step on that pine-needle-laden ground, every twisted root that popped out of the ground as if it were purposefully trying to trip her, every stupid stream that required rock-hopping (and usually ended with her getting her socks wet), was agony.

No, seriously. *Agony*.

Her feet ached. Her toes ached. Her poor burning calves were about to ready to give up and call it quits right then and there, while she collapsed into a very, un-elf-like, un-descendant-like, puddle.

Kate swatted the cloud of buzzing black flies that followed her like her own personal shadow. They got in her eyes, in her tangled blond hair. Didn't matter that it was pulled back in a ponytail; by the end of the day her hair seemed to have collected as many fly bits as it did twigs.

And her really cool cowboy hat? Complete with wide-brim and deep brown eagle feather stashed in the leather strap, a hat that she'd *insisted* Grandma get for her before going on this stupid trip? Totally useless. Seriously, it did absolutely nothing to relieve the heat. Sure the sun, when it managed to peek through the squished-in pine trees, was off her face and out of her eyes. That was nice. But the heat? Not a chance. Seriously, you'd think being up in Montana, so far up on the tip of some mountain that even Google hadn't mapped it, wouldn't be, you know, *hot*.

Except apparently it was.

In the summer. During the day.

And at night? Well, let's just say it was a good thing Grandma had packed thermal undies for this fantastic, and completely-forced-on-her, backpacking trip. 'Cause when that mountain wind got to blowing from those high peaks, with the permanent glaciers living up there, it got real cold, really fast.

Which, at the moment, seemed like a million years away.

All Kate could think of was putting one foot in front of the other and hoping to hell she didn't trip and have that fifty-pound backpack fall right on top of her (the odds of her getting back up were not currently in her favor).

The nonstop hours of hiking, of trudging up some mountain (and then another) with no end in sight. Her mud-splattered hiking boots so snug it felt like the shoelaces were about to pop. Sweat dripping down her knees and sliding over her wool socks. Don't even discuss the details of her armpits—thank God Grandma had considered deodorant essential when she'd done the packing.

Kate wasn't built for this, no matter what they all said about her.

Yes, she had finally accepted that her heritage was a bit...unique. A little, well, outside the normal. A descendant of a long-lost race of elves, the same elves who'd suddenly disappeared and, apparently, took all the magic with them. Not to mention there was the matter of some long-lost elven soul, Kátheryn Silverstar, parked right beside hers.

Yeah, life had gotten just a *tad* bit complicated. But all that? She could totally accept, albeit with some minor (and very much deserved) complaining. But this backpacking thing? Something that she was supposed to, you know, *enjoy*—seeing as how half her soul was some elf?

They were all crazy, including Grandma.

Kate wanted flushing toilets, running water, and the Internet. And not in that order, either.

Oh, and she really, really wanted a shower.

But she didn't have that. Instead, she'd been shoved into this trip with a grandmother she'd only known for two months, following a really, really good looking boy (also elf-descendant, also whom her inner-elf had the hots for—yeah, not confusing in the slightest). Oh. And his scary-ass, really powerful mom.

Talk about a real bonding experience.

And *why* this whole thing necessary? All so Kate could, *maybe*, get the approval of the Gathering. Apparently they, a bunch of local descendants, were none to happy with her, and she needed to (somehow) convince them she *wasn't* going to do something stupid like... bring down the barrier separating their world from like, every other one out there.

Kate somehow put another foot in front of the other. They were going up a slight incline and the dirt seemed to shift and roll beneath her feet, as if the whole mountain was having a huge laugh on account of her and how really, really bad she was at this elf-thing.

She reached up and grabbed a tree branch and managed to haul herself up and over the tricky, slippery dirt part. Not that they were on a path or a trail.

Nope.

That would be the *sensible* thing to do, and from what she had learned so far, elf descendants weren't exactly the sensible sort. But then maybe, that just went with the territory.

Oh, and those same descendants had totally left her in the dust—Grandma, James, certainly his mean-ass mom—while she scrambled and hauled herself up the side of the stupid mountain. They all apparently believed that she wouldn't do something stupid, like getting lost.

All because *Grandma* had said she needed training.

Grandma had said she needed to understand who she was, her heritage and all that.

To be fair, Grandma was probably right...but that didn't mean her mom hadn't had the right idea about hightailing it as far as she could from this life, and all the crazies and legends and magic that came with it.

Kate lifted a hand and traced the slight tip of her ear.

She couldn't help herself. She seemed to be doing that a lot on this trip, when it was just Alfeim Forest and her thoughts, no distractions of movies or phones or all that she'd left behind. Because...this really was her new life.

Everything from her oddly-shaped ears to her odd way of simply moving through the world, she was different. Not hugely noticeable, but enough. More than enough that no matter where she and her mom had moved to, Kate had always stood out, always stood apart. Never really welcome. Never really fit in.

Until now.

Mostly.

If she didn't count this whole trudging through the backcountry thing. Because really, as far as Kate was concerned, every rock, pine tree, and mound of dirt looked the same. As in, they passed that same tree, the one with the moss shaped like a bulldog, an hour ago and here it came again, only this time she saw Grandma's boot-stomping had taken her to the right and not to the left.

And after three days of seeing the exact same bulldog-moss covered tree, she was ready for a change of scenery—or more importantly, clean underwear and a flushing toilet.

But no matter how much she wished, dreamed, or fantasized, her companions kept trudging onwards.

Kate her heard Grandma before she saw her, barely picking out the shifting of boots on the ground, the slight bend of pine needles, a snap of small branch. Grandma could move so silently when she wanted to, totally leaving Kate in the dust when it came to the stealth factor. The fact that Kate heard her at all was so she wouldn't get freaked out by Grandma's sudden reappearance, which on the whole, was kinda nice of her. Kate had had a recent bad experience with her evil magi dad suddenly appearing and trying to kidnap her (it hadn't been the best first meetings as far as she was concerned; once was enough, thanks very much). So she was, understandably, a bit on edge with the surprises.

Grandma appeared then, sliding between a small grove of pines without a pause or a stumble, even with that big-ass backpack on. Slivery-white hair tied back by a string, a camouflage bandana stuck to her head, ready to catch any sweat. Not that there were any. Nope.

Grandma looked as if she'd just come back from a nice casual stroll and not climbing up a mountain with nothing but bare hands and feet.

It really wasn't fair.

But this time, she wasn't grinning from ear to ear when she saw Kate (who was still stumbling and falling, using another poor branch to get her up yet another slippery-dirt part).

Grandma didn't say anything as she waited for Kate to, once again, catch up. But then, she really didn't need to. It was pretty obvious from the way her mouth pinched and the loud sigh she let loose that she was disappointed.

It might come as no surprise, but Kate was pretty much a disgrace to all things elven.

"You can go on ahead, you know," Kate mumbled. "I'm coming."

She scooted her backpack higher up on her shoulders—shoulders she'd lost feeling in three days ago when this nightmare trip began.

Grandma shook her head. "It's better off to have me checkin' on you. Just in case."

"Look. My dad's not going to appear out of thin air. I don't need you to hold my hand."

"Maybe." Grandma shrugged, somehow not falling over with the weight of that backpack. "My old body is feeling tuckered out."

Bullshit. They both knew Grandma could run circles around Kate.

"Besides," Grandma said, "I like taking my time and walking in pairs. Not to mention it's just good hiking sense."

"Fine. Whatever."

But even with Grandma's grim, concerned looks, it couldn't stop Kate from enjoying Alfeim Forest. As much as she hated camping, the forest was truly beautiful. The way the breeze brushed passed pine needles, making the whole woods seem like a quiet chorus of whistles and chimes. The constant and steady hum of insects, the chirps and calls of different birdsongs as if each were saying hello to her, and not necessarily to each other.

And then the occasional sharp, piercing scream of a bald eagle high overhead, circling in arcs as he watched over her.

Eagle, her spirit guide.

Even if Grandma hadn't come back, Kate knew she wasn't alone.

There was also that part of her, deep within her soul, that could almost sense where James was. All she had to do was close her eyes, steady her breath and...she'd be able to feel him. Feel the warmth as he sensed her as well. As he reached and almost clasped her hand, squeezing it slightly.

He was still far ahead of her, on the trail-that-was-not-a-trail, and yet it felt as if he were right beside her.

The warm feeling in her chest spread, tingled. She heard a soft sigh, one that mirrored the chimes of pine needles and the wind, and she knew without a doubt that it wasn't her own soul sighing.

It was Kátheryn's. Her elven soul.

She was the one reacting to James's presence, not Kate.

But the warmth she felt from her chest, and the warmth she felt from James, crossing the distance like the wind or starlight itself, was so natural, so comforting, so perfect. All she had to do was let go and believe—

No.

Kate immediately snapped out of the sensation and tripped on a rotting branch for good measure.

Grandma glanced back, concerned at first, then, as if somehow seeing the scattered starlight around Kate, or whatever was left of the bond she and James (and their elf souls) had just shared, she simply shook her head. Disappointment. Sadness. It as all there, and the wrinkles road-mapping her face looked even more pronounced.

Kate blushed, but said nothing.

Grandma had a reason to be disappointed. And why not?

Kate had made a promise to herself, and to James. She'd been trying desperately to stick to it but it was as if she were fighting some huge current and it was all she could do to keep swimming, to keep her head above water and keep breathing. She'd told James they would be friends. Only friends. Oh, she was straight-up attracted to him, and she really, really wanted to kiss him and learn exactly what all these warm feelings in her chest, in her stomach, in her soul meant...but, she couldn't.

Couldn't fall in love with a guy when she didn't know if it was *her* falling in love or the elf soul living inside her. Both of their elven souls, hers and James, had bonded in their previous life and it was pretty darn clear that death (and then rebirth) hadn't dampened those feelings one bit.

He'd said he'd understood that. He'd agreed to, for cryin' out loud.

And yet...something had happened between then and now. Something she didn't understand and he wouldn't talk to her about. Grandma wouldn't either, telling her it was between her and James (though Kate was pretty damn sure *his* mom didn't share the same opinion and that it was most likely *her* who'd caused his sudden... distancing from her).

And that hurt. Hurt so much that Kate could barely see straight at times, could barely breath from this sudden pressure on her chest, squeezing until she was nothing but this awful pain.

And *that* scared the living daylights out of her.

"We're getting close, Kate," Grandma said. "Best pick up the pace if you want dinner."

"Yeah. Right."

Anything to keep from thinking about James.

Yet, even as she walked, she rubbed at that warm spot on her chest. Could almost feel the sprinkling of starlight falling from her fingers and dusting the pine needles and leaves dotting the forest floor.

They reached a small rise and the valley stretched out below them. Tall crags poked through clouds and snow clung to the dark, rocky surface. In a way it felt as if she were no longer part of the earth but some place else, some place...other.

Kate squinted her eyes and thought she made out the slow, circling flight of Eagle. Still beside her, still following.

Grandma pointed out the direction of Glacier National Park, which she said was actually part of Alfeim Forest, though the government didn't know any better.

"This place was our home then," Grandma said, "and will always be our home. Don't matter how far or hard you try and run, as your mom knows well, this is the only place we'll ever be at peace."

Kate took in the vast wilderness below her. Again, there came that settling feeling in her chest, a warmth that spread all the way to her fingertips and even down towards her toes. Could feel this...connection.

Between her and this place. The feeling was undeniable, like, if she closed her eyes, she could *see* how the clouds slowly moved across that vast blue sky, see just how those pine needles rustled against their trees in the wind. Could feel the small ground squirrel digging its way into some burrow.

A slight breeze picked up the ends of Grandma's hair, brushing it against her bandana. "It was also her home too, you know."

"Whose home?"

"Kátheryn Silverstar."

The very name caused Kate's breath to hitch, to pause in her throat. Fear and excitement mingled, intertwined.

She couldn't help it.

She was overcome with a sudden longing, an ache that swept straight to her heart and made her stumble backwards, far from the edge of the cliff, far from the edge of something else she couldn't put her finger on but knew with her entire being. So very close to falling over...to never getting back up?

She didn't know if this was *her* feeling this way, or the long dead elven soul inside her.

Kátheryn.

Her elven ancestor, an elf who'd died hundreds of years ago but who loved this world so much, who'd loved so deeply, she'd chosen to remain. To be reborn in one of the descendants. Kátheryn hadn't vanished like the other elves—the light ones, as they were some times called by Alfeim's inhabitants—had. Instead of disappearing like her kin, part of Kátheryn had remained.

Kate touched her chest. Felt the steady, thrumming beat of her heart. The beat that told her *she* was alive. Not Kátheryn. Kate. No matter what happened, no matter what anyone said, she was still and always would be Kate.

She hoped.

Grandma, not missing a thing, watched as Kate wrestled with these feelings. And Grandma, like always, didn't shy away about what this meant. She was the type of woman (though old) who stood up and acknowledged that life was hard and it sucked at times.

Kate saw all and more reflected in those eyes of hers, sorrowful yet steady. She was nothing at all like Kate's own mom...the mom who ran away.

"I know it's not been an easy journey for you," Grandma said, "any of it. But at least for this part, we're almost there."

But far, far from being done.

No, she couldn't focus on that right now. She needed to shift away from these feelings, the ones that fought in her chest. Too much had happened in such a short period of time; two months and her life had turned on its head. Now...now there was an elven soul in her slowly becoming aware of her surroundings...and of Kate.

Not to mention James—

"Thank God," Kate said. "My feet are killing me and I really, really need a rest."

"'Course, that's when the real hard part begins: getting those stubborn-ass folk to like you."

And that, Kate decided, was one of the reasons she hated her grandmother. It had nothing to do with having met the woman for the first time only two months ago and everything to do with her cryptic, otherworldly comments.

Whatever happened to straight answers?

"Fine, whatever," Kate said. "Nothing can be worse than surviving your idea of camping."

Kate turned her back on the beautiful view of Alfeim Forest, of Glacier and its great National Park just beyond her fingertips, and let her giant, heavy-ass backpack thump onto the ground. She slumped onto the nearest (and biggest) rock, leaving the small, pointy one for Grandma.

"And, by the way," she said, as matter-of-factly as she could, "this is *not* camping. Camping at least involves small bathrooms or heck, even outhouses."

Grandma settled on the pointy rock as if she were some fairy princess who didn't mind the uneven, uncomfortable surface she now placed her bum on. Must be yet another special elven trait that had conveniently skipped Kate. Like her sense of direction. Or balance. Or love of camping and all things forest.

Grandma merely shook her head. Again, disappointment clear as day on her face.

"I thought for sure your genes would have kicked in by now. And if not yours, well, Kátheryn might have helped out a bit."

"I do *not* want Kátheryn's help," Kate growled. "I am doing just fine without her."

"Sure about that?"

"Yes."

She crossed her arms and scowled at the no longer enjoyable view. Yet another superpower of her Grandma's—the ability to completely ruin even Kate's best of moods by reminding her, once again, just how much danger she was in. For just a moment, she'd felt herself, well, if not completely relax, at least welcome to the idea that there was some weird relationship going on inside her, two souls and all that, and for just a freakin' moment, it wasn't scary but just...

Different.

Grandma shot that feeling right in the foot, though, and in a single sentence managed to remind Kate of just how much trouble she was in. And most likely, how totally screwed she was with the Gathering.

And right on cue....

Grandma leaned towards her, hand wrinkled but as strong as Thor's hammer (not kidding), and squeezed Kate's knee (which happened to be poking out from the rip she'd put in her poor jeans yesterday).

"This is serious business, Kate. I know it's not your fault, how your mom had kept you in the dark, but I need you to understand. If you're not focused, if you can't prove yourself to the Gathering—"

"Prove myself? Gee, I thought telling my asshole of a dad to get lost or finding my shadow was proof enough? Oh! Or how about me crossing that stupid veil you're all so freaked out about?"

Grandma stiffened. "We don't talk lightly about the veil, Kate. Never."

"And how the hell was I supposed to know *that*?"

As it was, she'd been stumbling through her heritage, learning who she was and making mistake after mistake and still, they were *all* keeping secrets from her. Grandma. James. Certainly his jerk mom, Aila.

And all of it kept leading back to the veil. A misty place, a boundary between worlds, hers and all the others, including the magical one. At least, the one where the elves came from and the one where, according to her dad, lay a gate they were now locked behind.

The very last thing she wanted was some kind of special gift that let her touch another world. *Nothing* good would come from something like that. And so far, nothing good had happened.

Kate jumped to her feet.

"The only reason I'm on this stupid trip was because you told me it was necessary. Well, getting eaten by mosquitoes, nearly falling into a ravine, and then having a bunch of uppity, half-elven descendants like you *judge* me—was *not* what I'd signed up. You promised me answers. You promised to help me understand who I was. Guess what? You didn't."

She turned away, fully intending to go stomping off in some random direction (away from the cliff, though), when she nearly collided with a tall, and very powerful, Aila.

Everything about Aila radiated grace and comfort. From the way she stood, hiking boots planted firmly yet softly on the hard-packed dirt. Her soft tan pants flowed about her, catching in the slight breeze as if she herself were part of the wind when she willed it. Dark blond hair swept back in a complex series of braids that reminded Kate of the elven cast from *The Lord of the Rings*, and not a *single* strand had fallen loose. Certainly not a bead of sweat dotted her perfectly clear complexion.

And those gray eyes? Oh yeah, totally narrowed, totally displeased with her.

Again.

Not that Aila was very open about it, but Kate knew damn well what that narrowed, pinched mouth meant. She could also *feel* Aila's annoyance with her as her gaze swept over Kate, taking in her ripped jeans, the pink sweater her mom had given her and which Kate had insisted on taking (though certainly not practical) on this trip. The poor sweater was littered with small holes and snags from branches, but it was from her mother and even if she refused to be here in person, refused to be a part of this journey, Kate at least needed something of her.

Especially now when *everything* about Aila radiated displeasure. Disappointment.

And as usual, Kate hadn't heard Aila return. Nor had she heard James, either, who lingered just behind his mom.

Their eyes met briefly and Kate glimpsed his elven soul, half-hidden under the boyish, teenage face she'd become so familiar with. Dark hair that was suddenly long and tied back against his neck. A moment of longing and then James's normal gray eyes stared back at her....

Weighing her. Judging her, just as Aila had done.

Kate tried not to fidget under his gaze, under the same disappointment she felt from him. Again, that sorrow she felt in her chest, suddenly so overwhelming her knees shook and if she hadn't been standing in front of a super-annoyed Aila, she'd have let herself sink right down to the ground.

But in front of Aila, Kate refused to give an inch. That woman ate weakness for breakfast, then spit it back out when she was good and done chewing.

Then James dropped his gaze.

It felt as if Kate had been slapped, and she stumbled back a step.

But she refused to feel guilty, refused to back down. She'd told him her feelings, all of them, and if he couldn't accept that, then fine.

She lifted her chin, daring him to say anything. He didn't. He hadn't, in fact, spoken of what happened that first day on this god-awful trip, when she'd told him she might actually have feelings for him.

Meanwhile, Aila stood there, and Kate *swore* she felt glee radiating from that woman. What had she told him? What had she said that pushed James away so much?

No more joking. No more easy smiles or the comfort that they'd shared, that had come so naturally and easy between them.

It was like this giant gulf, this black-hole ravine had opened between them and nothing, *nothing* she said or did worked.

She'd at least thought they were friends. After all, right from the beginning, he'd done more than accept who she was, differences and all. He'd been the one who pushed her to understand, to listen…to both heart and souls.

She'd always thought he would be there, beside her, helping her through this, as scary as it was.

Apparently she was wrong.

And Aila was pleased as punch about it, the bitch.

Kate willed that stupid single tear away and glared at Aila. She'd had *enough* of people judging her.

Aila slid her own backpack off as if it weighed no more than a feather, and flicked her long braid over her shoulders. She barely spared a Kate a glance, even though she spoke directly to her.

"Your grandmother is concerned," Aila said. "As she has a right to be. As do we *all*. Fate, it seems, has brought us the one person who can cross the veil, who can find the light ones, who can save our people, our forest, from fading. Of course, you also happen to be the one person completely inept at all our gifts."

"Hey! That's not my fault."

"Your fault or not, if you're allowed to continue as you are, you'll injure not only yourself and us, but all of Alfeim Forest as well. We cannot afford any injury, not as weak and timid as we've become. As… compliant to this world and its…modern conveniences."

She said this last to Grandma, who'd gone straight and still as that pointy rock she sat on.

Aila swept past Kate. Not even her khaki pants made a brushing noise as she moved and her boots were silent as she stepped on pine needles and dirt. It was as if simply by moving, she wanted to prove a point.

And she had, damn it.

Kate spun to face the other woman, and she was pretty sure any creature within a mile heard her, the way *she* crashed over that same ground. It really, really wasn't fair.

Aila turned, her eyes lifting upwards and her face saying, *See?*

Kate couldn't help it; she blushed. Big time. Some elven descendant she was. Couldn't even move softly or gracefully without really, really trying (and even then it was a pretty woeful attempt).

She glanced at James, looking, praying for some support or hell, maybe even an encouraging nod or something, but...he wouldn't look at her.

He wouldn't meet her eyes.

She stumbled back, shocked.

James had always stood up for her, especially when his mom ripped into her. And now...now he acted as if he didn't want anything to do with her. He wasn't even trying to tease her.

His rejection...hurt. Hurt so much she nearly sank to the rock by her grandmother. But she wouldn't. She wouldn't give either of them the satisfaction.

Grandma got back to her feet, knees clicking and groaning as she stood. She placed a steadying hand on Kate's shoulder. It didn't matter how old she was, Kate could *feel* her strength. It was as if she'd pulled it right from the very ground. Stubbornness too.

"That is not the way we reach her, Aila. We agreed on this."

Aila's eyebrows lifted. "And? What else are we supposed to do, Emmaline? We are running out of time. *She* is running out of time."

Grandma's grip tightened and Kate flinched. Not from her strength, but again, from that disappointment. And it wasn't just from Grandma, but from all of Alfeim. As if the forest's gaze was suddenly on her, suddenly acknowledging that she stood there, among its trees and groves, the wild spirits it contained, and regardless of how far Kate had come, the respect she'd already earned, it didn't matter.

Alfeim was disappointed in her.

"It's not easy to hear this, Kate, and I'm...sorry. I'd been hopin' that once we got you out here, once we got you back to the place you'd, well, you were from, it'd all make sense. The parts of you that were lost finally would click into place."

Kate swallowed, her mouth suddenly dry. "Except I didn't."

"You didn't. And I'm not about to give up on you or what's happening. What happened with your mom, how she hightailed it outta here so fast, that's on me. I won't leave you, ever. But it doesn't change the fact that right now, you're a danger. Either we teach you how to use your gifts, how to safely cross the veil, or you threaten what little we have left."

"And everything we've worked for," Aila added.

"Worked for," Kate mumbled. "Gee, it'd be nice if you informed me what the hell that was."

Aila was suddenly there beside Kate. Just a breath, a passing of wind, and she was right beside her. Power flowing through her, an angry tempest barely held in check, in balance. Gray eyes flashing and, for a moment, looking like storm clouds.

She caught Kate's hand in a hard, tight grip.

Thunderbolts flowed from Aila, sparking right through Kate's fingertips as if the damn thing were reaching straight for her heart.

Kate bit down on her lip. She would not scream. Would *not* cry out. Never.

"We are preserving the old ways in every way we can," Aila's voice dropped, became…other. "We were charged with protecting and serving Alfeim, just as those before us have done. We will *heal* the forest; we will keep it, and us, from fading. Do you understand? Do you have any idea of what you threaten, the war that *you* can unleash upon us? The magi are right there, waiting to finish what they started. So desperate for revenge. So desperate to reach out and steal their magic back."

This whole time, James said nothing. But he was finally looking at her, at least. Sorrow and pain and…just maybe, guilt?

Aila leaned closer. "We will protect ourselves, our legacy. Even if it means silencing the one person with the gift to help us."

Before Kate could reply, before she could make this whole thing way worse by pissing off (even more, anyway) the really powerful woman, James *finally* stepped forward. Finally stood up for her, just as he'd promised he'd always do.

He lightly touched his mom's shoulder and that contact, *that* was also like a thunderbolt. One Kate felt even through Aila's touch, no joke.

Again came that feeling in her chest, the agony and her desperate need to breathe, to get him back on her side.

Back in her life.

James.

He wasn't looking at her; like, if he did, he wouldn't be able to say no.

"Enough," James said. "She knows the risks."

"Umm, no, I don't."

He didn't look at her. "She's trying, Mother. Leave her alone."

And for some reason, it actually worked. Kate watched, pretty darn shocked, as Aila's anger drained away. The power sparking through the woman, practically making both their hairs stand on end, slipped away, leaving behind a tired, worn out-mother and someone else...someone whose entire life had been focused on this one task and who had to suffer the presence of Kate—the one person who could screw everything up.

"James," Kate whispered.

She reached for him but he was already turning. His back, towards her, and he barely finished as she called his name. Her chest hurt so much, his rejection...but why? What had his mother said to him? Why wouldn't he even look at her anymore?

She didn't have a chance to ask any of it, to even relay how this felt, this feeling that desperately wanted to tear her from the inside out, because then he was gone. Boots moving silently over the thick, brown bed of pine needles. A simple breeze slipping between the handful of cottonwoods, causing the leaves to dance and sang, and he was out of sight. Again.

Another twist of her heart, and something more. Something...deeper.

Grandma gave her a comforting pat on the shoulder. "Let him go for now."

"But I don't understand. What happened?"

Aila glanced at Kate, with a smugness to her that made Kate want to deck the woman. "Nothing but what should have happened in the first place. You have no place in our world, Katherine Silver, as I've warned from the beginning."

Then Aila too was gone, following in the footpath of her son, as if *she* could see the way while Kate saw nothing but pine needles and rocks and a hard-packed dirt ground.

"Grandma..."

"I know, Kate. It's not an easy path we've asked you to walk—that *I've* asked of you. I'll try to answer your questions, prepare you. Let's keep walking, though; we've nearly reached the site. You can rest until nightfall and then the Gathering will meet."

Now, Kate had thought herself all hardcore and ready for anything, but actually hearing the words "the Gathering" and "meet" suddenly did strange things to her stomach, like make it knot up like crazy. And thank God, made her forget (at least momentarily) this messed-up business with James and their elven souls.

Kate picked up her backpack, nearly fell over backwards because of the weight, then managed to right herself and sort of catch up to her already-hiking, nearly eighty-year-old grandmother.

"James mentioned risks," Kate said. "I don't know what those are. Or even who this Gathering is."

All she knew was that they were a bunch of local elven descendants, who still followed the old ways, who believed in the stories, and who (apparently like Aila) weren't happy that Kate was stumbling all over "the way things were." Oh, and that Aila herself was the great and powerful leader of the Gathering (the *laulaja*, whatever *that* exactly meant).

Grandma sighed, a big, heavy breath expelling from her lungs. "I've been telling you from the beginning the risks with the forest, what happened to your mom when she rejected her shadow, all of it."

"You weren't exactly being clear there. You were also keeping a whole mess of shit to yourself."

"Yes...yes, I was."

And still was, *that* was as clear as day.

But now, with the Gathering finally meeting, there was no way Grandma could keep her in the dark. Not anymore.

"Tell me, please."

Kate followed beside Grandma as best she could, hopping over fallen logs and skirting trees when needed, doing her absolute best to listen with both of her slightly pointed ears. And not fall on her ass in the process.

But Grandma, finally, told her, and Kate actually listened.

Yet the more she heard, the more she wanted to wave goodbye and head the other way—even if she didn't actually know which way she'd be going.

The Gathering was going to eat her alive. No question about it.

"The first thing you've got to understand," Grandma said as she skipped over a tree root sticking out in the path, "is we're not a sociable bunch."

Kate thought about Aila. Sociable. Uh-huh, right.

"Now that's one hell of an understatement," she mumbled.

"Stop mouthing off and pretend like you give a shit that the Gathering might decide to silence your connection with your elf heritage. Unless that's what you want?"

"Wait...what?"

"That's right, Kate. *That's* what's at stake. You thought your life was off before, standing on the outside of everyone else, always being the odd girl, different and just slightly out of place? That's 'cause you *are* different. Your blood is different and hell, for you, your *soul* is different."

It was really, really darn scary how close Grandma actually came to, pretty much, describing Kate's whole existence thus far.

"Now," Grandma went on, "imagine if you *lost* that part of yourself. It was simply...gone. Ripped right out of you. You'd be walking around as half a person, half a soul. Something that you would never get back, an emptiness in your chest that would eventually, slowly, eat you alive. A darkness, a hollowness, you could never fill."

Kate was shaking.

"That's what they'll do to me?" she whispered.

"They might." Grandma's fists clenched at her sides. "If they believe you're too dangerous."

"And you'd...you'd let them?"

Kate was having a hell of a time talking. And walking. She kept stumbling on one rock after another, as if the forest itself was trying to slow her down or drop her right there.

High above, enjoying the warm currents, was her eagle. Circling, round and round. She spotted his brown form between trees, his welcoming cry like music to her ears. But there was something more in his calling to her...worry.

Agitation.

His presence had grown the longer they'd hiked, the deeper they'd gone into Alfeim, almost never leaving her side.

Grandma was telling the truth—about the Gathering, about their fear of her—and Eagle knew it.

Grandma followed her gaze and watched Eagle circling above them.

"Will I stand by and let them tear you in half?" Grandma asked. "No, I won't. The hell I won't let them take you from me."

She didn't look at Kate then. She didn't need to.

Kate knew darn well what was left unsaid...Grandma might not be able to do *anything* to stop them.

"Why have you kept this from me? Why wait until now? Why call the Gathering in the first place?"

Grandma stopped. Her boots kicked up a small patch of dust that spread upwards into the air and made Kate's eyes water...because, they weren't tears. Certainly not tears, or this feeling of betrayal.

"I had no choice, Kate. I had no idea...none...what you could do. Damn the light ones...I almost wish your mother had never brought you here."

Except that was never an option, not when Kate's heritage had come looking for her. That day hiking in Mount Rainer, how she'd gotten trapped by the forest there, in the misty place, a place that her mother had called Niflheim.

No. There had never been a choice for Kate. Certainly not to run.

Even as much as she wanted to right now.

Her heart was pounding fiercely; she could almost feel the coming judgment from the Gathering, as if each one of them were alive, their hearts tied to the forest, and each one of them watched her right now as she stumbled after Grandma, barely able to keep up, barely able to keep breathing at this high (and still freakin' hot) altitude.

Kate managed to swallow. "Okay, okay then. Who are they? What do they want?"

"A bunch of disgruntled locals who've been complacent for too long. Too long sitting in their homes, secure in knowing that life will just continue on as it. No one is happy about this Gathering, Kate.

Aila can say what she wants about finding the elves or healing Alfeim, but everyone's just fine with the status quo. Going about our lives, slowly fading away, and no damn magic war on the horizon with the magi."

"That's the second time war has been mentioned."

Not to mention, James's elven soul had also warned her about the magi, about wanting revenge on the elves for stealing the magic when they disappeared.

"So, there *are* more magi around, not just my dad?"

Grandma slowed, her shoulders bowing under more than just the weight of her backpack. "We thought they were gone, or maybe we'd just buried our heads in the sand for all these years. Only magi we'd seen in years was your dad, but now, after you went and lit a goddamn beacon when you crossed the veil, they're everywhere. You know all those calls I was gettin' before we left?"

"You mean, other than the Gathering members pissed at being dragged into the woods because of me?"

"Yeah, other than those folks. The rest were reports. Magi returning to the forest from about every direction possible, or maybe just climbing out of whatever hole they'd been hiding themselves in, the bastards. We haven't felt so many in years, not since the war." Grandma shook her head. Strands of silver hair stuck to her forehead. Kate couldn't believe that her grandmother might, actually, be sweating.

"They've been turning every tree and shrub they could get their grubby hands on, makin' dark, makin' them hate the light ones. And us. They've got spies everywhere now; we sure don't want them overhearing our plans."

"Overhearing?" Kate tripped on a root jutting up from the ground. "They're what? Are they following us?"

"Why do you think it's taken three days? We had to lose our tails." Grandma paused, craned her neck to look at Kate. "I thought you knew."

"Right. Of course."

Except she hadn't known, hadn't sensed it, and judging by the (once again) disappointed look on Grandma's face, she knew it too.

Kate frowned, concentrating on putting one foot in front of the other (and not face-planting in the dirt). The scent of pines and ever-greens surrounded her, and there was something about it, something that just kept on tingling outside of her senses, just, just out of reach. If only she could just focus, if only she was as good of an elf descendant as James or Aila, or heck, even Grandma.

She wasn't, and yet...the hair on the back of her neck tingled.

What was *wrong* with her? Why couldn't she do everything the others could so easily, like it was as natural as breathing? And here she was, stumbling through the goddamn forest, sweating like a pig, and she hadn't known for one *second* that they were being followed?

She was screwed. There was no way in hell she'd convince the Gathering, and survive whatever test they had cooked up for her.

The very thought made her want to turn back the other way and run home. Fast.

She didn't, though it felt as if her whole body, all the way to her insides, was shaking and shivering.

Kate tried taking a deep breath. Then, another.

At least she was still standing. At least she was still walking forward, without having pitched headfirst into the dirt and rotting leaves.

She needed to focus on what she *could* do, what she *could* control. And that was ask questions. Lots and lots of questions, even if they seemed stupid to someone who'd grown up knowing she was related to some long-vanished elves (and also happened to have a soul of one living right inside her).

"What I don't understand," Kate said, "is if their magic was sealed away, then how could my dad, you know, do all those things he did?"

The invisible hand grabbing her shoulder; the way he'd gotten the forest to turn against her, to try and trap her.

"Alfeim Forest still has a bit of magic left. Unfortunately, it's up for grabs to anyone who can use the stuff. Us, and magi, included. The magic, if you can call that tiny-ass dusting magic, ain't gonna last forever, which is why you've got everyone in such a tizzy."

"Right."

Made perfect sense. Kate was the only one who could cross the veil, who could *possibly* walk between worlds and find where the elves had gotten themselves to.

In some ways, what the magi and descendants wanted wasn't *so* different from the other. They both wanted magic back and they both wanted a return to the "way things used to be." At least, up until you considered that one side wanted to free the elves and the other wanted to wipe them completely out of existence.

Forever.

Eagle gave another shrill scream above, his voice piercing right through the birdsong and chirping bugs as if the sounds were butter. But it wasn't a warning call, just a reminder.

Kate took a deep breath. The sense of the forest filled her, comforting her. The evergreens; the way the breeze brushed through her hair, tickling her cheeks and bringing a fantastic relief to the endless heat.

"We'll get to them soon enough, Kate."

She felt Grandma's hand on her shoulder. Comforting as well, and secure. Grandma wouldn't turn away from her, not like James had.

Her heart again twisted at the thought, but she quickly shoved it aside. She had bigger worries than James right now.

Like surviving.

<hr>

To say Kate was exhausted from head to foot and right back to her soul was an understatement. A huge-ass understatement.

What she wanted, more than anything else, was to curl up in a super-hot bubble bath complete with scented candles and soft music. Oh, and a big-ass box of chocolate. Not the cheap kind from See's. We're talking Godiva here. From the sweet, mouth-melting white chocolate to the dark stuff that packed a punch and made you close your eyes in complete and utter contentment.

Since Kate had neither bath nor bubbles nor chocolate, she made do with what she had.

Which was a giant-ass boulder nearly three times her size. But hey, it was warm from the sun, and resting her back against it actually caused at least one or two of the knots in her back to loosen, even if just a tad. She closed her eyes and enjoyed the blissful warmth as it soaked into her sore, tired body. The sun's rays had done its thing, heating the surface and providing her the exact kind of relief she needed.

Relief for both her body and soul.

The clearing they'd stopped in was a natural depression along the side of the mountain, a spot where the trees had simply not bothered to grow, leaving a wide, circular opening.

Perfect, Kate guessed, for a Gathering of half-elf descendants.

She tilted her head up and peered into the tall pine trees, their branches now hiding the sun. She squinted, but couldn't make out any tree structures or rope bridges or, who knows, hidden palaces made of leaves. Nope, nothing cool like she'd seen in *The Lord of the Rings* movies, just trees.

Maybe the Gathering would bring regular old camping equipment, you know, and coolers filled with beer or something. Tents, that sort of thing. Hell, even Aila used a tent (though she'd sniffed like the Ms. Snotty she was when Kate had *actually* asked her about it).

Aila, James, and Grandma were doing the breaking-out-the-camp thing. They worked on a fire, collected water for dinner, and unfurled and raised the tents. They also didn't ask her for help (they'd given up on that by day two—again, it wasn't her fault she'd never been camping in her life). It was as if they couldn't stop moving—or, more specifically, they had the energy to keep moving. Which Kate so didn't have.

Not like Aila cared. Not if that glare she sent Kate was any subtle indication that Kate wasn't wanted or needed.

Fine. Whatever. It wasn't like this whole thing was her idea.

She tried to untie her hiking boots, eyes closed and one-handed. It wasn't going very well and she couldn't swell up the energy to give a real go at it. Right now, it was all she could do not to fall apart, not to pick apart how truly unfair her life was.

No one had said anything about being followed. Not James, not Grandma, not even Eagle. Eagle, who even now she sensed close by; very close, in fact. He was perched on the tree just above her head, though out of sight from the others. She could see his gaze, watching her, watching Grandma, and more than likely, watching Aila.

He was afraid.

But why hadn't he warned her about the magi or spies? Or...maybe he had and Kate just didn't have enough sense to understand.

But why hadn't anyone—Grandma or James—said anything? Why keep her in the dark? Why not tell her, "Hey can you sense this? No? Well, let's practice!"

You know, *try* to actually *teach* her to be what she was instead of keeping it to themselves, right along with their legion of secrets and half-truths.

Once again, she couldn't help but feel how much of an outsider she was. How no matter what she did or how hard she tried, she just didn't belong.

And she never would.

Kate sighed, giving up on untying her boots. Might as well try earning a few points with the *laulaja*. Not like it mattered. Aila would turn the Gathering against Kate before she muttered a word. Until Aila was convinced Kate was planning on leaving James and his elf soul the hell alone, she wouldn't stop until she destroyed Kate and her chances of walking out of here with souls (both of them) intact. Not to mention that Aila was one-hundred-percent convinced that Kate was a screwup.

Kate, somehow, with a strength and energy she had no idea she had, pushed herself off the boulder and went to help. Kind of. Because, again, she got in the way more than she helped. Even James was frowning at her by the third time she'd caused the navy-blue, two-person domed tent to collapse. For some reason those rods did not want to stay clicked in place and the whole thing just kind of, well, collapsed into a sad puddle of scratchy fabric tent.

Was it embarrassing?

Oh, yes.

And the look that James gave her? Let's just say he wasn't regretting the whole "not talking to her" thing. It was pretty obvious he was happy he'd been distancing himself from her and her complete and utter failure to be...to be someone she wasn't.

It was Grandma who'd suggested Kate, once again, go collect firewood (only the dead kind, as if she needed reminding by the third night).

So, she did.

And then tried really, really hard not feel the disappointment... from the others, and more importantly, from herself. Why was she having such a hard time? Why couldn't she just...just be a normal descendant like the rest of them and not another failure?

"Because it's not who you are," she mumbled.

She shuffled the sticks in her half-bent arms. Her second armful, and this time she'd found a couple that were still covered in sap and coated her bare arms in the sticky stuff. Well, that went along just great with the twigs in her hair and the sweat.

The day was slowly drawing to a close, the sun sinking beyond the trees and behind some mountain she didn't know the name of, and really didn't care. Wondering, yet again, why she was trying so hard when she would never, could never, measure up.

She fumbled with the sticks, nearly dropping half her load, when she felt another traitorous tear coming along and she swore that this time, *this time*, she would *not* cry.

Ha, as if she had any more control of her body as she did her elf senses.

There was another branch on the forest floor, this one a little buried by some brown, curled-up leaves. Bending down, still balancing what wood she had left, she wrestled with this...particularly difficult stick. Huh. Maybe it wasn't dead and fallen like she'd thought, 'cause it clearly had no intention of coming quietly.

Except, there was that tingling again. A slight brush of a breeze, of something more, but she was just so frustrated with everything, everyone, how they never believed in her, never gave her the benefit of the doubt, and just *judged* her—

Kate dug her feet into the soft dirt and yanked. She pulled with every ounce of strength she had left, let it all out into that stupid, stubborn stick.

The stick didn't move, but she did.

Backwards.

Yep. She'd pulled so damn hard that *she* fell backwards. Her fire-wood went flying and she landed in a nice heap right on her butt. A fall which actually really, really hurt.

"Oww!"

Her hands immediately flew to her injured bum, and she winced when she realized she'd actually landed on a nice pointy rock.

Wonderful.

"Perhaps," a deep, musical voice called from behind her, "you shall take heed of the forest next time."

Kate yelped and spun. She grabbed one of the bigger branches and held it like a bat, ready to pound the shit out of any magi who dared come near her. Except the voice hadn't been her dad, not at all seductive or promising; her subconscious picked this out slowly, over the hard pounding of her heart, the adrenaline that shot through her like a firecracker.

Kate's grip on the branch tightened, a sharp edge of wood digging into her palm, but she didn't dare move. She squinted, trying to see, trying to understand, but even her good eyesight was playing tricks on her in the twilight.

He was half hidden by the slowly darkening forest, by the trunks of trees that were both made of rough, coarse bark and shadows. Shadows that seemed to extend closer towards her, lengthening by the second as the sun continued to sink beyond the horizon. It was as if he was one with both forest and shadow, hard to see because he simply fit, belonged. Like a white-tailed deer startled while grazing. Or not a deer, because this man was far, far from being prey.

But...not predator (unlike her asshole dad). This man...he was other.

He stood there, watching her, completely still, fading into the woods even as she watched. He remained so still, so distant, it would be easy to pretend that she hadn't actually seen—or heard—anything.

Except she had. And she wasn't her mother, wasn't interested in running.

And more than anything, despite his tangled, long, dark hair or clothes that seemed to fall off his body, the stitching threadbare and pushed to the breaking point, she recognized him.

Or in truth, she recognized his son.

This, this was James's dad? What was he doing here?

Kate lowered the branch, but didn't let go. She was learning how to survive in this strange, elf-filled world, although slowly. A weapon should always be close at hand.

James's dad tilted his head to the side and he blinked, still watching her, studying her, as if trying to understand something just outside his reach. The movement seemed even more graceful than even James's, as if this man were a dance in motion, the twinkling starlight in a deep night sky.

Again came that sense of *other*. And she knew everything Aila and James had told her about him was true...this was his elven soul, and no mistake.

"You're James's dad."

"James."

He spoke the name as if testing it for the first time, unsure and yet curious all the same.

"James," he said again.

"You know, your, uh, son?"

Or did he know? Did he remember? If you gave into your elven soul, did you remember anything of who you'd been before?

A scary thought, indeed. Especially after Aila's warning about James and how easily *this* could happen to him. Not that it could happen to Kate, 'cause, you know, the whole Gathering was pretty much banking on ripping that part of her out, so hey, no danger there.

"You are scared," he said.

"No."

His gray eyes focused on Kate again and she tried not to shiver, tried not to show how really weird and really disturbing it was to come face-to-face with an elf soul. An elf soul living in a human body; a soul that shouldn't be staring out of those eyes. A soul who'd died a long, long time ago.

"I was too, for a time," he said.

His eyes closed and a peace settled over his face. For a moment she saw the elf fade and the man emerge.

"James. My son..."

Kate wished she knew more, wished she knew what had happened to him, and why he'd given up his own human soul to the elf. But she didn't. Neither James nor Aila had thought to inform her of *that* little detail, and she bet they were hoping she wouldn't come anywhere near him. Hell, she didn't even know the man's name, which was weird considering she'd almost been, you know, *dating,* his son.

Almost.

Of course, she bet Aila hadn't counted on him seeking *her* out.

"He is well?" James's dad finally asked.

"I think so. He's been distant with me lately because you know… our souls. And his mom, I mean, Aila, wasn't too thrilled about us spending time together. She talked with him about something, I don't…I don't know what, but now he won't even look at me."

The words sort of rushed out of her. Fear and frustration and again, a soul-deep longing. And hurt. James had walked away from her. But… could she blame him? Could she, when she staring face-to-face with what James could become? The part of him that she did care for her, greatly, lost forever?

"He won't even look at me," Kate said again.

Her words, barely a whisper in the slight wind that slipped between them, stealing those words before they found their way to prying ears.

She blinked. Where had that thought come from?

"Aila."

His eyes snapped open.

The man was gone. The elf soul had returned and there was nothing human in that sharp gaze, penetrating and all-knowing. A gaze that she doubted knew anything of kindness or empathy.

Kate felt heavy then, as if it was hard to breathe. Fear, maybe? Kate tried not to shiver at the sudden change, the realization—and the fear —that perhaps in this Aila was right. She didn't want to see James's elf.

All she wanted was James.

"Yes, Kátheryn," he said. "She would not wish the two of you together. Not then, and not now."

"Actually, it's Kate."

She realized she was holding the branch higher, her grip tighter, as if she was readying to deck the man if he came close. A big stick was probably next to worthless when it came to an elf, and this was, after all, still James's dad.

So, she lowered the branch. His gaze followed.

"And you are...?" she asked.

"Eolis."

"It's nice to meet you." Kate held out her hand.

He paused, considering her offered hand, before extending his own. His fingers were cool against hers and his touch felt...different. Not like Aila's, which radiated power, and not like James's, whose touch sent her stomach tumbling towards to God-only-knew-where. For some strange reason, Eolis's touch...felt like home. The same way Alfeim Forest felt like home.

"So. Are you here for the Gathering?" she asked.

"I no longer speak for the Gathering. Or more specifically, they can no longer speak for me."

Right. Which made total sense coming from an elf guy and all.

"Then, why are you here? I mean, right now. Did you come to see James?"

"I did not. My son will not accept me as I am. I came to find you. To warn you."

"Warn me?"

The words stuck to her throat. Her heart pounded. Her own instinct went into overdrive because she knew, knew right to both her souls, exactly what he was going to say.

"The Gathering cannot allow you to leave here, Kátheryn. Not with your souls intact."

She felt light-headed and steadied herself against the trunk of a pine tree. The rough bark scraped against her open palm, but it didn't hurt. Instead, she felt a warmth flood through her...which was also when she realized just how cold she'd become.

Freezing cold, actually.

"I know," she whispered. "They're afraid of me. Of *her*."

Of Kate's elven soul, Kátheryn.

How she knew, Kate hadn't a clue, only that the feeling, the sense had been there from the moment she began sensing Grandma's disappointment, her concern. And when James...James turned away from her.

Her allies, few as they were, slowly being taken away. Slowly, having stopped believing in her.

Had this been Aila's plan all along?

Again, as if reminding her that she wasn't alone, she heard Eagle. His cry echoing through the forest and straight to her heart. No, she was not alone, even if James had left her and Grandma was already giving up on her.

"Yes," Eolis said. "They fear you."

Kate's head snapped up. "How did you...?"

She gripped the tree hard; needing the support, needing its strength, and for some strange reason, the tree gave it back. She didn't feel quite as weak in the knees; her head, just a tad bit clearer.

"I cannot read your mind, young Kátheryn. But I can read the forest, and the forest, it reads you."

He nodded at her hand, touching the tree, then at her feet, where her boots stood in that brown and drying patch of pine needles.

"Oh. Well, okay then."

In truth, that was a pretty good explanation when you walked in a world with elves and chatted with one in the middle of a big-ass forest. Still, Kate removed her hand from the tree, but slowly, and not afraid either.

That was a strange feeling.

Along with a stirring in her gut. An uneasiness that weighed on her, like footsteps, light but true. Confident. Steps that were determined and radiated power and...anger.

Anger, at Kate.

Aila.

She was coming this way.

Kate stumbled back and managed to trip over something—either another damn rock or her own foot, who the hell knew, and would have ended up on her butt if not for Eolis. He was there, suddenly, not even the wind stirring as he moved—he was that good, and that freakin' quiet.

His hands were strong and cool as he steadied her.

"Aila comes. We most go."

"Wait, wait a minute."

"There is no time. Already she senses my presence. We must leave."

"Leave? But I can't, I mean—"

She didn't have options, not when her only allies were turning against her, one by one, as they no longer believed in her. Then there was her dad and the other magi, who'd be pleased as pie to force her to be their personal veil/world-jumper.

And seriously, she was not okay with the Gathering ripping out her elven soul. She might not understand this side of her, this Kátheryn, but Kátheryn *was* a part of Kate and it was up to *Kate* to decide what the hell she wanted to do with Kátheryn.

It was for both of them to figure out, without anyone else meddling with their grubby fingers.

"Okay, okay," Kate said. "I'll go with you, but, but I don't know what to do. I don't know how to be, you know, like you. Like them."

"Like Kátheryn?" he asked.

"Yeah. I'm not, exactly, very good at that."

Eolis froze then, body stiffening. "I have been watching you, as the forest watched you. I did not understand your challenges here, nor did the forest. You seemed out of step with yourself."

That was one way of putting the whole elf-thing she wasn't very good at.

Eolis was watching her, those gray eyes piercing. The sense of *other* overwhelmed her to the point where she no longer felt Aila's footsteps, their hurried approach.

Coming faster. Closer.

He glanced in Aila's direction.

"You cannot sense the danger?" he asked.

"Umm...sort of? They didn't exactly teach me. Anything."

Not her mom, not James, not even Grandma.

Eolis finally stepped away from the shadows and Kate made a surprised squeak. Holy crap, he did look like James—no, not like James, but the *elf* soul within James. The same facial structure, same intense, otherworldly gaze. The kind of gaze that made her knees shake and question her sanity because after all, what the hell was Kate

Silver doing backpacking in the middle of goddamn forest following her eighty-year-old grandmother to meet with a bunch of other Montana crazies and elf descendants?

"See for yourself, Kátheryn; use your sight to see *truth*. Let the forest speak to you."

"About that..." Kate waved a finger in the air. "I can't exactly *do* that. I mean, not really well. Or at all. On command, anyway."

Eolis's gray eyes followed her finger, then lifted slowly to the sky.

Eagle screamed, and she glimpsed a ruff of brown feathers. This time, unlike before with Eolis, he was warning her. About Aila. That Aila was nearly there.

Eagle feared Aila...but not Eolis. Kate filed the information away, trusting in Eagle, in her instincts; as undeveloped as they were, they were still hers.

But they had to move, they had to do *something* before Aila got there, but what?

Eolis watched Eagle circling overhead. He frowned. "You cannot sense Alfeim?"

She shook her head. "Only a little, but not enough. That's why Grandma's worried about the Gathering, about what's going to happen."

"I see, then. So that is her plan."

"Her?"

But Eolis didn't answer. "It is no matter. I will show you."

"You, uh, what?"

And that was about all Kate was able to say before Eolis wrapped his arms around her waist and ran. Between one blink and the next, her throat filling with either a scream or a really angry curse she was sure would offend the delicate sensitivities of a long-dead elf, she was swept away from the clearing.

Away from Grandma and Aila.

Away from James.

Not that he'd notice, or freakin' care.

Except...he did. She felt it. Just as he felt the instant she disappeared deeper into Alfeim Forest.

But what other choice did she have? What other choice had they given her? She was *not* about to allow any part of her to get ripped out.

But being cared around like a sack of potatoes was also not okay.

Kate tugged on Eolis's iron-clad grip. Nothing, not even a slight hesitation. She opened her mouth to shout at him, then snapped it shut when she got slapped with a bunch of leaves.

Above them, she heard the distant beat of wings and the shrill cry of Eagle. Following her, looking after her, like always. Instead of fighting, Kate let herself fall limp. She wasn't alone. Eagle was with her.

Eagle clearly agreed with Eolis, certainly about Aila. And he'd been increasingly agitated as they got closer to the Gathering. Eagle had known what they might do, just as Grandma had, as her fear had grown the longer they'd hiked and Kate continued to remain her boring, Kate-like self (meaning, not elf-like).

They'd run far enough that James was barely a feeling in her soul, still there but...distant. Which seemed fitting considering that was what he'd been doing since that first day of hiking, since Aila had warned him away with whatever it was she'd said.

Apparently, Eolis decided they had gone a safe enough distance, and he slowed.

Which was a really, really good thing 'cause she was starting to not feel so well.

The world stopped zipping by like she was on the Mad Tea Party ride at Disneyland (not that she'd ever been, but clearly she had a pretty good imagination), and hopefully this also meant her poor stomach would have a chance to settle before she lost her lunch of jerky and peanut butter sandwiches.

Eolis, clearly sensing her imbalance, propped her onto a half-dead log. She spared enough of a glance to ensure she wasn't sitting on a spider's nest before sinking down—very ungracefully and un-elf like.

And, of course, Eolis noticed.

"You are not familiar with our world," he said.

"Gee, you think?"

"I am not...familiar with this phrase, Kátheryn."

Maybe because she'd been tired of being strung along on this whole trip, maybe because she felt like throwing up, or maybe because she was tired of this whole elf thing, she let Eolis have it.

"Yeah, well, you used to be familiar with it back when you were James's dad and not Eolis, whatever your name is. And for the last time, my name is Kate. *Kate*. Not your elf friend or whatever I was to you, and I'm doing the best I can, all right? Just because I don't have a rock-hard stomach to zip through the forest doesn't mean I've failed as an elf."

Which was exactly what Aila and James had been making her feel like. Even Grandma, too.

A failure.

Eolis stepped back a moment, the movement as graceful and at ease as if were one with the wind, which really, really wasn't fair. She *was* trying, goddamn it.

He considered her words. "You have not failed. If you had, you would no longer be connected with your eagle. You would no longer touch the soul of the elf I knew as Kátheryn. You would be dead, Kate, if you'd failed."

She blinked at her name.

Oh. Maybe dead elves could learn new tricks.

"I guess that's one way to look on the bright side," she said. "I'm not dead."

Yet.

'Course, if Aila and her stupid Gathering got ahold of her now, that would certainly change. And fast. Grandma had warned Kate the Gathering would prefer life to remain as it was, which Kate could understand. A lot of people hated, or feared, any kind of change. Good or bad.

Her head spun just from thinking about it, making the whole need-to-vomit feeling come back.

So, she focused on where they'd stopped, a small glade hidden by the mountain's shadow, with a nearby stream trickling through. The trees seemed to have pulled back here, allowing this patch of ankle-high grass with a sprinkling of purple and blue flowers to grow. A soft breeze, gentle, almost, blew through here, tickling her cheek, pulling on her hair as if...as if it was playing with her.

And smiling.

The sense of *other* returned, but also something more... something...right.

Drawn to this place, pulled by a feeling that went right to her soul —both of them—she slid off her improvised chair.

There was something about this place.

It wasn't a small glade, a sliver, a patch of openness in an otherwise dense forest, like she'd first thought. Except the appearance, the sense, of this being small, of being unimportant, remained. As if the glade itself was telling her to look away, to keep moving, to not look back.

But she couldn't stop looking, couldn't help but be pulled forward.

Kate let her eyes wander. She noticed the way the sun's fading light trickled between the pine needles like a wave of gold dust until it settled on the moist, tall underbrush. And yet, still the feeling wouldn't leave her—that there was something more here, something that, if she would only close her eyes and believe, she would truly *see*.

It...it felt like home.

The feeling in her chest warmed. She wanted to reach out with her hand, to brush her fingers over the grass, allow her whole being to touch this place, touch it and remember.

The sound of water filled her senses, washed over her and through her until she felt completely surrounded by it and the golden light.

Kate sucked in a lungful of air. Tears filled her eyes and the feeling of longing, of returning, was so real, so overwhelming she couldn't *help* but feel it.

"Where...where are we?" she asked.

"One of the few havens left in Alfeim, but I do not need to speak of this, do I?"

She turned, tearing her gaze away from the glade, to face him. "What do you mean?"

"You recognize this place, Kate. Or I should say, Kátheryn does."

Kate buried her hands in her jean pockets, fisting them tight together. He was right. Kátheryn knew exactly where they were.

"This was her home, wasn't it? This is where she lived?"

Eolis didn't smile, didn't show any joy from what Kate could see, and yet the presence in the glade—the feeling of home—shifted. She felt the joy from the glade itself, as if it shimmered in the air, so powerful and real it nearly knocked her on her ass.

"This was her home, and Alfeim, even now, remembers her touch."

It took all of Kate's concentration, all her hard-fought control to wrench herself from this pull, this need to toss her arms up in the air and sing. She would *not* give in. Couldn't allow herself to be controlled by anyone, not even Kátheryn. She couldn't trust without asking questions. She was done with that.

Not for the forest and sure as hell not for Kátheryn, an elven soul she didn't understand, didn't know.

The person who she was, was *Kate*, not some long-dead elf.

And yet if that were true, then why wouldn't she let the Gathering do their thing? Why not just let Aila rip out her elven half and be done it with?

Because...because Kátheryn was a part of her, had always been a part of her.

Kate reached up, touched her ears, the slightly pointed tip that had haunted her since she was young. Always different, always apart, and now...now she knew why, even if she still didn't understand.

She lowered her hand and looked Eolis right in the eyes. "I think you better start explaining. From the beginning. Who was she? Kátheryn. What happened to her?"

"I am sorry, but I cannot tell you."

Kate nearly took his head off. She was so *done* with people feeding her that crap.

"At least," Eolis said, calm as day, as if he didn't care at all that she was ready to tear his head off, "not in the way in which you'd like me to. You would not believe me, and Alfeim, Kate, needs you to believe."

Which equaled to about as cryptic an answer she had ever heard before. Hell, he'd even topped Grandma with that one!

She crossed her arms, tried to ignore the dropping temperature as the sun continued to disappear (her poor, beat-up sweater was back at camp and really, it was getting *cold*), and glared at the elf.

"And is that supposed to be helpful? Is that supposed to somehow help me see this *truth*, as you keep calling it? Because the only thing I know is you warned me, snatched me up from everyone else, and plopped me here, some place in the forest that's trying really, really hard to not be noticed."

He gave her a small smile.

"You know, nowadays we call that kidnapping." Ha. As if he knew what that meant.

His smile faded. Maybe he did know.

"You said they have not trained you," he said. "Have you not asked yourself why?"

"Of course I have!"

Or…maybe not. At least, not as much as she should have.

"It's complicated," she said instead. "Grandma can't do it, the training, and she said I needed the Gathering's approval to cross the veil, to learn—"

"Which they will not do. Ever."

Eolis moved away from her, turning his back on her and the glade and Eagle, who had silently landed on a branch near her and the pine needles swayed underneath from his weight. Eolis's steps barely disturbed the ground, his leather boots simply parting the moist grass that somehow still clung with this morning's dew, even though that had been, you know, like twelve hours ago. Not to mention a blistering hot day—the sweat still clung to her shirt and armpits—although now it was turning pretty cold, pretty fast.

Kate wrapped her arms around her middle and shivered.

Eolis moved so gracefully and without pause, as if he was content in the quiet of the forest, compared to Kate who was itching to fill the silence with some kind of sound. As if she was afraid of what she might learn, or uncover in the silence.

He turned towards her and Kate saw a resolution in his eyes. Whatever he'd been thinking about, he'd come to a decision.

"They cannot train you to see *truth*," he said. "They cannot train you to learn your gift, to cross the veil, to walk between worlds. Nor would they, if they could."

"But, that's not what Aila said. She wants to bring back the elves and apparently I'm the only who—"

He touched a finger to her lips.

She immediately quieted. Felt the power from him, then, so similar, almost like a twin to James's. And again, she felt that stirring in her chest, the longing to have him back, to have *him* touch her lips, not his dad.

James.

"I brought you here," Eolis said, "because you cannot control your sight. You cannot see on your own the truth of the forest, of memories long gone. You cannot do this, not even with your spirit guide beside you. But this place, though, these havens, they shall help you."

He removed his finger and gestured to the glade, and Kate was only mildly distracted by the flapping brown cloth that was slowly unraveling from his arm.

"A haven?" Kate asked. "I don't understand. Grandma never mentioned anything like that."

"You've been told the light ones have disappeared—that their presence is gone from Alfeim—and yet they are still felt. Is this not true?"

"Uh, yeah. I mean, that's what I heard. But...what the hell? Where are *you* getting this information from?"

"The forest."

Right. Talking trees.

Kate opened her mouth to ask about Yig (the only talking tree *she'd* met), but Eolis cut her off.

"How I learned of you and your blindness to your gifts is irrelevant. Can you feel Alfeim here? Can you feel the forest? The birds resting down for the night, the stirring of bats and others in the dark places and in the shadows? The earth as it slowly shifts, allowing the smallest worm to continue its path?"

Kate really, really wanted to make some biting, sarcastic comment. She didn't, though, because Eolis was actually trying to help her, which was more than Aila had done. And if she found a way to *see*, that would only help her with the Gathering, right? Maybe she could actually convince them that she could do this...and then they'd let both her souls in peace.

"I'll try," Kate said, finally.

Eolis nodded and gestured her forward.

She turned in a circle, taking in the glade, the dripping dew from the nearby brush, the stream gurgling as it moved...still cold, she knew, as if she'd gone and dipped her fingers in it. Freezing, actually, the glacier-fed waters still strong even in the middle of the summer.

She closed her eyes, letting the glade slip past her never-ceasing thoughts.

She felt it, then. The forest. Here. In this place, and just as Eolis had said. Felt the small shift in the ground...earthworms, perhaps, or maybe beetles or centipedes. There was a fluttering above her, and then the spread of wings as an owl took flight without a sound, without a sign of his passage.

All the while, she felt Eagle and Eolis watching her, guiding her.

Bit by bit, Kate lowered her shields. Didn't know why she thought of them in that way, just that they were there. Giant guardrails surrounding her mind, her heart, her soul. She'd put them up years ago to protect herself. To keep out the never-ceasing disappointment from her mother, the cold, harsh looks from other children and their parents.

Now, though, she lowered them. One after another.

"She lived here," Kate whispered, "and the forest...Alfeim...remembers her. It remembers me."

The words slipped from her. Part of her wanted to deny it still. Those last guardrails still up, still so high and tall, and she wanted to slam them all back into place.

But she didn't.

Alfeim Forest knew her. And in this exact spot, right here, it sang for her return.

Kátheryn's return.

Tears swelled in her eyes, and she quickly wiped them away. There was no time for crying, not now when she was actually getting somewhere.

Kate opened her eyes and glanced at Eolis. "But I still don't understand. Why did you bring me here?"

"To help you."

Eolis reached for her hand and turned her towards to the sun, the last glint of yellow before it faded completely behind the mountains, its lingering gold rays and dust.

"You cannot reach your spirit, your eagle, without help," he said.

"This place shall help you and when you can, you will see. *Truth* and memory, that is your gift, that is what Alfeim wishes you to see, what it has always wished. You shall see what Alfeim showed me."

Even though she followed, let him pull her along, she still didn't believe. Couldn't.

"But why? Why are you helping me?"

"I made a promise to my human half, my human soul. A promise I intend to keep even if it means I must stand against my kin. You must let go, Kate. Trust Kátheryn. Trust in what you feel for Alfeim. She shall not harm you, nor shall the forest. You are too important. We cannot lose you, not to the Gathering, not to my son or my wife."

"No, no. I...I can't." Kate pulled free. "If I let her in, I'll lose myself. I'll disappear. That's what Aila told me, that's what James told me."

And no, even though Aila didn't exactly wish her well, in this, Kate knew, she hadn't been lying.

Kate shook her head, the end of her ponytail slapping her cheek. She backed away from Eolis and the golden light.

"That's what happened to you. You forgot where your human soul ended and Eolis began. You *lost* your soul. I'm not doing that."

She glimpsed movement from the corner of her eye. Eagle! But he did not flap his wings in agitation or cry out for her to run. Instead, his perfectly white, perfectly beautiful head tilted to the side. His dark eyes blinked at her. Watching...encouraging, even?

He wasn't afraid, wasn't trying to save her.

"You do not need saving," Eolis said. "He knows this. He knows what you need is guidance. I swear to you, young Kate, you are in no danger form me, nor from Kátheryn."

"Bullshit."

This time it was Eolis's turn to blink.

"I do not know this word."

Figured.

"Okay, whatever," Kate said. "Say I do this thing—what guarantee do I have I'm not going to lose myself? Because I really, really like just being me."

And she also liked dressing like a normal human being and not someone who'd stepped out of *The Lord of the Rings* movie, with that tunic that was barely held together. Or, okay, maybe the clothes looked a heck of a lot closer to Tarzan than those really beautiful robes in Peter Jackson's movies.

Eolis held out his hand to her, but this time waited for her to take it. "My human soul did not lose himself to me. His name was Aaron. He made a choice, a choice and a promise I've honored ever since."

A choice? That didn't sound like what Aila had made it out to be. Which...should really be no big surprise by now.

"You mean you chose to give up your human soul? Why the hell would he do something like that?"

It didn't make sense. None of this did.

Kate's head spun. She rested her hand against a nearby tree, a tree that instantly felt warm and comforting at her touch. She decided to just go with it, the tree liking her, instead of being freaked out by it.

Figuring out this elven soul thing was a hard enough challenge.

"Aila warned me away from James because our elven souls, and the love they had for each other, would take control," Kate said. "This really, really doesn't make sense. You gave up your humanity because you loved Aila's soul so much. You *chose* to walk around with clothes falling off you? I expected the elves to be a bit more...sophisticated. Careful of their clothing and perfect hair. Not the slightly crazed jungle-man look."

Now, Kate had expected a range of reactions.

Laughing, however, was not one of them. Beautiful laughter, almost like wind chimes, was definitely not one of them.

"Ah, Kátheryn, your humanity truly is a gift, one I hope you fight to keep."

Eolis shook his head, the laughter still tugging at his lips. "But no, young Kate, I do not love Aila nor the Áila soul within her. She is too cold, too powerful to be loved in such a way. Love must be warm and joyful, otherwise the love goes only one way. No. It is Alfeim Forest that both Aaron and I love, love more than the passing of time, it seems."

He lifted his hand higher, gesturing towards her and then to the glade.

Again she felt its pull. The warmth spilling from the tree she touched, filling upwards from the ground and through her hiking boots. The forest wanted her to see, wanted her to understand.

"This," he said, "is what you must see for yourself. You shall never lose yourself to Kátheryn because neither of you wishes it. But so long as you fight your heritage, so long as you refuse to accept who you are —who Kátheryn is—then you will never see either Alfeim or the veil."

"But why should I want to see the veil? Why would I *want* to cross the veil?"

It was the one question no one had answered for her, not truthfully anyway, not without selfish reasons. Her dad wanted revenge on the elves and Grandma...well, who knew what the hell Grandma wanted.

But she would get an answer from Eolis. "Why do *you* want me to see the veil?"

"To know what happened, young Kate. To find the lost ones and, if I can, to help them find peace."

Her mouth dried. "But, but I thought you knew what happened?"

"I...died before my kin disappeared. I do not know what happened to them and no matter how I ask Alfeim, it does not know either. Please, Kate, help me. Help Alfeim."

For a moment, Kate didn't move. Couldn't. She could only stare at Eolis's offered hand, the skin cracked and riddled with callouses. Nothing like Aila's soft yet powerful hands. And for some reason, some strange, weird reason, it was enough. Enough to convince Kate to close her eyes, and for this one second, reach out to the elven soul within her.

The elven soul she had been born with.

Please, Kate thought, hoping Kátheryn would listen. *Don't take over my soul.*

She felt a quiet, relaxing warmth in her chest and thought she heard the beating of wings. She didn't give herself a chance to question or second guess or run away, like her mother would have done. The sense she'd had when she went in search of her elven spirt, of walking closer to an edge, of taking that final step and falling.

She could never be able to turn away, never be able to forget, to go back to the life that her mother had tried so desperately for them to have.

Instead, Kate reached forward, her eyes still closed, and took Eolis's hand.

"Kátheryn shall guide you. Follow her lead."

Again with the cryptic answers, but this one time, it made sense.

She felt Kátheryn, felt a second presence, like a warm, glowing candlelight inside her. It brightened, glowing stronger and stronger.

She felt hands covering hers—not Eolis's—these were smaller, but not delicate. They were hands like hers. Hands that liked to dig in the dirt, to pull up weeds, to plant and water new life. Kate accepted those hands, curling her fingers around the other's, and finally, let the last of her guardrails down.

Kátheryn guided her, showed her how to open her mind.

And for the first time, Kate didn't fight her. She took a deep, long breath and let go. Let go of worry and fear and everything that'd been holding her back from truly understanding...herself.

Kátheryn showed her the way, showed her how to reach into Alfeim, to hear and to see, to feel and become one with the forest. To see its memories.

The feeling...it was like the very first day hiking, when she'd stood beside Aila and for that one, brief moment, had seen out of Eagle's eyes. How she'd seen into the veil itself, a sight that had allowed her to see the *truth*—that Aila was afraid of her, of her and James, of the connection they shared.

But this time Kate felt more.

She felt the pulsing of the earth, the way the ground rose and fell, how it *breathed* in and then *exhaled*. She felt the wind brushing through pine needles and heard the birds' calls, welcoming her home.

It was...amazing. Breathtaking.

And terribly frightening because now Kate felt Alfeim Forest itself, felt its vastness, its age, and how deep the very roots went into the ground. The lingering...hum that settled about the place, the last dusting of magic that kept the trees alive and aware, both welcoming and frightening.

The feeling was so strong she nearly collapsed, nearly broke the concentration Kátheryn and Eolis were passing onto her. But then she felt Kátheryn holding her up, preventing her from falling.

"You must first see. See the Truth, my Kate."

And before Kate could swallow, protest, or utter a prayer to get out of this vision in one piece (with two separate, very individual minds intact), Kátheryn shifted Kate's focus from the forest and into a Memory.

Alfeim's Memory.

She spiraled down into the forest, trees and branches whipping by her face, slapping at her cheeks, though not a single one actually touched her. Kátheryn took her down, and further down still, until they finally stopped, a hairsbreadth above the ground. A ground that was completely covered in snow. Hard-pack and flurries both, as if a recent storm had sent down a small dusting before moving on. The night sky, though, was gray and cloudy, with the moon and its accompanying stars trying desperately to pierce through, and failing.

But Kate knew, right down to her soul, that she was still in Alfeim, though where exactly was anyone's guess.

But this was clearly not the July she'd just left, as the only snow to be found nestled in those high-ass mountain peaks with glaciers that held on, somehow, despite the climate change and all that. Not to mention it was now full night and not the twilight that she and Eolis had stood in.

But those were all the thoughts Kate had time for before Kátheryn and the Memory pulled her away to focus on the reason, and the who, of why Kate was here.

Here, in fact, to see her father, Severi. There was no mistaking *that* jerk.

He stood there amidst the snow, arms crossed, his dark pants and shirt stretching across him as the wind tried to shove him back, as if this place, this part of the forest, didn't want him here. His deep brown, piercing eyes narrowed and he said some word that she didn't know or understand, and after another moment of the wind slapping even harder, fighting him, flattening his dark blond hair against his head, it suddenly stopped.

The wind died, completely.

Even from here, there was no mistaking the menace that drifted from him, right next to the allure and the temptations, the desires he could wrestle from you without a second thought.

The Memory pulled back a moment; Kate felt Kátheryn within her, guiding Kate to see even more, to see beyond her father....

And she saw that he wasn't alone, either.

Kate's heart thudded, her breath freezing in her chest if it could.

A woman stepped forward from the shadowed woods, her leather-bound feet not leaving a single trail or mark on the snow. A cloak, one as dark as the shadows surrounding her, snapped at heels. She lowered the hood and for a moment, the night's shadows pulled back, the moon and what small light there from stars piercing that cloudy sky, just enough to show her face.

Not that Kate needed it.

Aila stood there, with her beautiful silken flowing hair (so nothing at all like Kate's and the tangled mess it preferred to be). She was perfectly poised, perfectly calm, and no less menacing. Her power, even from the Memory, was nearly blinding.

The phrase "why, that traitorous bitch" came to mind, but Kate wasn't in control right now. Kátheryn was, and she didn't seem inclined to break with the Memory to have some swearing thrown in as commentary.

"You are sure she's the one, Louhi?"

Her father's—Severi's—lip curled up. "That is not my name."

"It is the name you wear. No other suits you, though perhaps trickster. Traitor. They might suffice."

"And you?" Severi asked. "Perhaps we shall call you the same? Traitor. You are the one who's turned your back on your people, not I. You, who are willing to give up the savior of your precious forest, the chance to re-find your light ones."

He stepped forward then, all grace and all menace, temptation in his very movement, his voice. He plucked a strand of her long, unbound hair and curled it between his fingers.

She slapped his hand away. "The light ones are gone. My husband is not. You say you can do this? You can bring him back?"

"I can, but you asked me another question first: Is she the one? Yes. She can cross the veil, she can open the gate between worlds."

"How do you know this?"

He shrugged. "I tested her, of course."

When Aila said nothing, just glared, he shrugged again.

"Her and her mother recently went on a little hiking trip, to Mount Rainer."

"That was you? You stole that magic from Alfeim?"

"Borrowed it, I prefer to say. Besides, it achieved what we both wanted. My daughter is awakening; she crossed into the misty world, into Niflheim, and she survived. Her mother can no longer deny her heritage. They will return to Lighthome."

"You swear? You will uphold your promise?"

Kate's father, the man Aila called Louhi, bowed low. Blond hair fell across his eyes, but even from here Kate could see the malice, could see the lie.

"I swear," he said, "on my soul before the light ones."

"Finally," Aila breathed. Mist blew out her mouth. "And my husband?"

"I shall bring him back...if, of course, you bring me my daughter. Unharmed and fully intact."

The world, the Memory, suddenly shifted. Became fuzzy like the mist from Aila's breath, clouding over, blocking what Kate could see. Only mist and gray and clouds.

Somewhere behind her, someone was shouting. No...just a really loud, really pissed-of string of curses—which, she realized after a moment, were coming from her.

The Memory snapped back completely and Kate found herself standing on the glade, her hiking boots squishing the long blades of grass, the water of the trickling stream nearby, and more swear words that would make even Grandma blush.

"Son of a bitch!"

Kate stomped her feet. She was back, in the here and the now, complete with shivering from the day's earlier sweat, back with Eolis and Eagle, with Kátheryn was nowhere in sight (unless you counted within her).

Which was fine. This was exactly where she needed to be.

"Bitch?" Eolis's eyebrows quirked up. "Yes. That fits my wife's personality perfectly."

Ugh. Kate felt sick. More than sick—like she needed to kick some serious, powerful elven ass before she felt normal. As if she ever could.

"I trusted her. Mostly. But, but my *grandmother* trusts her. Oh, oh no." Kate's mouth clicked closed. A sudden thought swept through her. "Unless, unless Grandma's in on it too?"

The thought was too horrifying, too frightening to think of—which alone was surprising. Only two months of knowing her and the thought of Grandma not actually caring for her, loving her? It hurt way too much to think of.

Eolis, however, shook his head. "Your grandmother knows nothing of this. Nor does the Gathering."

"Wait a minute. This doesn't make sense. She wants you back? I thought you said she doesn't love you."

"She does not."

Eolis shifted his shoulders, which Kate accepted as a shrug though it was way too graceful to be anything as simple as that.

"The world of elven descendants is complicated," he said. "What you saw, you cannot fully believe. Aila's purposes go beyond what she admitted to your magi father. She does not care to have Aaron back, but she does wish me, Eolis, gone."

"Why?"

He lifted his head to the sky, the growing twilight, the first sparkling stars gleaming so high up in that never-ending sky.

"Because she desperately cares for those who are lost, for the magic and the power she cannot ever have until they are returned. I threatened that desire, and I always will."

Kate shivered. She brushed her hands over her arms, trying to warm up, knowing she never could.

"So this whole time...the whole reason I came here, was because of my dad. That day, when I went hiking with Mom, when I got trapped in that misty world..." A world of no color, which slowly leached away your life, your happiness, your hope. "That had been him. That whole time."

Kate squeezed her eyes closed. She didn't want to believe, but she knew she had to.

It had all been planned, right from the beginning. Between Aila and her dad.

She felt Kátheryn stirring within her, a warmth, like a warm glow from a candlelight. She did not intrude, but she was present. Just enough to remind Kate that she wasn't alone in this.

Kate looked at Eolis, who studied her in this quiet way as if he, too, sensed Kátheryn...and knew that Kate now did as well.

He nodded at her.

"So," Kate said, "if all Aila wanted was to hand me over to my dad, why did we just spend three days trampling through a forest? He nearly caught me in town. Why go through all this trouble?"

"Because he failed. And because he did, he inadvertently awakened the one being both he and Aila fear."

"Kátheryn."

"And, you must remember, young Kate, Aila is the *laulaja*. She is still the Gathering's leader and must at least appear to exist by those rules set down. She has her own place, her own purpose. She must convince the Gathering—"

"That I'm not good enough," Kate finished. "That I'm a failure. That they should deny me access to the veil. And..."

Her voice trailed off.

"And destroy Kátheryn forever," he said. "Or, you may run and go to the one person who would accept you without question, you and your gift of the veil."

"My dad."

He nodded. "You would go to him, willingly."

Oh, she'd go willingly all right. *If* she had the chance to slug him in the nose for trying to kidnap her. While that might be satisfying, it still didn't change the problem at hand: What was she going to do?

"The story of my life," Kate mumbled.

Eolis looked at her oddly, but Kate shrugged him away. To think the only true ally she had was (to everyone else) a half-crazed elf who'd rather run about the forest half-naked, with clothes falling apart at the seams, than deal with his bitch of a wife. Well, it was probably a good thing she learned all about the quirks of James's family before she actually, you know, went and fell in love with the guy.

Kate's chest tightened at the thought of James, and she knew for a fact this feeling came both from her and Kátheryn.

"What about James? What will happen to him?"

Eolis shook his head. "I do not know. Aila loves him, but more than her power? Her position? If she does not deliver you as promised, Louhi will expose her."

Which means Aila had no choice, regardless of how much she loved James, to sacrifice her son if necessary.

But it was more than that. Kate, and Kátheryn, both knew that Aila feared their two elven souls reuniting. Why, exactly, Kate didn't know, but she felt it...felt it in the same way she could feel the earth shifting under her boots, the breath of the forest as the wind sighed between them.

Again, her chest tightened, and it felt as if her heart actually ached. Hurt. Longed. Kate rested a hand there, then closed her eyes and reached within herself.

Towards Kátheryn.

Again came that feeling. A single last warning.

She could still walk away. She could run from the forest right now, rejoin her mother and find a way to live with an elven soul besides hers. Lonely, yes, cut off from this world, this...this Alfeim that she loved, that she felt drawn to and a part of.

Or, she could accept her fate and the path she found herself on. Not one she'd chosen, but one she'd been born to.

This, though, *this* was her choice.

To stay.

To go.

She'd need Kátheryn's help. She'd need Kátheryn's sight, her ability to see Memories, to read the forest, if she had any chance of surviving the Gathering. Not to mention a pissed-off Grandma when Kate unexpectedly returned from her unexpected disappearance.

Kate felt an answering light, the same glow from earlier. Acceptance. A promise.

She didn't know Kátheryn, didn't know the elf soul and just how much she could trust, but...she was willing to try. Willing to trust because...she didn't want to be her mother. She didn't want to run and hide and run some more.

She wanted to be herself, even if that meant a life with Kátheryn beside her.

Kate nodded. "Okay then."

"Okay?" Eolis echoed.

"I'm not going to run away anymore. I can't run from who I am." Not when the "who" part was inside her. "I'm going back."

He frowned. "Did you not see the Memory correctly? You realize the Gathering itself will stand against you so long as the *laulaja* has been comprised?"

"Nope, I got that part."

"I...I do not understand."

"Actually, I'm pretty much screwed even if Kátheryn manages to do her thing and helps me out some. But I'm not running anymore. I'm going to face this head on."

"You think James will listen to you? Do you think he'll believe your *truth* over his mother's?"

"You tell me. He's your son."

Eolis's eyes narrowed. "I have not known him for many years."

But there was one thing Kate did know. "He said it himself: he's known me my whole life. He'll listen. I have to believe he'll at least listen."

Would he?

She didn't know. Not now.

But she had to try, and hopefully she'd figure out some brilliant plan along the way because she really, really didn't want to die yet. And if she did? Well, Kátheryn didn't seem too upset by the whole after-death experience and Eolis seemed to be doing rather good himself.

But more importantly, she wasn't about to let someone like Aila boss her around. After all, that's what grumpy old grandmothers and hopeful future boyfriends were for.

Kate slid her feet into a wide stance and propped her hands on her hips. "Now. Which direction is the Gathering again? I was trying not to throw up on the way here and got a little turned around."

Eolis didn't bother to answer. Instead he pointed towards Eagle, who launched himself off the branch, his large, brown wings extended in flight. "I will watch from the shadows, young Kate. I will do what I can to aid you."

Well, that more help than she'd expected, and it was better than nothing. Now if only if she had that genius plan figured out...

Kátheryn stirred within her and Kate could only nod. At least they agreed even if there was no plan, they still had to try—try to save James from his own mother.

Not to mention her own elven soul, who might possibly get ripped right out of her.

"Are all elven souls and their family issues this screwed up?" she asked both Kátheryn and Eolis.

Eolis, as helpful as always, answered. "Only those foolish enough to love this world. And to love humans."

That sure sounded about right. Not that Kate had much experience in love, especially since James happened to be her one and only up to this point. Perhaps it was best not to think about *that* right now. One issue at a time.

Falling in love with her potential elven soul mate was a problem for tomorrow.

Kate took off at an easy run, smiling when she realized she couldn't actually hear her feet slapping against the pine-needle-covered ground. Maybe she was getting better with this elf thing...

Her chest tightened, warmed with a light separate from Kate's own.

Okay, with *Kátheryn's* help, she was doing better.

She shoved her worries over Kátheryn and James to the back of her mind. Right now, she had to survive a Gathering and outwit a nasty Aila because her odds really weren't looking so hot.

But hey, she had two elf souls on her side. That had to count for something. Right?

Either way, she would try. Try, and find out just where her heritage, where her path, was going to take her.

An Elven Heritage Novel

CHAPTER ONE

Kate took another slow step, her hiking boots pressing into the soft, spongy grass. She shivered as a cooling breeze drifted up and around the tall trunks of pine trees and larches and a whole bunch of others whose names she didn't know (and frankly, didn't care a whole lot about either).

She wanted to stay.

To sit on that boulder right there, overlooking that slow-moving creek, with water that had a hint of aqua to it. Fresh and cold from all the glaciers melting way off and up there in the distance, nestled up in those dark mountain peaks. She'd sprawl, arms and legs stretched out on that rock, with its mix of pink and black and ruddy-brown specks. Close her eyes. Feel the last bit of warmth from both the rock and the sun until, finally, she fell into a comfortable, peaceful rest.

After all, it *had* been a long, long three days of hiking. Camping. Trudging up some mountain in the middle of nowhere Montana, in the middle of July, sweat pouring out of just about every pore, all to help her understand her heritage.

Oh, and totally skipping on the showering bit. Or the simple washing of her hair.

Ugh.

Her hair *used* to be this darker blond color, nice sunlight gold streaks, about the only attractive feature. Now though... well, her hair looked more like the forest floor, what with all the twigs and leaves and tangles she'd acquired since she'd started this oh-so-lovely camping expedition into the wilderness of Alfeim.

And yet, even with her missing all those oh, so important amenities, she wanted to stay.

Stay right here, in this small glade with its trickling creek and canopy of pine needles, the way the trees and their branches bowed to her, their bark and joints creaking as if they'd been asleep for an age, but finally, because of her, were waking up.

The glade didn't want her to go either.

She felt it.

Felt the trees, who were sad to see her leave. Even the grass, somehow still holding onto moisture from the morning dew all those hours ago, and how the heck there was any moisture at all was certainly some kind of magic (she had the sweat-soaked T-shirt to prove just how damn hot and dry it got during the day). That grass though, magic or not, with all its small individual blades, gave her a final, wet tickling along her ankles, right where her wool socks couldn't quite reach.

The last of the setting sun cast a dusting of gold specks in the air as if it, too, were waving goodbye.

Above her, circling high up overhead in the hot thermals and wind currents, was Eagle. His great brown wings stretched out as he rode the hot thermals and wind currents of that endless sky, with all those purples and pinks blending until finally fading into darkness.

Simply beautiful. All of it.

Kate breathed in, feeling the peace of this place, the peace she was finally feeling within herself. About her unique heritage. About the warm, new candlelight glowing within her.

And there, right in the middle of that endless sky, stretching out across the whole it seemed, was Eagle. His brilliant white head a beacon, ready to lead her home.

Eagle gave a sad, shrill cry.

He knew her well, her spirit guide. Always there for her, always watching out for her. And now, telling her it was time to leave.

Kate's stomach twisted.

Just a little, but enough. Enough to know that, by taking this one last step, she'd be leaving a part of herself behind.

Which, in a way, she was.

This wasn't her glade, exactly. It was Kátheryn's.

Kátheryn Silverstar, the warm candlelight within her.

The soft pink and gold flame. Still small, just like an actual candle flame, but growing stronger. And Kate had a feeling that the real Kátheryn probably felt more like a high school bonfire.

But now, more than ever, Kate understood why she'd always felt so different. So weird and strange.

She *was* different. Yes, she was an elf-descendant, just like her mom, just like her grandma, and also, a bit more. Like, an actual elven soul living right beside hers.

That's right. Not just one, but two souls.

Cause her life couldn't get anymore complicated with it just being *her* in there.

Her, the recently-turned seventeen-year-old who'd been seen as odd and weird everywhere she went, every house she'd lived in, every school she'd been forced into. The reaction, the treatment, by her classmates, teachers too, always the same. Her slightly pointed ears and crazy-good hearing really didn't help. Then there was her mom, Queen of Denial and Running, who'd pretty much dumped her out in the wilds of Montana with a crazy Grandma who, while she was crazy, had a certain fondness for shotguns and a history that you'd never, ever find in history books.

Like tales straight out of myths. Probably legends, if you believed in that sort of thing.

Like... well, like Kátheryn.

Kátheryn Silverstar who was the other part of Kate, the part that had *really* made her seem 'other' to just about every person she met. Except for Grandma. And James.

Kátheryn, the long-dead elf soul whose glade Kate now stood in.

This place had once been her home... a really, really long time ago, but it was pretty apparent that the glade, and the trees, probably even the ants crawling up that branch not two inches from her head, remembered her.

Kátheryn, that was.

Not Kate.

And she had to leave. Had to leave this beautiful, peaceful place. A place where she could well and truly hide, where all the bad things out there couldn't get her, from her evil-ass dad to the sore heart she just knew she'd feel the second she caught a glimpse of James again.

Because... she had to get back to camp. To warn Grandma about James's bitch of a mom and the war she wanted to start between the magi and the elf-descendants. A warning Kate had gotten because of Kátheryn and her magic, and the memory from Alfeim Forest itself.

There was still so much Kate didn't know about her heritage, about who she was, or heck, even what she could do. And Kátheryn, she'd shown Kate just a little bit more. How to connect with Alfeim Forest, its consciousness, to feel the actual shifting of the earth as it breathed, the small worms and bugs digging down there amidst the roots. And by doing so, she'd been able to see the forest Memory. A memory as if she'd been standing right there, watching the whole thing unfold.

A memory and a warning, one that she needed to share. She had to tell James, even if he'd end up hating her for it.

Eagle called to her again. Urging her and a little... uneasy it felt like. Like he needed her to move. To hurry.

Yes, it was time to go.

"I'm sorry," Kate whispered.

Though, she didn't know if she spoke to the glade or that slight tightening in her chest. An ache that she felt like it was splitting her in two.

Not that she could blame Kátheryn. After all, just waking up from a really long sleep and learning the person whose eyes you stared out was actually a pretty pathetic version of an elf-descendant, who was bad at just about *everything* elvish.

Like magic.

Especially magic.

Which was just another truth she couldn't run from. Not any

longer. Couldn't be her mom, who just kept running and driving and hiding. Oh, and lots of denying.

Not Kate. Never, Kate.

At least, not anymore.

Eagle flew on ahead, straight into that sunset. Kate followed him, followed the golden strand that always connected them. She took one last look at the glade, this place that felt like home and called to just about every inch of her being. The sun finished its descent, giving her one last, golden wink.

She took that final step—

Her boots sank straight down into a giant mound of freezing, brilliant white snow. And her connection to Eagle, her beautiful spirit guide, with his constant warmth and love, who believed in her when no one would, snapped.

Go to ChrissyWissler.com or your favorite bookseller.

bowl of ice cream. Double-scoop of huckleberry, cookies n' cream, sprinkles, river of hot fudge.

No problems at all.

Except for her backpack zinging with magic. And the impatient, unhappy tree tapping at her window.

Ignore an angry forest? Not a good idea.

Hidden in Darkness, a story about a reluctant girl coming to terms with herself and the magic living inside her—whether or not she wants it. The "In-Between" Elven Heritage Story, set some time after the events in *Hidden in Time*.

By joining my list you'll receive wonderful benefits such as being notified of upcoming book releases as well as the never-before-published short story and special gift for fans of the series: *Hidden in Darkness*.

To enjoy your free copy of *Hidden in Darkness* and keep up with the latest news and releases, go to https://dl.bookfunnel.com/yk3ksnyz29 and chrissywissler.com.

Chrissy Wissler's writing has garnered praise both from readers and professional writers. Readers love her characters and the emotional grip she engenders.

About her novel *Home Run*, *New York Times* bestselling author Kristine Kathryn Rusch said: "Wonderful book, chockfull of unexpected surprises. If you like sports novels, you'll like this—even if you don't like romance. If you like romance, you'll like this—even if you don't like sports novels."

Chrissy's short fiction has appeared in the anthologies: *Fiction River: Risk-Takers, Fiction River Presents: Legacies, Fiction River Presents: Readers' Choice, Deep Magic,* and *When Dreams Come True.* She writes fantasy and science fiction, as well as a softball, contemporary series for both romance and young adult.

Before turning to fiction, Chrissy also wrote nonfiction for publications such as *Montana Outdoors, Women in the Outdoors,* and *Jakes Magazine.* In 2009, *Inside Kung Fu* magazine awarded her with their 'Writer of the Year' award.

Follow her online at ChrissyWissler.com, as well as her blog on being a parent-writer, at ParentsandProse.

To enjoy another story by Chrissy Wissler and to keep up with the latest news, releases and more, go to: chrissywissler.com/free-book/

For more information:
www.chrissywissler.com
chrissy@chrissywissler.com

ALSO BY CHRISSY WISSLER

Elven Heritage Series

Hidden in Mist

Hidden in Truth

Hidden in Shadow

Hidden in Fire

Hidden in Flight

Hidden in Spirit

Hidden in Desire

Hidden in Memory

Hidden in Time: Novel

Hidden in Lore: Collection #1

Hidden in Myth: Collection #2

Hidden in Legend: Collection #3

Little League Series

Swing Away: A Little League Novel

Prom Dates & Softball Bats

Throw Like a Girl, Catch a Date

Fly Away

No Crying in Softball

More to Life than Softball

A Pitcher's Unexpected Date

A Catcher's Christmas Wish

Stolen Bases, Stolen Kisses

Softball Baby

Off-Balance

Batter-Up Pucker-Up: Collection

Everlasting: Collection

All or Nothing: Collection

Home Run Series

Home Run

Romance Video Game Series

Second Chance: Novel

Anything Possible

Changing Perspective

Enchantment Avenue

Searching for Sanctuary: Novel

Dragons in Preschool: Short Novel

The Blessings Bridge

Pixie Dust Cupcakes

Christmas Weather Witch

Unfreeze a Heart

More than Nurture